MAN CUFFED

MAN CUFFED

SARINA BOWEN & TANYA EBY

TUXBURY PUBLISHING LLC

1 RENAISSANCE STRIPPERS

 "The world breaks everyone and afterward many are strong at the broken places."

ERNEST HEMINGWAY

Meg

My long skirts swish around my legs as I stride toward the king's throne, a bottle of wine in one hand, a silver chalice in the other.

I've wanted to be an actor since I was four years old. I love shiny lights, passion, and costumes. So you'd think that the Renaissance era wench's costume I'm wearing—with my boobs hiked up to my chin—might possibly be a highlight of my career.

But no. I'm not dressed like this to meet a knight, or wrestle dragons. This isn't a low-budget *Outlander* knockoff. This is my day job. I'm a serving wench at Ye Olde Tavern.

Five nights a week, I lace the tight bodice up over my puffy-sleeved blouse and sell tankards of beer. Some days it's fun. When I'm in the right mood to play the bar wench, I bring out my English accent. Or Scottish when I'm feeling extra feisty.

Tonight, though, it's just a chore.

My thirtieth birthday has just come and gone, and I'm still waiting for my big break. Acting is a hard profession, and I'll admit that I'm a little depressed. My agent called today to let me know that I was passed up for another role.

At least this job pays well. Ye Olde Paycheck has bought me some time to figure out what I'm going to do with the next act of my life. I'm in the midst of a wicked midlife crisis. Pre-midlife crisis? Let's just say, a crisis. And it doesn't help that my sister suddenly has her entire life figured out. She's married to a knight in shining armor. Am I jealous?

Hell, yes.

I'm also a little sick of rejection. I've been *this close* to landing role after role for a decade now. I'm starting to take that shit personally. And that's no way to approach a career that you love.

"Wench!" calls an aggravated voice from the private room.

I'm a little sick of that, too. Ye Olde Tavern is particularly rowdy tonight. And not the good kind of rowdy. It's the bad kind, where the kitchen is slow, the bartenders are in the weeds, and chaos reigns freely. There's a bachelorette party going on in the private room, where a dozen young women are getting drunk and crabby in equal measure.

I grab some Ye Olde Pretzel snacks and a couple more pitchers of beer. Then I gird my loins and head back there.

The bride-to-be is your basic definition of a bridezilla. I can easily picture her stomping on all the tiny townspeople around her. She zeroes in on me right away. Here we go. *Smile, Meg. You're an actress. Pretend you give a shit.*

"This is a *disaster*," she sneers, getting up close and personal. I set the beer and pretzels on a table and prepare to take whatever she's about to throw at me. I'm hoping it's not a punch. "We're starving and we're supposed to have turkey legs and all we've got is pretzels and bar cheese and I'm pretty sure they didn't have that in the Renaissance. And my strippers are late!"

It's time to whip out the British accent.

"Oh! Don't play the daft cow! Pretzels pre-date Christianity," I say with a giant smile, so she won't realize I just insulted her. "And I know those skivers will turn up before you know it!"

The truth is that the strippers are *usually* late. They like to get baked before they turn up with their old-fashioned boom box and cheap costumes.

A half hour from now, Bridezilla won't care, though. All will be forgiven as soon as they rip those costumes off and gyrate their backsides.

Also? I'm pretty sure they didn't have male strippers in the Renaissance. Not that I'm going to point that out.

"There's an event at the arena," I point out. "Your gents are likely stuck in traffic. And your turkey legs have just arrived." Thank goodness. My coworker has just entered the room with the platter. He's quickly swarmed by the bride's drunk and starving girlfriends. Legs are grabbed, and elbows are thrown. It's Ye Olde Feeding Frenzy.

As I watch one of the women rip into a turkey leg, I have a brief flashback to working as an extra on a popular zombie TV show. I was a highlighted extra. And I can still taste the intestines.

"Finally," Bridezilla growls. "You ought to at least comp those legs for me."

"I'll give you a free dessert," I counter, sans accent this time. "And the bar cheese."

She glares at me. Her green eyes hot and angry. I have the sudden impulse to wrestle her to the ground, pin her arms behind her back, and make her cry for mercy. This costume is starting to affect my personality. And I've always been impulsive.

But that has to end. I'm the new thirtyish Meg. The responsible Meg. The younger me would've tackled this bitch already.

Thankfully, the beaded curtains part again, and three guys in cop uniforms step into the back room.

Hooray! I'm saved by the strippers.

And I must say they're looking fine tonight. Holy shit. Rent a Gent has hired some new talent. These cops...they're fucking hot.

Especially the one in the middle. His blue shirt can barely contain his muscles, which I'm pretty sure are rippling. They're either rippling or the collective lady-sighs are causing a warm breeze to drift over him. He's got sandy hair, cool gray eyes, a strong jaw and shoulders that I could sit on.

I'm not the only one who notices, either. Moments ago the room was a cacophony of drunken screams and turkey noshing, but a startled silence claims the room. The air is suddenly heavy with anticipation.

Except for one big problem. The hottest stripper I've ever seen is apparently new at this gig. The newbies forgot their boom box. There's not a bad 80s rap song in sight.

But it's all right. I got this. There's something to be said for improv training.

I make a beeline for the sound system and crank it up, then head over to the hunk of man and his two buddies. Clearly, Mr. Square Jaw is in charge. *Alpha* just rolls off him in waves.

Leaning in close, I say, "You're a little buttoned up for tonight, aren't you?" Then I undo the top button of his shirt. I feel something hard against my leg. Hard enough to turn me on. But then I realize he's got a walkie talkie radio strapped to his hip.

I wonder what else he's packing.

"Can you guys dance to this?" I ask, demonstrating with a bump of my hips. Although they don't really need to dance. They just need to take their clothes off. Right now, preferably. "The woman in the white spandex unitard is the bride-to-be," I add.

His jaw clenches. Gosh, he is the strong and silent type, isn't he? But he just isn't moving. Neither are his buddies.

This is going to get awkward fast if they don't find their groove. So I decide to show them how it's done. "All right ladies! Are you ready to get hot?" I scream.

"*Yeah!*" they scream back.

"Are you ready to get wet?" I call to them.

"Yeah!" they say.

"Who here is a bad girl?"

They all raise their hands. It's a fucking frenzy of estrogen. Someone in the back actually passes out.

"Then check out these hard bodies!" I reach up to rip off Mr. Square Jaw's pants. They're velcroed up the sides, so they should come off really easy.

Only they don't. So I give another tug.

Huh. That's weird.

And that belt he's wearing? It looks awfully heavy. That must be the problem. I start to reach for the belt to undo it, and a realization starts to creep over me.

This uniform is not a costume.

This dude is not a stripper.

This dude is an actual cop.

And I'm about to be arrested.

———

LUCKILY, I avoid arrest. I'm saved by two things. The first is the immediate arrival of the real strippers, striding in with "Baby Got Back" blaring and their sequined cop-pants sparkling under the disco lights of Ye Olde (Not Authentic At All) Tavern.

The second is the debilitating laughter of the *other* two real cops, doubled over, struggling for breath. "Maguire? A stripper?" one of them gasps as if it's the funniest thing on the planet.

I realize my hand is still resting on his belt buckle. Oh, if only...

"Knock it off," Maguire snips. "I'm not a stripper." Then he does something I'm not expecting. He leans close to my ear and whispers, "At least, not for hire. Only when I volunteer."

And now I'm frozen, in what I'm pretty sure is a spotlight, that declaration reverberating through my body.

That's when Officer Maguire and his buddies move into cop action. "All right! Everybody out! There's a main gasline break down the block, and we need to clear the premises!"

Bridezilla, who's sitting in a chair, one turkey leg in each fist, surrounded by four gyrating sets of, um, junk, suddenly looks crazed. "I'm not leaving until this lap dance is done! I'm getting married and I earned a lap dance! And I demand that I get these turkey legs for FREE!"

That's when my patience for her finally dies. Did she not hear that *our lives are in danger?* I'm about to pounce on the bitch with: "I'll give you a free turkey leg and put it right up your..."

When Maguire squats down next to her and *lifts her chair right into the air.* Then he heads for the exit.

Once again I'm not the only one who notices how incredibly impressive this guy is. There's a frenzy of iPhone camera activity punctuated by the heavy breathing of drunk women swooning over a very sexy cop. Maguire's muscles pop and strain as he strides outside carrying Bridezilla as if she weighed nothing more than a turkey leg.

I hate Bridezilla.

I want to be his turkey leg.

These are my thoughts as I find myself standing alone in a room that was crowded only moments earlier. I'm still frozen in place, a little breathless from that show of pure manliness, and possibly experiencing an adrenaline crash from my close call with being thrown into the hoosegow for molesting a police officer.

A deep, burly voice shakes me awake. "Hey, serving wench."

My head swings toward the doorway, where Maguire is standing. "I don't like being addressed that way," I hear myself say. But it comes out breathy and weird.

"Then maybe you should put something different on your name tag."

"Well, sure. If you want to be technical about it." My hand covers the name tag in question. Moving home to Michigan was supposed to help me become a grown-up. Only I don't feel like one right this second.

"Come on," he says in that gravelly voice. "It's not safe here. *You* gotta vacate the premises too."

This probably means the Tavern will clock me out early, those bastards. But hearing the news from Maguire's sexy lips, in that deep voice of his, makes me feel like it's almost worth it.

I follow him outside. No wonder I thought he was an entertainer. Ordinary people don't have muscular asses and long legs like those. I'd be willing to follow him anywhere at this point.

But this is real life, and not a movie set.

So it's another six months before I see him again.

There's an important thing I've learned through my years of acting. Comedy or drama, it doesn't really matter...but the impact of a line depends on the perfect timing of delivery.

My timing with men is already terrible.

My timing with Maguire will prove to be even worse.

2 NEVER, BASICALLY

Meg

"Well, it doesn't feel like home yet. But the kitchen is unpacked." I close a white cabinet door and turn to face my friend Cassidy.

"It's..." She struggles to choose an adjective for my new, spartan apartment. "It's so *clean*," is what she goes with eventually.

The giggle starts like a tickle in my belly and then erupts.

"What? Clean is good, right?" Her pale, freckled brow wrinkles with uncertainty.

"Yes!" I gasp. "But can you imagine us using that same standard for men? He's boring, but he's so *clean*."

"Oh." Cassidy closes a drawer and then covers her mouth to laugh. "Fine, so it's faint praise. But good hygiene in a man is important."

"Then we're setting the bar pretty low." I snicker.

"I grew up with three brothers!" she protests. "Boys can be so gross and sweaty."

Because I'm me, the image of a sweaty man isn't enough to scare me off. A strong, sweaty man—preferably one who's just helped me set up my new futon bed—sounds pretty good right now.

But I'm not sure Cassidy and I can agree on this point. She and I don't have the same taste. Or the same personality. Or the same goals. I'm thirty. She's still in her mid-twenties. I'm a drama queen; she's analytical and practical and, fine, kind of a nerd.

When I met her at a party for her brother Liam—who is now my brother-in-law—we hit it off immediately. And we have one big thing in common. We're both at a crossroads in our lives. She's just home from a fellowship abroad that didn't go as she planned. And I'm trying to decide whether or not to give up acting.

Actually, we have more in common than that. We both have pushy families with deep opinions about what we ought to be doing with our lives. Hers are a pair of slick lawyers. Mine are actual rocket scientists. No joke—my dad works for one of the new private launch companies who are changing the shape of space exploration. My mom teaches astrophysics at a college in Oregon.

They worry about me. And so does my only sister.

For example, my sister, Sadie, is worried that this new apartment costs too much. "You could find new roommates again and save a wad of cash," she said only yesterday.

But Cassidy understands, which is why she's the one pulling my graphic novels out of the box and placing them carefully on the shelves. I know it's a risk to spend money on this place. But thirty-year-olds don't have roommates. I'm tired of living like a starving artist.

Although I am a starving artist.

And Cassidy is right about my new apartment. It *is* clean, and was recently constructed. The walls are painted white. The floorboards are pickled to a nearly white color. The countertops are a shade of dove gray chosen to never offend anyone. They are practically invisible.

In other words, I'm moving into an apartment with all the warmth and character of a recently built mental institution. But, hey. At least it's *my* mental institution.

And anyway, I'll liven up the place soon. Paint isn't very expensive. Groovy lamps will be sourced from secondhand shops. Fabric. Beads. I have ways of brightening up an interior that don't cost much. Plus, my sister gave me a cast-off couch—the one she had in her guest room, which is now the baby's room.

I've already chosen fabric for the slipcover I'm making in bright orange. That ought to brighten things up. And then I'll need pillows, though. Throw pillows make all the difference, and great fabrics aren't cheap.

Space isn't an issue for me, luckily. This will do. There's a tiny living room, separated from the kitchen area only by a countertop that serves as a preparation space and my only table.

But there's a bright bedroom and a (very clean!) bathroom that I don't have to share with anyone. The not-sharing part is key. That's why I moved here. To live like an adult.

"You should see some of the dumps I rented in Atlanta and LA," I tell Cassidy. "I'm ready for something clean and quiet, even if it is a little out of my budget."

"I totally understand," she says, giving me a smile. "And this is a very safe neighborhood."

"Again, something we wouldn't look for in a man."

"Safe? Why the heck not?"

"Oh, honey." I just shake my head. "Safe turns into boring, usually by the third date. If you don't feel a little whiff of danger, what's the point?"

"Hmm." She gives me a squinty, slightly confused look. "I'm not sure it all adds up."

"What do you mean?"

"We have a pact," she says in a grave voice. "We're both going to find good, decent men."

"I didn't forget." This is the other thing we have in common—a pressing need for better male company. We're both coming off of romantic disasters. So last night—over a pitcher of margaritas—we made a deal to only date decent men.

"But you *just* said you need a man to have a whiff of danger!"

"A *whiff*," I emphasize. "Not a stench. It's different. There are some very decent bad boys in the world. Good men who like to have a fun time. There have to be."

Cassidy does not look convinced. "How can a man be both good and bad at the same time?"

"Oh, honey. There's this thing called sex..."

She throws a wad of packing tape at me. "Don't talk to me like I'm a child. Everyone does that."

"Sorry," I say quickly. Cassidy is some kind of statistics genius. But she's also sheltered, and a little sensitive about it. "I was just making a dumb joke. But our needs are *not* funny. There have to be men in the world with good hearts and dirty minds. There just have to be."

"I hope so. I asked someone out today. On a date."

My hands freeze on the box I'm folding up. "What? Already?"

"Yup. I told you we can't waste time. So I just went for it in the dentist's office."

"The...really?" God, I hope she didn't proposition the dentist. If he's a bad kisser she'll have to switch dentists. That sounds really inconvenient.

"He was waiting to see the hygienist at the same time I was. His name is Greg."

"Greg," I repeat slowly. "He sounds very clean."

Cassidy laughs suddenly. "He *was* very clean, now that you mention it. Silly me, I took that as a good sign. And maybe it is. Maybe he has straight teeth and tidy hair and a wonderfully dirty mind." Her eyes are sparkling. "You're going to be so jealous."

I laugh because it's true. "When's the big event?"

"Well, we're going out on Friday."

"Wear the nice lingerie on Friday!" I chirp.

But Cassidy looks scandalized. "No way! That's the first date. He doesn't get to see my undies until at least the third."

"The third?" I don't know if I'm cut out for dating like a responsible adult.

"The third," she repeats firmly. "If he won't even wait a couple weeks for the main event, then how could he possibly be relationship material?"

"I suppose you have a point. Although this process is going to take longer than I thought."

"What do you mean?"

"If responsible dating means three dates before nookie, how are we going to weed out the losers? The two-pump chumps? The sixty-eights?"

"The—what?"

"Can't quite be bothered with sixty-nine?"

Cassidy blushes furiously. "It's not a perfect system," she admits. "But impatience hasn't worked for us. So I think we have to try a little restraint."

She's making plenty of sense. It's just that restraint isn't my strongest attribute. "Hey, speaking of restraint?" I drop my voice and point at the living room wall. "My new neighbor tied up his girlfriend last night. With handcuffs."

"What?" Cassidy whispers back. "How do you know?"

"Thin walls." I move closer to her and sit down on the floor, so we can't be overheard. "I had some music playing, so I didn't hear them getting started. But when the playlist ended, I heard moaning."

"No way." My friend's eyes are as wide as dinner plates.

"Way. And after a while she said, 'Go get the cuffs, tough guy.' And I guess he did, because she sounded very satisfied with the results."

"H-how satisfied?" Cassidy squeaks.

"She's a screamer," I whisper. "If I ever meet them in the elevator, eye contact is going to be a challenge."

Cassidy giggles. "Is he a screamer, too?"

"No, but..." I pause, wondering if I can even do him justice. "He has this deep, growly voice, Cass. He was ordering her around. I couldn't hear the words, but..." I shiver. There's no way to describe the effect that voice had on me. It was so masculine and commanding.

Not to mention the deep, agonized groan at the end. I get another shiver just remembering it.

"Who lives there?" Cassidy asks.

"No idea," I admit. "But he *sounds* hot." There was something a little familiar in his voice that I just couldn't place. But that was probably only wishful thinking.

"Now watch," Cassidy says. "They're both, like, seventy-five years old."

I howl. "God, I hope they are. Because that means I have another forty-five years to find a guy like that." And speaking of time. "Don't you have to go?" Cassidy is supposed to have dinner at the Evergreen Club with her family.

"Yeah," she sighs. "Good times."

"Free food," I point out. Then I swat her on the butt. "Go. You've been a huge help to me. Thank you for giving me your Saturday."

"Anytime! You know I don't exactly have a packed social calendar."

"Except for Greg from the dentist's office. I expect a full report."

"Don't worry."

I walk her to the door. "Give my love to Liam and my sister!"

"Will do." She turns around after pressing the elevator button. "You could come, you know. There will be room at the table."

"Maybe another time. I have to...shampoo my cat."

She rolls her eyes because I don't have a cat. Then she gives me a friendly wave and leaves.

I head back inside, congratulating myself for dodging that invitation. The McAllister parents aren't exactly party animals. But that's not really the issue. My sister and her husband will be there. And I just can't deal with them today.

Don't get the wrong idea. I love them both. But—like Cassidy—I'm a member of the Lonely Siblings Club. My sister Sadie just married Cassidy's brother Liam. They also just welcomed my sister's third child into the world—a little boy. Alfred. They named him after Hitchcock, their favorite filmmaker.

They are happy in that exuberant way that seems unfair to single people. And they don't even have the good sense to be smug about it. Which makes it hard to hate them. I shouldn't be so irritated with them finding love and happily-ever-after and all. That's what I want, too.

But there are days when I don't think it's going to happen for me. Especially after my last relationship. That was my last really optimistic moment with a man. I'd begun imagining an alternate future for me. Instead of Meg The Famous Actress, for a brief moment I thought I'd be Meg Who Is Famously Married To A Podiatrist.

Unfortunately he was *already* married. A fact he'd failed to mention.

That's when I knew I had to get out of Atlanta. He was the last bead on a long string of disappointing relationships and even more disappointing acting gigs. I wanted a different life. One more like my sister's life, honestly. Even if it kills me to say it. I want a little hit off the happiness and contentment pipe she's smoking. Hell, she even has a great job, and the respect of her peers.

I've got a tiny rental apartment I can barely afford, a waitressing job, and a string of unsuccessful auditions.

With these irritable thoughts, I walk all the way through my apartment, my footsteps echoing because I can't afford adequate rugs. When I get a little money, though, the first room I furnish won't be a room at all. Cleanliness aside, what really drew me to this place is the deck.

In my kitchen, I open the back door and step outside.

Like the apartment, the deck is small. My outdoor space is maybe twelve feet by twelve feet square. But it looks out onto a neatly trimmed lawn, and then to a line of trees concealing the neighborhood bike path. I can see in two directions. The third is obscured by a six-foot fence that divides the space between my next-door neighbor and me.

Mr. Deep Voice. I haven't met him yet. I've been dreaming about him, though. I hope he has a fascinating accent. I love accents. I can make myself a cocktail and sit out on the deck, eavesdropping and improving my Scottish brogue. Something like: *Hello, laddie, I'm ah-bout to sit on yer face*. Or maybe my neighbor is Australian! That would be great to practice because Aussie accents are hard.

On second thought, maybe I don't really need any more accent training. I might give up acting altogether. I think. Maybe. We'll see.

It's June, so I take a deep breath of fragrant spring air, just to clear my brain. *Ahhhhh*. There's enough space out here for a small dining table and two chairs. *And* a chaise lounge—the sturdy kind, with a cushion and a cup holder.

It's not a seat at the Academy Awards. But it still sounds great.

All I've got at the moment is a folding chair. So I sit down on it anyway. A cold beer would be really nice, too. But I haven't been shopping yet. My new (and very clean) fridge is empty. So I sit on my folding chair and mentally compose a shopping list.

I don't know how long I've been sitting there when I hear someone step out onto my neighbor's half of the patio. I glance up in spite of the fence. But of course I can't see who's there.

"Bring the wine, hot stuff," a woman's voice says. "It's hot out here. I hope there aren't bugs."

I roll my eyes. Who steps out onto a deck on a lovely spring day and immediately finds two things to complain about?

Then I hear the deck boards creak as heavier footsteps emerge, too. "Move over, sugar," says a gruff voice.

Ooh! I sit up a little straighter. Now things are getting interesting. He doesn't have a Scottish accent, sadly. But now I can hear him properly. His voice is still glorious—deep and raspy. This will be fun. Also, eavesdropping is a professional necessity. The more voices I can absorb into my soul, the better my repertoire will be.

"You like white wine?" the woman asks.

Whoa! A clue! They don't know each other well, then! It's not something a wife asks a husband.

"It's okay."

Riiiight. He's just being nice. "It's okay" probably means "white wine is vile, but I still want to get under your skirt." But, God, that voice. There's something about the timbre that gives me a tingling sensation in my chest.

"Let me guess, you're a beer man."

"Sure. Usually."

Usually. I never knew that word was sexy until right this moment. But he draws it out nice and slow.

"What else—" the woman makes her voice sound impossibly breathless—"do you *usually* like?"

He chuckles, and that sound turns me inside out, too. "You want a demonstration? I thought we went over this. Last night."

"You'd better show me again," she breathes.

Whoa! I lean forward in my chair. But all is quiet, until I hear a little gasp and then a whimper. And then the snick of a kiss. Times four or five.

Then that voice, pitched so low that I feel it in my breastbone. "Is this what you were looking for when you asked to come to my place today?"

"Y-yes," she sighs.

"Better hand me that glass." He chuckles. "I don't think you can hold it upright while I—"

She whimpers.

"That's right, sugar. You don't need these."

When I hear the quick but telling sound of panties being ripped, I nearly whimper, too. This man works fast! I eye my apartment door, knowing that I should go back inside. On the other hand, they'll hear my door open and shut.

And I was here first!

"Oooh!" she cries. "Oooh!"

He growls. A true growl. And I feel it in my nipples.

But then she starts up again, with more "oohs" and "aahs" than a doo-wop group on tour. "Yes! Yes!"

He growls again, and I feel it in my toes.

Okay, maybe it is hot out here. *Whew.*

"Need you," he grunts.

I sigh inwardly. When is the last time anyone needed me like that? Never, basically. Not with that hungry rasp, anyway. The last man who said he needed me was a podiatrist and a philanderer. He didn't need me specifically. He just needed a distraction from his life.

It was a low point, I'm telling you.

But the guy next door...he doesn't sound distracted at all. He sounds very focused. Very.

She lets out a little shriek, and then they're on the move. His screen door opens and shuts with a bang.

And I'm a hundred percent sure it won't be the only thing getting banged. I'm so, so jealous. With a lonely sigh, I rise from my chair and head inside, taking care not to slam the screen door. As if those two can hear me.

Alas, the only sound I can hear in my living room is my own ragged pulse. I need a distraction. So I walk into my bedroom to put away some of the clothes Cassidy helped me carry in.

I've just put my nicest sweater on a hanger when I hear that growl again. And—good lord—I practically jump. Because it sounds so close. If I close my eyes, I can almost pretend he's growling at me.

"Baby," he grunts. "*Yes.*"

Instantly, my nipples are back to full power. Like headlights on the high-beam setting.

So I guess the walls of this apartment are paper thin. They'd have to be. For the next five minutes, I can hear every grunt and thrust and whimper they're making next door.

And, wow. There are a lot of thrusts and whimpers. I'm rooted in place, a cashmere sweater in one hand, a hanger in the other, while a lucky woman on the other side of the door makes sounds like a hyena in heat.

I want to be a hyena in heat.

When she quiets down, I assume it's over. I take a steadying breath and hang the sweater in the closet with a long exhalation.

That's when I hear the finale begin. First a low, masculine groan. And then another. There's a thump—the sound of a piece of furniture hitting the wall. It repeats and grows faster. I stop breathing as it builds to a crescendo. My eyes fall closed and my mouth goes dry as he roars his approval.

And then silence.

I force myself to take a breath. With a shaky hand, I pick up my phone to try to distract myself, or at least remember my own name.

Hey, how's the new place? my sister has texted.

It's breathtaking, I reply immediately.

———

LATER THAT WEEK, I finish unpacking all my possessions and arranging them in my new apartment. And I've made some strides in decorating. The sofa slipcover is done. But I need better lamps, and those aren't cheap. So I've strung up some fairy lights in the meantime. Instant ambiance!

I've moved the furniture around a few times looking for the best flow. Besides, there's feng shui to consider. If you want to prosper in a new home, you can't just ignore feng shui.

For example, I know I need to have something living and green in my space with me. Wherever I place that living, growing thing will essentially bring more life into that area. So, if I need more money, I should put a houseplant in the money corner. If I need more peace, I should put a potted cactus in the peace corner. And if I need a good banging like I've heard at my next-door neighbor's *three days this week*, I should just ditch the plant and go knock on his door.

But no. I am more sensible than that. He could turn me down, and then I'd have to pack up everything and move, just to avoid the humiliation.

Also? I don't even know if he's attractive because I haven't seen his face.

But *someone* finds the man attractive. Moaning, biting, screamingly attractive. Last night I swear the wall was in danger of caving in. That's how hard the headboard shook. *There goes my security deposit*, I thought.

Why not me was my next thought.

Since I can't have sexual satisfaction right now, I go to the garden store instead. I gaze at the outdoor furniture I can't afford and then buy a bushy plant.

It's only when I get home that I realize how big the plant is. I can barely hold onto it. It's taking all my strength—carefully cultivated over the years by pursuing camera-ready muscles—just to wrestle the plant into the lobby. I poke the elevator button with my elbow, and I am immediately rewarded by the doors opening.

Hallelujah.

"Hey, hold that?" a deep voice says before the doors close.

"Well..." If I had my hands free, I'd be happy to. But all I can manage is to balance on one foot and thrust the other one out to stop the halt of the elevator doors.

"Ouch! Fuck," rumbles that voice as my foot collides with something hard.

I experience a strange little shimmy in my chest before it dawns on me that I just hurt someone. "Sorry! I'm trying. Couldn't see you."

My arms are starting to shake. And the plant's green fronds are so dense that I can't see a thing in front of me. Basically, I've become a plant with feet.

As I tuck myself into the corner of the elevator, I realize two things. One, there's a heady scent of masculine aftershave in the elevator. Like leather and strength. I sense the dude's attractiveness the way that characters in movies sense dead people: I just *know*. And two, I can't push the elevator button.

"Could you punch five for me?" I murmur. I hope he can hear me through the pounding of my heart and the rustling of fronds.

"I'm on five too," he rumbles. And I mean *rumbles*. I feel his voice in my loins and that's when I suddenly understand. *Holy shit*—I'm sharing the elevator with my neighbor. The one who has loud sex with great frequency on the other side of my wall.

"Five," I breathe, as if it's something sexy. Because right now it is.

"You must be my new neighbor," he says.

How does he know that? Has he been listening to me too? I do a quick inventory of the week's activities. I ate a lot of Greek yogurt and watched some TV. It could be worse, I suppose. There was also that reenactment of a fight scene from *Star Wars*. Hopefully he didn't misinterpret the grunting.

"How'd you know?" I ask.

"There's only one other apartment on our floor, and that one belongs to Miss Havisham."

Ohhhhh. He's literary. "Miss Havisham?" I ask.

"Well, I don't know her real name. She doesn't introduce herself when I say hello. But I've only ever seen her in slippers. You're not wearing slippers."

"Of course not." I'm wearing kickass fuck-me boots. Just, you know, what I wear when I'm running out to get pizza or an enormous plant for my sad, blank apartment.

"Look," he says. "If you hear comings and goings in my apartment at night—"

I freeze. Are we going to discuss his sex life right now? Omigod!

"—Just know that I'm a cop. I work weird shifts, okay? I'll try to be quiet, but sometimes I roll in at five a.m."

"A cop..." I breathe. And then something clicks. That voice. That heady, masculine scent. The elevator lurches. I readjust my grip on the plant. But I'm losing my grip on reality. Because now I know who my new neighbor is.

"The name is Maguire. Or just Mac." He then parts my fronds with his big hand.

Mmmm. He parts my fronds. That sounds dirty.

Focus, Meg! He wants to shake hands!

But I can only stare at the big hand in front of my face. "Kinda holding an enormous plant here."

I hear him chuckle, and then the weight of the plant is lifted away from me as he grabs it with only one arm. Then he offers me his hand to shake again. And I notice his foot is already holding the door of the elevator open, ensuring that it won't close on us.

What a great neighbor I have! This dude has the sexiest voice on the planet, he grunts while fucking, and his limbs are multitalented.

Our hands clasp. And that's when I feel it—that crackle of tension. We have the kind of instant chemistry that's hard to ignore. I'm too young to have hot flashes, but when his thick fingers close around my hand, I feel a surge of heat and awareness. An actor's first job is to notice people, so I know chemistry when I see it.

And so does he. Our gazes lock, and his is very familiar. But now there's recognition dawning there. "It's *you*." The words come out soft and low. "The Wench."

"Hi, Chippendale," I whisper.

He grins. He's still holding my hand. Neither one of us wants to let go. I look down at our joined hands, and he does that trick with his thumb, where he slips it past the pulse point on my wrist.

Oh my. This is wonderful. This is also terrible. My neighbor is a sexy cop. A sexy cop with a *girlfriend*.

Just like that, I take my hand back. As we both step out of the elevator, I whip out my keys, so I can reclaim that plant and cool my head. And other body parts.

When I moved home to Michigan, I vowed never to date, screw, or flirt with anyone who was attached in any way. My ex turned out to be married, and I'm never making that mistake again. This is new Meg. Meg 2.0. Meg who-is-thirty-and-done-with-losers. And I'm ready for a real commitment.

I unlock my door in record time. "Thanks for holding that. I can take it from here."

"Nah, I got it," he says, stepping right into my apartment, uninvited.

Dammit! Now he's in my space. He's going to leave behind some of the testosterone that rises off of him like a mist.

"Where were you putting this?" he asks.

"Right there," I snap, pointing at the spot under his feet.

"Really?" he scratches his chin. "The feng shui can be better optimized over here, I think." He carries the plant to a corner of the living room.

I blink. "What quadrant is that?"

"Health, career, and luck with parking spaces."

I blink again. My neighbor, the hot cop, knows about feng shui? *Swoon!*

No! No swooning. He *has a girlfriend*. Of course he does. I think I might cry. "Okay," I say with a gulp. "Better put 'er there. Thank you."

"Anytime," he says in that gruff, wonderful voice.

I'm doomed.

3 SHE MIDDLE-NAMED ME

Maguire

What's wrong with me? I'm actually looking around for reasons to keep standing here in my neighbor's apartment? She blinks at me, her expression cool. I've outstayed my welcome already. "You have a good day, now," I grunt.

"You too, neighbor."

Lordy. And here I thought I'd left my teen years behind more than a decade ago. But apparently not. I give her one more longing glance, and an awkward wave. The stunning serving wench from Ye Olde Tavern is my new neighbor?

I am shook.

The effect she has on me is inconvenient, to put it mildly. There's a naughty sparkle in her dark brown eyes. There's something about the way she tosses her head, sending her corkscrew curls swinging against the smooth brown skin of her kissable neck...

It's not easy to make neighborly conversation when your libido is firing up like a 400 horsepower engine. It's lucky I didn't mispronounce my own name. All I can think about after I see my new neighbor is ditching my current hookup and taking this woman to bed instead.

Maybe we wouldn't even make it that far. Her coffee table looked sturdy.

I saw it in her eyes, too, if only for a second. She feels the pull. If we'd met under different circumstances, I might already know how much weight that table could bear.

But I do the sane thing and make myself scarce.

Back in the hallway, I try to shut that shit down. *It's just an impulse*, I remind myself. And I can't afford to live by my impulses. That's my brother's strategy. He lives by impulse and nearly destroyed me in the process. I have to be the better man.

It's just rotten luck that my new neighbor is the unforgettable serving wench from Ye Olde Tavern. The one who within five seconds of meeting me tried to rip my clothes off. What kind of man is immune to that?

Not this kind.

She'll never know that I've been looking for her. My partner Lance and I have a deal. We take turns choosing the bar we go to after work. And I've chosen Ye Olde Tavern three times, hoping to run into her. Lance is probably onto me. "What's with your sudden love of turkey legs?" he asked me last time.

"They're...meaty," was all I could think of to say. He'd laughed.

Oh, and I've endured a mountain of ribbing over my neighbor's assumption that I was a stripper. But it was an honest mistake. And after my last turkey leg, I finally asked the waitress if she knew where the dark-eyed beauty with the fake English accent had gone.

"She quit," I was told.

But here she is again, just as sexy and startling as the first time I saw her.

I still don't even know her name. Just now, I was too startled to remember to ask her. So I'm just going to call her Trouble, because I can just feel like that's what she is. For me at least. Because a guy who doesn't like attachments can't boink his neighbor. If things go badly, you gotta move out of the building. Maybe even the whole neighborhood. I like this neighborhood. It's close to work. And the breakfast special at Hot and Crusty is only $3.99.

These are my thoughts as I unlock my own door. Whatever fire is trying to ignite between me and Trouble is not important. I should just blow that shit out.

Of course, now I'm thinking about blowing.

Those legs, though. And that smile. If my dick had any say in the matter, I'd already be peeling those jeans off her.

I open my own door and remind myself that I have a fuck buddy already. It's casual, of course, but we're a good fit. I close my eyes and think about her for a second. Nicole Nicole Nicole.

Maybe I should call her. I mean, she just left my apartment a few hours ago. So that would probably be weird.

A cold shower it is, then.

Grumpy for no reason, I step inside my apartment. It's clean and orderly, just the way I like things. I tug the mail out of my back pocket and toss it onto the countertop. I pull a beer out of my refrigerator, open it, and then sort the mail so it doesn't become clutter. There's a cable bill and a postcard offering me a free tire rotation with purchase of an oil change.

But the third envelope is the one I really don't want to open. It's fancy, which is the first clue that I'll hate what's inside. It's also made from paper with little bits of flowers and seeds trapped in the weave. I didn't even know that was a thing.

My name is swirled across the front in calligraphy, which seems like a waste. My own sister paid someone to write my name so that I look like the king of England. MACKLIN JAMES MAGUIRE.

She even middle-named me. And everyone knows that when your family uses your middle name, there's no getting around them.

With a sigh, I use my thumb to tear open the fancyass envelope, ripping it open to reveal two fancyass cards and yet another envelope inside. The cards are edged in gold, too. There are villages somewhere that could eat for a week on what this piece of mail cost.

And none of that would offend me at all, except for one simple fact: I really do not want to attend my sister's wedding.

Don't get me wrong, I love my sister. I see her every week for lunch. I don't know much about this guy she's marrying, but he isn't the problem, either.

It's the rest of my family. Ten years ago I excused myself from family holidays and events. That was necessary to save my own sanity. But now that Rosie is getting married, I will probably have to show up to this thing and be civil.

My beer is half gone already. Huh.

The wedding date is in a couple of months. That gives me a few weeks grace period to pretend like it isn't happening. Or does it? There's a reply card, which I will probably fail to fill out. Rosie knows I won't blow off her wedding. But aside from the "will attend" and "won't attend" boxes, there's a line to enter the name of my date.

I don't have a date.

Christ, I *need* a date.

I cannot show up to this thing alone.

In addition to a date, I also need a new suit, a promotion at work, and probably a new personality.

The first thing is doable. The second is possible. The third is a nonstarter.

There's one more slip of paper in the envelope, containing instructions. *Place your seed paper on soil, and cover with 1/8 inch of additional soil. Give it a good drink of water! After that, make sure it's always moist and in a sunny spot. You should see sprouts within 7–10 days!*

Fuck me, now I've seen everything. This wedding invitation is inviting me to bury it in the ground. I scoop it up—including the response card and its envelope—and carry it out onto my deck. There's a pot of dirt there already from last year's petunias.

Good enough.

Two minutes later I've buried the wedding invitation. After draining my beer, I refill the bottle with water and soak the whole business.

That was seriously therapeutic. Now if I could also repurpose my asshole brother the same way...

My phone rings in my pocket. The caller is Nicole. That's a little weird. We don't know each other very well, and we don't usually call each other. "Hello?"

"Hi, Maguire," she says. "I'm really sorry to bother you. But I'm having a bit of a crisis."

Uh-oh. I do have a weakness for a damsel in distress. "What's the problem?"

"When I got home I found that my apartment is flooded. A pipe broke upstairs."

"Oh hell." I shudder in sympathy. I hate chaos. "You need help moving something?"

"Not exactly. I spent the last couple hours getting the property manager involved, and the cleanup has already begun. But I can't stay here tonight. They're ripping out all the carpeting and drying the place out. My renters' insurance is offering me a night at Motel 72 on Division. Is that a safe neighborhood?"

"Well, no," I growl. "A woman shouldn't stay there alone. That's all they'll do for you?"

"It's eight o'clock on a Friday, though. They said I could call back on Monday and ask."

I can't stand the idea of her staying in that shithole all weekend. We see drugs and prostitution at that motel all the time. "Come here instead," I hear myself saying.

There's a silence before she speaks again. "That's really generous, Maguire. You don't have to do that."

"I know," I say, wondering if I'll regret it later. "But it's okay. Couple 'a nights, right? We can be roommates." She doesn't even have to know how weird that will be for me. I haven't had a woman stay over in my space more than a few times in ten years.

But it's the right thing to do. Even if Nicole and I aren't going anywhere as a couple.

"You're a good man, Mac Maguire."

Good enough, I suppose. And it's just occurring to me that I'm about to have a lot of sex. Nicole and I don't hold back when we're together. And sharing a bed for a couple of nights? "Come right over."

This good guy is going to have a fun and dirty weekend.

4 THAT'S NOT A LEG

Meg

"Do all the McAllister kids know how to cook?" I ask Cassidy as she peeks into my oven at the chicken she made. She mixed it with a dry rub of Indian spices before roasting it. Then she made a cucumber salad with yogurt and cherry tomatoes.

I keep her wine glass full and just watch.

"Yep. We all cook because our parents can't. No lie." She closes the oven door and rolls her eyes. "They hire everything out. In the days before Grubhub, that meant paying a personal chef or sending the nanny to fetch takeout. So we all grew up wishing for the home-made food on our friends' tables. And now we all cook. Liam is prob-ably the best, though."

I've seen Liam in action in my sister's kitchen. It's pretty sexy, I have to admit. There's something about having a man cook for you.

"Are your parents excellent cooks?" Cassidy asks.

"They are," I admit.

"That's probably why you aren't. Just saying."

"Oh," I say slowly. "Is that also why I'm not an overachiever? Oh, wait—my sister is, though." She's a shrink with her own practice. "Can achievement skip a generation?"

"That's an interesting question, but…" Cassidy breaks off. "Did you hear that?" she whispers. "It sounded like moaning."

Ooh! It's showtime, apparently. I clap my hands together, then beckon, urging my friend closer to the screen door.

Cassidy's pale eyebrows lift. "Omigod," she whispers. "Are they starting up?"

In the two weeks I've lived here, I've heard more sex than a sound tech on a porn shoot. Clearly the cop next door and his girlfriend are sex fiends. She lives there now, too! I've spotted her in the hallway, arriving home from work, a shiny new key in her hand and a happy smile on her face.

I'd be happy too if I were getting it from Mr. Stamina every few hours. I swear, they're like rabbits on steroids. Every night as I lay in bed, I can hear all the dirty things he whispers to her. *Put your hands up. Do as I say. Ride me, sugar.*

Just thinking about his deep, gruff voice makes me feel all tingly.

And that nickname? *Sugar.* He must really love her.

Sigh.

Cassidy has heard all about the sexual soundtrack in apartment 503, although she hasn't experienced it. She won't right now, either. Because the sounds next door aren't sex. There are a couple of unfamiliar bumps to the wall. And I hear the girlfriend's voice.

But not his voice. Hot Cop is disappointingly silent. Ah, well.

"So tell me about your new man," I say, wiping down the countertop.

"Oh." Cassidy's face is solemn. "Date number two is coming up."

"God, could you look any less excited?"

"It's early," she says flatly. "We don't really know each other yet."

Oh dear. Her lack of enthusiasm tells me everything I need to know. But I can sense that Cassidy isn't ready to hear it. "Well, if you've snagged a good man in your life, it's my turn next."

"Deal," she says.

"I could make the thin walls shake, too."

"Loudly," she agrees.

Although that only makes me think of Maguire next door. Would it be too much to ask if the man I end up dating looked like him?

———

WHEN DINNER IS READY, I plate everything up and carry it ten paces to the living area, where I've set out napkins and silverware on the new coffee table. "Thanks for cooking. I feel spoiled."

"Anytime." Cassidy sits down on the couch beside me. "Well? Tell me how it tastes. And then tell me what's happening with the Chicago audition."

I take a bite of chicken. It's succulent and spicy. "This is terrific. Wow." The cucumber salad is a nice contrast, too.

"You didn't answer both questions."

"I'm avoiding my email, to be honest. My agent sent something, but I'm afraid to read it."

Cassidy sets down her fork at once. "Where is it? I'll look. I have a good feeling about this one."

If only I did, too. Right before I moved into this apartment, I drove to Chicago to audition for a tampon commercial. Don't laugh. A single tampon commercial can earn enough for a house if it gets enough airplay. Cassidy rode along with me for fun, and to do some shopping.

We ended up staying an extra day, though, because I got a callback. And then another one. By the time they were done with me, it was down to three women, and they said they'd be in touch.

Today.

I take another bite of chicken and sigh. Then I fish the phone out from under the couch cushion, unlock it, and open my email. While it's tempting to make Cassidy read it for me, I'm a big girl.

A big girl staring at bad news.

Megan, we loved meeting you! And we were impressed with your poise. But ultimately we went in another direction.

Wordlessly, I hand the phone to my guest.

"Oh!" she gasps. "No! I was so sure. This is awful. How *could* they? I mean, when you were pretending you had those cramps, I totally believed you! I tried to give you ibuprofen and rub your head, remember?" As I watch, Cassidy's eyes get red.

Mine don't, though. I've had a good ten years to get used to this kind of rejection. "It happens to every actress. Even Emma Watson."

It must. Or at least it used to. Maybe.

Though I can't really see Emma Watson selling tampons.

Cassidy tosses the phone onto the couch between us. "I'm disgusted for you. Those other women were so *boring*. I wouldn't buy a sandwich from them. Let alone something *intimate*. Don't you think?"

"I think…" I set my fork down, too. "There's no way to tell you what I think without sounding like a crazy person. But it's starting to get to me."

"What is?"

"I'm tired of wondering why I don't get cast. Is it my talent? Is it my preparation? Or is it my skin color. I mean—they say they want diverse casting, you know? But what they really mean is a really tan white girl and not an actual woman of color."

"Shit," Cassidy whispers. And this girl never swears. "I think that would make me crazy, too."

"Sometimes it's all I think about," I confess. "Leading roles are very white. It's even more true for women than men."

Cassidy chews slowly. "But Meg. You're *so* beautiful. And talented! I just don't understand why you're not cast in anything you show up for."

"That is a very nice thing to say. But beauty is subjective. And it's also making me crazy."

It was my choice, though, to pick a job where looks matter so much. As a consequence, I probably spend more time looking in the mirror than your average accountant or veterinarian. When I do, I see features that are a really nice blend of my mom, who is a white Dutch lady, and my dad, who's Jamaican American. I'm a striking mixture of the two of them. And my gut is 90% sure that it's holding back my acting career.

But it's even more complex than that. Sometimes, casting wants someone who is ethnic but not *too* ethnic. Take my sister, Sadie. People think she's Indian, or Spanish, or just really tan. She has a golden hue that's quite popular in Hollywood right now. She's ethnic in a way that, to them, is interesting without specificity.

But I look more like our father. I press my hair for auditions, but it naturally has a lot of texture. And my skin tone is darker than

Sadie's. My gut says that a pharmaceutical executive somewhere decided not to alienate his white tampon consumers by putting me in that ad.

Or maybe my audition just wasn't as good as I thought it was. I don't know which. And the soul-killing truth is that I never will.

But I know two things for sure. One: I'm not supposed to say these things out loud. Because it sounds like whining and blaming other people for my career failures.

And two: this kind of circular thinking can really drive a girl insane. Which I know because I'm already there.

"I don't think..." Cassidy says slowly. "I don't think I ever want a job that depends on someone's biased opinion of whether or not I'm pretty."

"You're..." I almost say *you're beautiful*. Because she is. But that's not the point. "You're wiser than I am, then. Because it's a real drag having to trade on your face. And that's why I'm trying to find something else to do with my life. I need to get off the audition treadmill before I lose my mind."

We both pick up our wine glasses at the same time. I take a deep gulp.

"What's the weirdest thing anyone ever said to you at an audition?" Cassidy asks.

I let out a sigh. "Usually they don't bother telling you why you didn't get a callback. They just say 'Next!' But one time I handed over my audition card and the woman said—'We already have a black girl.'"

Cassidy makes a horrified gulping sound and then chokes on her sip of wine. So I pound her on the back.

Me, I don't choke anymore. I just get sad.

When I was in my early twenties, rejection didn't bother me so much. I knew success wouldn't be easy, and I was prepared to wait. But lately I'm just tired. I'm no longer sure if I'm auditioning out of love or out of pure stubbornness.

How do you know when it's time to give up? What should I do with the rest of my life?

I don't think those answers are going to find me tonight. Right

now I just want to drink this wine and eat good food with my friend.
It's a good start.

"Oooooh."

When the first moan arrives, I don't even hear it. I've grown
accustomed to living in a sex palace.

"Aaaaaah! Aaaaah!" the woman next door says. She sounds like
she's stepping into really cold water.

But Cassidy sits up straight, her eyes popping wide.

"YES! YES! YES! YES! HARDER!" screams the woman next
door.

"Oh my," Cassidy says, blinking behind her glasses. "That's...loud."

"Trust me, it's louder in my bedroom. Or on the deck." And I
should know.

Cassidy fans herself. "Maybe we should leave. I feel like a pervert
right now."

"Pfft!" I wave away her objection. "Finish your dinner. Besides,
you're just walking a mile in my proverbial kicks. It's like this *every*
night, and some of the daytime hours, too. Just wait until the finale."

I get up and head for the kitchen to bus my plate. The sound of
Hot Cop's lucky girlfriend grows even louder.

But I don't hear his voice this time. That's unusual. Where are his
gruff commands? The manly grunting? And then the panty-dropping
moment of silence before his satisfied moan?

And—sue me—I miss it. That voice stars in all my dirty fantasies
these days. I don't even feel guilty, either. If he didn't want me to
hear, he'd keep it down. He's lived here longer than I have. He must
know how sounds carry.

Then his girlfriend starts barking. Actually barking. Cassidy and I
look at each other, wide-eyed, and then bust out laughing.

"Oh, wait!" I say, barely being able to speak. "That's an actual dog.
I think."

Cassidy surprises me then. "Let's go find out for sure!"

I look at her for a beat. This is not the Cassidy I've grown to
know and love. Cassidy is a rule-follower. A good girl. Then I notice
that her hair is starting to come out of its topknot. And her cheeks
are flushed. This is drunk Cassidy. All hail drunk Cassidy!

"Okay, let's!" I agree.

———

FIVE MINUTES LATER, they're still going at it. Which is good, because that is how long it's taken me to convince Cassidy to strap on my old rock-climbing gear. I'm holding the pulley system with a carabiner. The plan is that I'll hold onto her, secured with climbing gear, while she leans out as far as she can around the divider. With the binoculars, she should *just* be able to see into the apartment. If the windows are open.

Please, lord, let them be open.

"Oh, I don't know about this," Cassidy says as I check the straps.

"Shush. Drink this. It's Courage Juice."

"It's wine," she says, clearly not fooled.

"Whatever. It's Friday night and this is the most exciting thing to happen in either of our lives since *Aquaman* hit the theaters."

Cassidy nods. It's go time.

"Climb over the railing now," I whisper.

She puts a foot on my folding chair and lifts herself up.

I might be officially drunk right now, but it's okay because I've secured the climbing gear around my own body. I have so many questions. Did Hot Cop get a dog? Or are they doing a little bit of role play? And why is he so quiet?

Wait. Maybe the girlfriend is home alone? Is there such thing as a barking vibrator?

Ew.

"Cassidy," I whisper. I'm in a deep lunge and Cassidy is slowly leaning over the balcony. "Cassidy!" I try again. I'm straining all my muscles to hold the rope in exactly the right position.

She's carefully focusing the binoculars. When Cassidy is on task, there's little that can distract her. Not even earthquakes or orgasms, or both.

"I can see them!" she whispers back. But it's one of those stage whispers that's actually incredibly loud. Drunk people aren't subtle.

"Is it just her?" I ask. This lunge is starting to burn. I really need to work out more. Or at all. I give a little more slack on the rope.

"Nope. There's two of them! And hooooo boy!" Cassidy gives me the thumbs up.

I have never wanted to see anything so badly.

"Your cop friend is really skinny," she says. "Or is she a giant?"

"What?" My cop...my next-door neighbor is not a small man. He's huge. I imagine all of him is huge.

"So scrawny! I thought you said he was hunky?"

Even though I'm drunk right now, something clicks into place. There is sex happening next door, in Hot Cop's apartment. But Hot Cop isn't the one who's having it.

Holy hell! Hot Cop's girlfriend is cheating!

"Omigosh!" Cassidy cries. She's really leaning out over forty-five feet of airspace, now. "Is this what it's like to watch porn?"

"You don't *know?*" I ask, forgetting to whisper. We have got to get this girl some more life experience.

She leans out a little farther, and now I'm starting to question our life choices. "You have to come back now," I say, straining in my harness. "You're heavier than you look." She has a glassy look in her eye, though. "Cassidy, don't go toward the light."

"He's got three legs!" She sounds overjoyed.

"Three legs?" What the...

Then Cassidy realizes her mistake. "OH MY GOD THAT'S NOT A LEG! It's not a leg!! Abort mission! Pull me in! Pull me in!!"

I'm using all my strength to pull her back. But that's difficult when you're both drunk and dying of laughter. Who is this skinny, little man with a penis so large that Cassidy thought it was another appendage? There's no way that it's my cop.

I give one final heave, and Cassidy reels back toward me. I try to catch her. I really do. But momentum is a scary thing. The moment she lands in my arms, we both just crash to the deck, a jumble of ropes and limbs and shrieks of laughter.

That's when I hear the skitter of claws coming toward us on the other side of the fence. "ARF ARF ARF ARFFFF!" yips a dog.

"YES YES YES!" screams the neighbor lady.

She doesn't even care. She's banging a skinny dude with a dog, while her boyfriend is at work, and I am not okay with it. Does she not know how good she has it? Does she not know how hard it is to find a gruff-voiced dirty talker who holds your plant in the elevator?

Is she out of her mind?

I stand up and dust myself off. I'm disgusted for Mac Maguire. But on the plus side, I think I've finally figured out what I want to do with my life, at least short-term. There's something rare in Hot Cop's gray eyes, and it makes me want to help him. I know what it feels like to be lied to. He needs to know the truth. And she needs to go.

My new mission in life: take that bitch down.

5 TOO ABRUPT

Maguire

"She's not my girlfriend," I say for the hundredth time to Lance. "Eyes on the property."

We're on stakeout in a quiet neighborhood. Not my favorite job duty. We're sitting in an unmarked car outside a car repair shop. My boss is waiting on a search warrant for this property, and it's our job to make sure the perp doesn't leave the premises with stolen goods or light the place on fire before the search can begin.

It's an important job, but not an exciting one. And worse, it gives Lance a lot of time to hassle me about my personal life.

"Does she stay overnight?"

"Yes," I say reluctantly.

"Does she sleep in your bed?"

"Define sleep?"

"In the middle of the night, if you wanted some action, could you move your hand between her velvet thighs and stroke her quivering core until she's begging for your thick, throbbing..."

"HEY!" I bark, shutting him up. "This is my real life, not one of your books."

Lance has not had a girlfriend in a while. He listens to erotic romance audiobooks instead. Sometimes, he plays me excerpts of his favorites.

"But hypothetically," he presses.

"Hypothetically, no," I grumble. "She's staying in the guest room. We only share a bed when we're gettin' it on."

"*What?*" he gasps. "You made that girl sleep in the other room? For this long?"

"That's not weird," I say. "We're not playing house."

"Dude." He shakes his big silly head. "That is super weird. But it doesn't matter. In the next chapter, you'll realize you're fooling yourself. It will happen any second now. Maybe when you're trapped in an elevator together. Or it might happen when she defends you from your crazy ex."

"I don't have a crazy ex," I say pointlessly.

"Um, yes you do." He gives me a pitying glance. "Anyway. It might happen when you rescue her from a warehouse fire, or from the alpha dog of a neighboring wolf pack…"

I groan. His taste in genre fiction is far-ranging. "If she was a shapeshifter, I would already know at this point."

"That's what you think. Have you ever been together during a full moon?"

This is what I have to deal with on a daily basis.

"Either way," he says. "One day soon you'll look at her and it will all fall into place."

"Nope. Sorry." I'm not fooling myself at all. Nicole is not my girl-friend, even though her two-night stay has turned into a couple of weeks. But it hasn't made me have any Big Realizations. It's only made me itchy. "She's very fond of my handcuffs, though. Honestly, my whole life is a cliché."

"Clichés are not all bad," Lance says. "I could use me some heaving bosoms right now. They'd be more fun than your grumpy ass."

He's right. My ass is grumpy, because I'm living with someone I don't really love. I need to break it off with her, which is a shame because I still need a date for my sister's wedding.

But I can't. I realize that now. It would send the wrong signal to Nicole.

I can feel my anxiety start to ratchet up. I need a good work-out. Or a good fuck. And not with Nicole. Somehow, when I'm with her, it's sorta like being alone. We aren't connecting at all, except, obviously, in the physical way. Truth is, I need my space back.

Maybe I just need out of this damn squad car.

If I get the promotion I want, I wouldn't have to do stakeouts anymore. In fact, it might change the entire trajectory of my life.

"Hey, I have a question for you," I say to Lance.

"And I have an answer! It's true. I *can* actually fuck a woman three different ways AT THE SAME TIME. This is why you need to stop reading that dipshit Whatshisname, and start reading some real books. You'll actually learn something."

There's a lot to unpack there.

The "dipshit" he's referring to is Hemingway. I read Hemingway. I read classics in general. Actually, I read something from the canon, and then I read something from the NY Times Bestseller list. It's all about balance.

"That was not my question," I say, though I've almost forgotten what my question is. "Why do you think they keep passing me over for the taskforce promotion?"

I assume Lance will mull that one over. Chew on it a little bit. But nope. Big nope. "You're Mr. Closed-Off. You're too abrupt. You have the social intelligence of a cardboard box. You don't think inside the box...you sit in a box, then draw a box around yourself then you think inside THAT."

Huh.

"But none of that matters. I'm a cop. Cops report facts. I do it well."

Lance shakes his head. "You are a terrific cop. But if you believe that's the only thing that matters, you're super gullible. And I bet you believe them when they say *Oh, I totally came!*" Lance makes his voice go all feminine like and then he starts laughing.

Me? Too abrupt for a promotion? Thinking inside the box? That is a lot of bullshit. And *they totally came*. I'd know.

Although...one hookup complained that I wasn't "emotionally available." I told her all my emotions were located in my dick and if she sat on it, she'd know everything she needed to know about me.

For the record, I was joking.

A cop does not need to be emotionally available. I don't know what the hell Lance is talking about.

I also sort of want to know how to fuck someone three ways at the same time. Seems like that would require imagination. Or dexterity.

Just as I'm trying to picture it, three cruisers roll down the street, lights on.

"The warrant came through," Lance says.

"You think?" I roll my eyes as the radio crackles, and my boss's voice starts giving instructions.

We're relieved of our duties.

"Lunch?" Lance asks.

"Sure."

"Where do you want to go? And don't say Ye Olde Tavern."

"I'm done with that place," I promise him.

If only I was done thinking about my neighbor.

6 BOXERS, CUFFLINKS, AND A LITTLE B&E

Meg

Life sure is a lot more interesting when you have a mission. Or a role to play. That's one of the reasons I've always enjoyed acting. It gives me purpose. Makes me feel more alive.

It's two days after the big discovery, and I'm on my way home from work. My new job is at another restaurant—The Hip Burger. It's the same grind as at all my other food service jobs, except here I get to wear shorts and a T-shirt and tennis shoes. It's all about comfort now. And tips, of course. It's a high-turnover bar, so what I lose in huge bills for bridal showers, I gain in serving quick meals to people who leave obnoxious piles of cash behind because they're too drunk to calculate the tip.

My bank account had a good night. And I'm still a little wired. So instead of heading straight home, I hit the 24-hour Meijer for a little late-night shopping. After all, a good theater production needs props. Tomorrow could be a big moment for me.

Operation Sting the Bitch is on.

I'm more determined than ever to ensnare Maguire's cheating girlfriend in her own trap. These past two days, I've seen two different dudes make their way to Maguire's apartment when he's not home. Don't ask me how I know. Let's just call it research for the moment I eventually play someone creepy on a Lifetime movie.

And let's just say these men aren't watching TV with Maguire's girlfriend. Those visits have a soundtrack of their own.

It seems odd to me that Maguire doesn't know his cherry is banging a bunch of sundaes. He's a cop, right? He should pick up on these things. Maybe he's just too in love with her to be able to accept reality.

So I've decided that reality will accept him instead.

At Meijer, I take my time picking out a few items that will serve as clues. Surely, as a cop, he'll be able to read the story I'm telling. Just to be safe, I choose a pair of boxers with *HOT TAMALE* printed on the crotch. This is no time for subtleties. He must understand that something is up. And it's not him.

I also grab a few other key props, including a slingshot. Don't judge me. I have a plan. I've spent many hours devising my strategy, and it's brilliant.

Also, I really need some direction in my life.

———

THE NEXT MORNING, it hurts to wake up. But I've set my alarm for the ungodly hour of seven, when I can be sure to catch Hot Cop at home.

And sure enough, I can hear the low rumble of Maguire's voice through the wall. It's my favorite sound these days, so I manage to peel myself off the bed and make myself vertical.

Since I've laid out my tools ahead of time, it takes mere seconds to silently open the door to the deck and assume the attack position. But first, some recon. I can hear Maguire's voice clearly now. It's a warm morning, and his deck door is open, too.

He's on the phone, I think. "This perp has a system. He steals keys from the valet stand. Uh-huh. When the garage guy steps away. Yeah. Pull the camera footage. Bet you anything it's the same guy."

Oh, swoon! My favorite cop is going to nail a bad guy. If he won't nail me, I guess this is the next best thing. I feel some flutters down below already. I can picture him right now, his shirt sleeves rolled up on muscular forearms. His cup of coffee in hand. He drinks it black, of course. He's pacing around his apartment, pecs rippling...

My fantasy life might be running away with me. It's time for action. I pick up the slingshot and load it with the hot tamale boxers. Then I listen carefully to that sexy voice. The moment it dampens—meaning he's turned his back to me—I stand up, lift the slingshot over the fence and fire.

Then I move to the one spot in the fence where a knothole leaves a peeping space in the fence, to see how I've done.

Success! The boxers have flown about eight feet through the air, and fluttered to a landing on the deck boards. Meanwhile, Maguire's voice does not break rhythm. I've launched my attack undetected.

I'm just congratulating myself when I hear the enemy approaching. She announces herself with the tap tap tap of high heels crossing the floor.

Crap!

I hold my breath and continue to peer through the knothole. It's a terrible view, but it's enough to see a pair of pumps cross the deck. I hear a gasp. And then a hand plucks the boxers from where they landed.

There's a flurry of movement. And that bitch chucks the boxers right off the railing. Then she leaves the deck.

A moment later, when I look over the railing, I see them on the ground, four flights down.

My first attack has failed. But this is far from over.

"See you at the shift meeting," Maguire's voice says. "Yeah, I'm on until four. Later."

This isn't over.

It's time for coffee, and then I'll plan the second wave of my attack.

———

"THE BOXERS WERE TOO BIG. Too obvious," I tell Cassidy. "But it's fine, because he gets off work at four. And I have more props."

"What now? Briefs? Tube socks? A used condom would really get the point across."

"Ew! Cassidy. I'm running a classier operation here. The cufflinks are up next."

"Wait, cufflinks? Really? So, in this scenario, she's banging a seventy-year-old Frenchman. Or the best man at someone's wedding."

"Honey, you need to get out more. Plenty of men still wear cuff-links." Don't they? The romantic in me sure hopes they do. "Cuff-links are classy. And this is subtle. I have a good feeling about the cufflinks."

"Go easy on the slingshot," Cassidy advises. "If you're not careful you could launch that sucker into next week."

"I have a plan for that."

"Of course you do. I'm going to need a full report."

"You'll get one." Of course she will. This is more fun than I've had in ages.

My plan has to wait a couple of hours, though. There's a guy mowing the lawn behind our building. He's wearing earphones and chewing gum like maybe it's his first day off cigarettes. He doesn't glance up at me once.

But still, I have to be careful. Bystanders would consider my actions suspicious.

Because—fine—it's not exactly normal behavior to push a stepladder up against the fence and study your neighbor's deck table. And when the landscaper leaves, I do exactly this. With one of the cufflinks in my hand, I brace myself on the ladder, gripping the fence tightly. I take a deep breath. Then I extend my arm and use a low, underhand toss to send the cufflink toward the table.

Plink. It gives one heart-stopping bounce on the surface of the table before landing a few inches from the edge.

"Yes!" I squeal, admiring my work. It's glinting in the sun. In a few hours, my guy will come home, get a beer out of his fridge, and come outside to enjoy it.

Then he'll *know.*

My fantasy spools onward, and it goes like this: Hot Cop will confront his girlfriend tonight. She will tearfully confess. "I don't deserve you," she'll weep.

"No, you don't!" I'll say to myself in the living room. Because surely I'll be able to hear everything.

Maguire will do the chivalrous thing and pass her his handker-chief. Sure, handkerchiefs are even less common than cufflinks. But this is my fantasy, dammit. She'll wipe her tears and promise to remember him always. And then she'll take her things and leave.

He'll walk her out to her car. He'll kiss her on the cheek. But that will be it for them.

Pause here for a time lapse. The man needs a few weeks to heal, right? If this were a movie, there would be a montage of Maguire running a few extra miles, sweating out the sadness. And getting drunk with his buddies.

The montage cuts to scenes of me lonely on my sofa, waiting for him.

Then, one day soon, we'll bump into each other in the laundry room. I could speed this up by doing a lot of laundry over the next month. Maybe I'll even volunteer to do Cassidy's. Maguire will show up to launder his cop uniforms.

I'll smile and lend him some fabric softener, while I amuse him with my rapier wit. He'll invite me in for a drink. But before we even leave the laundry room, we'll give in to the chemistry that crackles between us. He'll kiss me up against the dryer stack.

Then he'll do me on the washer during the spin cycle.

It's all taking shape in my mind as I stand there on the stepladder congratulating myself. So at first I don't even notice the crow. He comes in for a landing on the railing of Maguire's deck. Better his than mine, right? Bird poop is no joke.

But then it all goes wrong in the flash of an eye. The crow flaps right onto the table, picks up the shiny cufflink in his mouth and takes off again.

For a second I'm too stunned to react. My jaw hinges open, and I can only stare at the spot where the cufflink was a moment ago. But then I let fly a little shriek of outrage. "You asshole!" I scream at the sky. "You ruined everything!"

And now I'm that crazy lady, standing on a ladder, peeping into her neighbor's deck, and yelling like a banshee.

Hastily I climb back down onto my own side and haul the ladder into my apartment. But I'm steaming. So close to victory! Ruined by a bird whose brain is smaller than a walnut.

On the kitchen counter, I find the other cufflink. I could do the same thing again. But what if the toss goes wrong? Or the bird comes back? Or the bird has friends?

That's it. No more Ms. Nice Guy. I'm going to get this done for good. My heart rate is elevated, and my ovaries are ready to claim the man who is rightfully mine.

I want justice. And I want to kiss Hot Cop in the laundry room. So I'm going straight to the nuclear option before common sense steps in to stop me.

In my living room, I toe out of my shoes and socks. Then I unlock my door and open it slightly, leaving it ajar. I park my sneaker behind the door, to keep it from swinging wide open. Less than two minutes from now I'm going to need to come back through here.

Tucking the cufflink into the pocket of my shorts, I walk barefoot back through my apartment, grabbing the stepladder on my way. On the deck, I do a quick scan of the property. No landscapers. No neighbors.

It's now or never, then.

I prop the stepladder against the fence and quickly climb it. Bracing my hands on the top, I pop my body over and jump down onto my neighbor's side, landing with cat-like ease.

Or at least that's how I envision myself landing. That's how I'd land if this were a movie. The truth looks more like hanging on for dear life at the top, questioning every choice I've ever made, and then sliding down the other side while trying to avoid splinters in my belly.

I land in a heap on his side of the deck. Ouch.

But never mind. Even if my heart is pounding, I have survived the trip over the fence. If this acting thing doesn't work out, maybe I should consider stunt work?

I cross the deck in a couple of quick strides. As I reach for the screen door handle, I have one moment of terror. Would he lock it? Have I just trapped myself on his side of the deck? Without food or water or shade or—

The door latch opens easily. Phew! I've successfully broken into Hot Cop's apartment. And, wow, it's *very* clean. I knew he was a keeper. There's no clutter at all. Marie Kondo would be impressed.

I take a moment to just stand here and take it all in. Maguire's apartment is very white, like mine used to be. But it looks good on him. There are white bookshelves filled with hardcover classics. *The Sun Also Rises. The Old Man and the Sea.*

My neighbor reads Hemingway! This is shocking and completely obvious at the same time. Hemingway writes gruff, manly stories. He and Maguire could be soulmates. Or at least drinking buddies.

Maguire also has a wall-mounted TV and a video game controller. (Of course he does.) But there's no hulking macho sofa. There's modular, contemporary seating in midnight blue, with dove gray pillows.

If I'm honest, the throw pillows are a revelation. My sister and I have a thing for pillows. It's one of the few proofs that we're related. And here's a man with accent pillows! I feel tingles. I can't wait to tell Sadie.

But, no. I won't be telling Sadie any of this. I've broken into my neighbor's apartment to place evidence of infidelity where he'll find it. Normal, well-adjusted adults probably don't do this sort of thing. So I guess I'd better do my business and get out.

Now where to put the cufflink? The kitchen counter would work. His counter is so freaking clean that it would stand out like a beacon. Unless the cheater comes home first and removes it. Maybe his bedside table is a surer bet? It would reduce the chances of *her* finding it.

So I'm off in search of Maguire's bed. But this causes me a moment of confusion, because I expected this apartment to mirror mine. It doesn't, though. Maguire has two bedrooms. Fancy! The first one is standing open. And I can see a cop's hat on the bureau, so I know it's the right room. I tiptoe inside to choose a bedside table and—

I die. This is not a complete exaggeration. My heart definitely develops a brief arrhythmia because Maguire is *lying on the bed.* He's here! I've just broken into the home of a napping cop.

Omigod, I'm in so much trouble. This is the kind of mistake I might not be able to bounce back from. Is breaking and entering a felony? Will I serve jail time?

At least I look good in orange.

I'm lightheaded suddenly. It's the fear and also the not breathing.

I'm literally afraid to breathe. I take a slow step backward. I can just ease out the way I came. No—not the way I came. I need to leave by the front door.

The escape route is just taking shape in my mind when The Doors start blaring "Light My Fire" from a nearby location. That organ riff shoots right through my consciousness at high volume.

And I scream.

Maguire knifes upward in bed with a warlike shout.

"LIGHT MY FIRE" scream The Doors.

I scream again. It's a real ear-piercer, like the young Drew Barrymore in *E.T.* I drop the cufflink, too.

Maguire is off the bed and in front of me. "What the hell, hot neighbor? Is there a fire?"

"No!" I shriek. "Why?" Should I still run for it? I lean down and grab the cufflink. I can't leave behind any evidence of my insanity.

But he catches my hand in his, the thick fingers making a vice-like grip around my wrist. "What the hell is this?"

"What?" I yell over the music. Playing dumb is my best strategy here. I'll say that I walked into the wrong apartment by mistake. It's ridiculous, since I don't even have a key on me. But if he's sleepy from his nap, I might be able to talk my way out of this.

Maguire lets go of my wrist and steps over to the bureau. The one with the hat on it. I should have known! If he was at work, he'd have his hat with him.

Good lord, this will not end well. I wonder how high my bail will be set? I can already picture the disappointment on my parents' faces when I call them in Oregon for the cash to bail me out.

The blaring music stops suddenly.

There are a number of things I could do in this moment. I could make like a deer and freeze, in the hopes he won't see me. The fact that I'm even considering this is evidence of my instability.

And I was already caught. Literally. He had me by the wrist. Which was strangely nice. I've dreamed of his touch. Although I didn't picture it quite like this.

I basically have two choices: run for it, or flirt my way out of this. Yeah, that second thing. I'm going with that. "Maguire. You called me hot."

And it almost works. He blinks at me, clearly flustered. Or I just scared the shit out of him by waking him up from a dead sleep. It just takes him a second to clear his head. "I did call you hot. That's a truth. But what the fuck are you doing here?"

"Trick or treat?" I ask feebly and then hold out my hand to see if he'll take it again. He doesn't.

Instead, he glares at my hand. I can see something start to burn behind his eyes. And I bet it's indignation. So I decide to come clean. "Look, Copper. Your girlfriend is boinking other men when you're not here. Different men. One of them has a dog, and they let it bark while they boink. And you seem really nice, and you're pretty hot yourself, and it just doesn't seem fair that a nice, hot cop should be treated so poorly."

He blinks. "A dog?"

"Yes!" I shriek. "But, seriously, that's what you take away from all this?"

"I'm allergic."

I throw up my hands in frustration. "Omigod, I'm trying to tell you something important."

"But why break in?" he demands. "You could have knocked on my door like a sane person."

"I. Like. You." I grind out in a crazy voice. "I didn't want to be the one who ruined your day!"

"Aw!" He actually cracks a smile. "So you decided to commit a crime to tell me this? That's so special."

"Ha! No!" I laugh. As if anyone would ever understand my convoluted brain. "I decided to plant evidence so that you would find it and figure out that she's cheating on you. You weren't supposed to know I was involved at all."

His forehead wrinkles. "How'd your plan work out for you?"

I think about it. "Not well. The low point is getting caught. And when I threw the hot tamale boxers over and your princess grabbed them and hid them. Oh. Yeah. And when the crow stole the cufflink..."

"Who wears cufflinks anymore?" he asks.

"Plenty of people! Plenty!"

He grins, but goes silent. I realize he's studying me. No. Wait. He's doing more than studying me. He's performing some kind of cop Jedi magic. I know this because I recently auditioned for a pilot called *Pierson of Interest,* starring Katie Pierson, a cop who gets framed for a murder and... Never mind. It's not important. But I learned that cops like to wait you out, making you so uncomfortable that you confess everything.

Except I already did. "Can I go now?" I ask feebly.

He holds up a finger. It's a nice finger. Sorta strong and sexy. I could do a lot with that finger. "Just a second," he says. "I'm processing."

This time I wait him out. I feel like I should start humming the *Jeopardy* theme song.

"First of all, what's your name?" he asks. His voice is all serious-like. Very *coppy.* The hairs on my arms stand up. If I had a penis, it would be standing up too.

"Meg," I say. I try to say it challenging-like, like a 1930s Film Noir Dame, but it's hard to pack all of that into one syllable. I give it my best shot.

"You realize you are not very good at jumping to conclusions. Or into people's apartments."

My questioning look says it all.

Then he continues. "Think about it. The first time we met, you thought I was a stripper."

"Hey! That does *not* mean I jump to poor conclusions. You *should* be a stripper. You've got the bod for it."

His eyes flare, and there's another awkward pause. He's processing that too. "No," he finally decides. "Not in a million years. I have no sense of rhythm."

I'd like to dispute that, because I've been listening to him have sex over the past month and he's got plenty of rhythm. He's got Fred Astaire rhythm. I hear Fred Astaire had really big hands.

I check Maguire's. He's got really big hands too. *Nice.*

"But the worst conclusion you drew is about Nicole," he says. "She's not my girlfriend."

Oh.

What?

"What?" I ask.

"She's a friend."

"A friend you frequently fuck?" I'm incredulous.

"That is a thing, yes. Although I wonder why even a live-in fuck buddy doesn't bother staying faithful. I'm fucking cursed," he says this last bit more to himself than to me. Then he seems to focus on me again. "I could put you in jail, you know."

"For thinking she was your girlfriend? That's kind of ridiculous. I mean she sleeps here and you have a lot of sex and…"

"How do you know I have a lot of sex?"

I decide to just show the man. I didn't get a BA in theater from Northwestern for nothing. "Oh!" I cry, in a perfect imitation of Nicole. "Baby! Baby baby!! YES YES YES!" Then I put my hands on my hips and grin.

"Wow!" he looks alarmed. "That's eerie."

"Thin walls in this place, Maguire."

"Jesus." That throws him, but not for long. "Still, I could arrest you for breaking into my apartment."

He's got me there. "Would it help if I didn't actually *break* in but more like *fell* in?" I think he's a guy who can appreciate details. I'm trying.

He seems to consider this. He scratches his iron jaw. There's a raspy sound. Suddenly I want to drag my tongue over his jaw and down his neck, rip open his shirt, and…

Why does being around Maguire turn me into a hot mess of hormones? I feel just slightly out of control whenever he's nearby.

I decide to go back to the Film Noir idea. "Listen, Copper," I try, pretty convincingly I think. "Don't lock me in the slammer. Give a dame a chance. Maybe I can do something for you in return. A favor."

The hokey voice I'm using is going to be really embarrassing if he doesn't play along, but suddenly he's all Bogart to my Bacall. "What kind of favor?" he asks smokily.

A sexual favor. I don't say it aloud, because Maguire is the kind of standup guy who wouldn't really ask that. But the idea hovers right there in the room, and neither of us is appalled. Suddenly we're having a sexy staredown. His pretty gray eyes are dilated. Nobody breathes. There's so much electricity here that you could power a small city with it.

Wow. I know I should say something to break the tension. But I'm not sure I want to. "I could..." I swallow hard. "Feed your cat. Do you have a cat?"

"No," he whispers, amusement in those cool eyes.

"Wash your car?" Unzip your pants?

"Just did that myself yesterday."

"Damn." Nobody blinks. "I could make you a sandwich? Lettuce and mayo only, though. It's the only thing I have in my fridge."

He throws back his head and laughs. That finally does it. Now we're both laughing. "Oh, you are trouble, aren't you?"

"Maybe." I wipe my eyes. "But I mean well."

"Actually, I do need a favor."

"Really?" I perk up. "Lay it on me."

His eyes flare at my choice of words. But then they cool again. "You're going to think it's weird."

"I like weird."

"I sensed that."

"So try me." I wait, my curiosity piqued.

He sighs. "I need a date for something. It's a big ask. But you do owe me for all the chaos you've brought into my day. And also for making my colleagues laugh at me that time when you tried to take off my clothes."

"What? You should be laughing at *them*," I argue. "After all, I didn't have the slightest impulse to take off *their* clothes. Just yours."

There's that flicker again. A spark of lust before it's quickly concealed.

I lick my lips. "So what is this date?" It comes out a little breathy. No need to be acting now. It's all natural.

"It's a wedding I've got to attend. And I need a date. Do you think you could convince people we're a couple?"

I inhale quickly. A date with Hot Cop? And all I have to do is *act?* "Honey," I breathe, "if there's one thing I'm good at, it's convincing people to believe in things that aren't real."

And guess what? It's always easier to make the audience believe a fairy tale if it's based on the truth. In this case, it won't be a stretch to pretend to find him attractive.

Another glance at Maguire confirms that he'd be onboard with that, too.

But I do have a question. "Why do you need me to go to a wedding with you? Why not your girlfriend? Er....fuck friend?"

"Nicole?" he asks. "Nah. She's a nice girl, and totally down with the casual thing we've been having. But our thing has run its course. The wedding isn't for a few weeks, anyway. Besides, I'm not sure my family would buy me settling down with her."

"Your...family?" I'd assumed he was trying to impress his cop friends. What's he trying to prove here? I have so many questions. "Why do you need to convince your family that you're in a relationship?"

"I don't want to convince them I'm in a relationship. That's not good enough. I want them to think I'm in love. Or better yet, I'm with a hot chick who fucking adores me. Worships me." He pauses. "Can't wait to rip my clothes off."

"I feel like I've auditioned for this already."

"Auditioned?"

"It's your lucky day, Maguire. Not only do I work as a server, I'm an actor. An actor who pays the rent waiting tables. Big shocker, I know. My life is a cliché."

"Just like mine," he says. He seems like he's about to say something else, but he stops himself.

So I press on. "Why do you need to convince your family that a hot chick worships you?" This guy could have any girl he wants. "It helps me to understand motivation," I offer.

He crosses those tough guy arms. "I just do, Trouble."

"Trouble?"

"That's you. Trouble. And don't ask nosy questions."

Oooh. That means it's serious. Maybe the Maguire clan has a dark secret.

Or maybe I'm just a drama queen. But I'm okay either way. I like Maguire. I wanted adventure. Going with him to a family wedding is like being cast in a live improv show. I fucking love it. Plus, it would be nice to be in love for a night. Even if it's only pretending. And hopefully he'll pretend he worships me too. Goes all moony over me. Every girl deserves a little moon.

"Maguire," I say, lowering my voice just a smidge.

"Yeah?" he asks.

I take a step closer. Reach out my hand and then tug him by the collar so I can whisper in his ear. "I would love to go to your family's wedding with you. Just don't lock me up."

I see his jaw clench so I decide to finish the scene. "But you can cuff me later if you want."

I smile.

He growls a little.

I feel tingles. But I let him go. Step back. Wait.

We just stand there, simmering in our own tension.

"I have to go to work," he says eventually.

"Right now?" I yelp.

"Of course. Hence the nap. I don't get off until—"

"Four," I say, remembering what I overheard earlier. "A.M."

"That's right." He frowns. "The walls are really that thin?"

"They really are. Didn't you ever notice?"

"Your apartment was vacant for a while before you moved in."

"Oh." That explains so much. "So...do you think I could leave out the front door instead of the way I came in?" I ask.

"I think," he says, barely hiding a smile tugging at his luscious lips, "that's probably a good plan."

7   IS THAT A EUPHEMISM?

Maguire

I don't see Meg again for a couple of days. Or, rather, night shifts. Probably a good thing, too. There's just something about her that makes me crazy. I don't know if it's her knowing smile, or her walk. She has swagger, with a side of attitude. I can't get enough.

Every now and then, I imagine walking into my sister's wedding with Trouble on my arm. In my mind, she's wearing something silky and clingy and her nipples are alert beneath the fabric.

I shake that thought off.

And adjust myself.

Ahem.

Now it's Sunday, and my day off. I'm drinking coffee out of a mug that reads: *My bark is worse than my bite*. My sister, Rosie, gave it to me for Christmas. She's on some kind of mission to convince me not to be so grumpy.

By the time you hit thirty-five, though, I'm not sure these things can be changed.

These are my thoughts as I take my famous lemon coffee cake out of the oven and set it on the counter to cool.

The coffee cake is for my sister, at least indirectly. She's having a bridal shower today. The words *bridal shower* pretty much make my balls wither and retreat into my body. But I love my sister so I promised to stop by.

The coffee cake needs to cool for ten minutes or so before I can unmold it from the bundt pan. That gives me just the right amount of time to make the glaze, except for one problem. When I pick up the canister, there's only a trace of sugar left inside.

Fuck.

I suppose a coffee cake doesn't really need a glaze. But it's just so damn good with the lemony, sugary topping. My mouth waters a little just imagining it. But I really don't feel like running all the way to the store right now.

There's one other possible solution, though. A solution with long, tawny legs that have been walking through my dreams all week. And big brown eyes that are always wearing a sassy expression.

Before I can think better of this idea, I open the screen door to my deck, where the radio has been playing all morning. I've been vaguely aware of it as I make my coffee cake.

If by "vaguely" you mean that I've spent the last hour picturing my neighbor sunning herself in a tiny little bikini.

The truth is that my side of the fence has been awfully quiet this week. Nicole left three days ago, moving back into her freshly painted apartment. I never bothered to call her out on her extracurricular activities in my guest room. There was really no point. We shook hands when she left, agreeing that our thing had run its course.

I did vacuum really well, though. And there *were* dog hairs, dammit.

Lately, when I'm trying to sleep at night, it's not Nicole who's keeping me awake. It's a certain perky actor with boundary issues and a big attitude.

That attitude really gets me going.

So here I am standing on the deck like an idiot, wondering how to get her attention. "Hey, Trouble!" I call. "Meg!"

I hear the scrape of a chair as someone rises. With my luck, it will be someone else over there today. She probably has a big brother who is going to wonder why a guy is yelling over the fence like a loon.

But no. Her beautiful face pops over the top of the fence a

moment later, earrings swinging, smile wide. "Officer? Is there a problem? I've been a very good girl."

I choke back a groan. If only she could repeat that statement in my bed. Under me.

"Um..." She must be standing on something right now, and it bugs me that she's now taller than I am. So I overturn a metal flower pot that my sister gave me and step up onto it. Now her bottomless brown eyes are level with mine. "Can I borrow a cup of sugar?"

Her smile grows mischievous. "Is that a euphemism? Please say yes."

I laugh suddenly, and the sound is like a rusty engine coming to life. "No, it's not a euphemism. I'm legit baking a cake and I ran out of sugar for the glaze."

She sniffs the air. "Ooh lemons."

"Exactly. You gotta use fresh, or it's no good."

Meg considers me. "You are a study in contrasts, Copper. I might have some sugar, come around to the front door while I check."

"Yes ma'am."

Her eyes flare, but then disappear as she steps down and away from the fence.

A minute later I'm standing in her apartment, trying not to check out her ass while she rummages through a cabinet. "Aha! Found some! It wasn't a given. In my apartment sugar is only used for Jell-O shots."

"You don't bake?"

She shakes her head. "Not that I should admit this to a cop, but I'm pretty sure the last thing I baked was a pan of pot brownies. But that was when I lived in Atlanta. Not your jurisdiction." She puts her hands on her hips and dares me to judge her.

"Thank you for that helpful clarification." This woman's sass is going to kill me. I want to punish her for her crimes. With my tongue.

"Go on, then." She pushes the sugar toward me on the counter. "Do I get a piece of cake when it's done?"

"Unfortunately, I only made one. And it's for my sister's—" I actually shudder— "bridal shower.'

"Oh well." She shrugs. "Next time. I should go grocery shopping anyway."

"Yeah, you probably should. You don't cook at all?"

"I cook eggs." She shrugs.

"How do you avoid starvation?"

"Takeout food, sandwiches, and eggs." She steps into a pair of ridiculous platform shoes that make her legs look even longer. "See you later, Copper."

"See you later—" I stop myself before calling her Hot Neighbor —"Meg."

———

AND I DO SEE her later. About a half hour later.

As I'm carrying my nicely glazed lemon coffee cake out to my car, I find Meg leaning against her own car in the parking lot. "Everything okay?" I ask her.

"Sure." She hastily wipes something away from the corner of her eye. "No problem."

Oh shit, it's a tear. *Mayday!* I'm inclined to call dispatch and ask for an emergency vehicle. I can't handle it when women cry. It kills me, and I never know what to say. Not that I'm all that great at talking to them when they aren't crying. But I digress. "What's the matter, honey?"

She shakes her head. "Flat tire. It happens. No big deal." She flicks a tear away from the other eye. "I'll just..." she turns away from me. "Have fun today. Bye."

"Wait," I hear myself say. "Do you know how to change the tire?" It's not like I care if I'm on time for a bridal shower. And changing a tire is nothing.

"Yep. I know how." Her shoulders sag. "It's just that I don't have one."

"Not even a donut?" I ask. "They're not the best, but they'll get you to the tire shop."

Her expression is bleak when she turns around. "After my last flat, I drove on the donut until it gave out. And then I got the tire replaced. But I..."

"...Never replaced the donut." I sigh. This is exactly the sort of thing I lecture my little sister about. "Don't you realize you could have gotten a flat somewhere in the dead of night, in a shady neighborhood?"

"But I didn't!" She cocks a hip. "Somehow I got one right here at home, thanks. Now you run along to your party and I'll deal."

Aw, man. I can't leave a teary woman here alone with no groceries and a flat tire. "Where do you buy your tires?"

"At Discount Tires on 28th Street. They're open on Sundays."

"Tell you what. You come along with me while I stop in at my sister's thing. I have to buy a gift on the way, but I don't have to stay at this party. Then we'll swing by Discount Tires on the way home and pick up a new tire for you. And a new donut."

"Really?" Her face brightens up immediately. "You'd do that?"

"Sure," I say, and my voice goes gruff. "It's no big deal. Let's go." I gesture toward my car.

"Two minutes," she says, walking quickly in the wrong direction. "I can't meet your sister in short shorts and a tank top."

I freeze in place. It hadn't occurred to me that Meg would *meet* Rosie. Even before I knew Meg was coming along, I saw myself tossing the cake in the general direction of a dozen women, pecking Rosie on the cheek, and getting the hell out of there.

That was probably just wishful thinking.

So I wait.

And wait.

Ten minutes later I'm still sitting in my car, waiting for Meg, and questioning all my life choices. Just when I'm wondering if someone has kidnapped her, Meg finally appears. "Sorry," she says, breathless. The car door slams. "I'm ready now."

I turn to glance at her, and it's a mistake. In place of the short shorts, Meg is wearing big shades, red lipstick, and a yellow dress that shows just as much of her smooth legs, if not more. She's like a leggy goddamn flower that I really want to pluck.

And pluck.

And pluck harder.

"Do you have a siren?" she asks. "I want to play with it."

I close my eyes and groan.

"Or not," she says quickly. "What are you giving your sister for her shower?"

"Not sure," I say, starting the engine. "There's a registry, so I don't have to think too hard about it."

"Uh-oh," Meg says as I pull out of the parking space.

"What now?"

"You can't buy off the registry on the day of the shower."

"Why the fuck not? That's what registries are for."

She gives me a patient look. "All the good stuff will be taken already. You'll be left buying the caviar spoons."

"The what? Nobody buys caviar spoons." I accelerate toward the store just in case, though.

"Weddings make people a little crazy," Meg says. "Trust me."

The store is called *Coq de la Cuisine*. When we get there, I find a salesperson and give him my sister's name. "Oh dear," he says with a disapproving frown. "The shower is today? I believe she still needs the caviar spoons. And perhaps the *brosse de toilette*."

"The...what?"

"The toilet brush," the man says with a patronizing smile.

And now I feel like one of those Instapots with the top loose. I might explode. "I'm not buying a goddamn toilet brush as a gift! This is for family that I *like*."

"Surely you can find something to your taste?" The salesman lifts a hand and makes a game-show gesture toward the vast selections on the shelves.

"Christ," I grumble. I can't *choose* something for Rosie. It's supposed to work the other way. She chose literally everything in my apartment except my clothes and underwear.

"Deep breaths, Copper," Meg says. "I'll find something."

"Would you?" I gasp. "Shopping makes me itch."

Meg claps her hands like I've just promised her Redwings tickets. "What's your budget?"

"Try not to scare me. Bonus points if we're out of here in ten minutes."

"Challenge accepted!" Meg bounces off toward a section marked *"vaisselle,"* whatever the fuck that is. In fact, the whole store is in French.

Just take my service revolver and shoot me.

Luckily, Meg beckons only moments later. "Found it!" she says. "And it's only two hundred dollars."

Considering how badly I want to get out of here, that doesn't sound so bad. "What is it?"

"Ooh, mademoiselle has fine taste," the salesman says. "The cocktail cart is *très populaire!*"

"What is a cocktail cart?" I bark. I see some shelves on wheels. And an ice bucket.

"It's a shelf on wheels, with an ice bucket," Meg says. "Perfect for entertaining. The hostess can move around on the patio."

"But..." What planet is this? "I wanted to get her something she can use. Like, more than once a year."

"Sure," Meg says, and her tone suggests that's a weird idea. "You could do that. But weddings aren't about reality. They're about being a princess for a little while. The cocktail cart is glamorous, it says: I live to enjoy elegant cocktails with my friends. But if you don't like it, there's always the *brosse de toilette.*"

Beaten, I just hand over my credit card.

———

FIFTEEN MINUTES later I'm standing in my sister's kitchen, shoving big bites of chicken salad in my facehole while a dozen women coo over a cocktail cart. In between bites, I take longing glances at Meg. Specifically her legs. And cleavage. That yellow dress is killing me. Every time she laughs, her chest bounces pleasantly...

"We have to talk," Rosie hisses in my ear.

"About what? I thought you liked the cocktail cart."

"*J'adore* the cocktail cart," she says. "I fuckin' love it. But we have to talk about *her.*"

Uh-oh. I look quickly out onto the patio. But the woman I'm so eager to avoid is nowhere in evidence.

"Mac," my sister says, her voice softening. "I didn't mean Julie. They're not here today."

"Oh?" I try and fail to sound casual. The "they" she's referring to are my brother and his wife.

"They're not. They're in Chicago for the weekend. He has a work thing. That's why I insisted you come *today*."

"Oh." Now I feel like an idiot. But I always feel a little idiotic around my family.

"I meant, we have to talk about *her*," she whispers, her eyes flickering toward Meg. "You suddenly have a date for my shower? And I haven't heard her name before? How is that possible?"

"Well..." I hesitate, wondering what to say to my clever sister. I glance in Meg's direction to see how she's holding up. She's somehow the center of attention, talking and gesturing wildly. The women around her burst into laughter. Seems Meg is just fine.

"Who is she?" my sister whispers. "How long have you been dating? And when is the wedding?"

I can't process any of that. Too much too fast. "Say again?"

Rosie puts her hands on her hips. "Just who is Meg to you?"

"She's my neighbor. Don't get so excited."

Her eyes narrow. "Just a neighbor? I hope not."

I don't get a chance to answer, though. The kitchen door flies open, and a tornado whirls inside. "Rosie! Macklin! Help me with this thing!" There is a swirl of color, like a bunch of colorful scarves caught in a windstorm. Looks like she picked up another Dress Of Many Colors at an art fair or something. She's also wearing big earrings that she fashioned out of tin cans. *Reuse! Recycle! And Redazzle!* she likes to say.

Our mother has arrived.

And somewhere in the near distance is Dad. Wearing a handknit sweater that mom made for him. My dad's a fucking saint to wear that thing. First off, the arms are different lengths. Secondly, it's summertime.

My sister and I both set down our plates without argument and troop outside. Because nobody crosses mom. She's not a monster, but she is a force of nature. Arguing with her is like arguing with a grizzly bear. She doesn't bother arguing back, she just mauls you.

She opens the back of her monstrous, gas-guzzling car to reveal... I don't even know what. I see a bunch of flowers. Some kind of white board. And pictures of a bunch of strangers grinning at me. It's like they've been plucked from a freakish catalogue of healthy living or something.

"This is your shower gift!" Mom bellows. "It's a collage of your future happiness."

Huh. Sounds like I was right on the money.

I take a closer look. "Collage, huh?" I ask mom. "I thought you were into crochet these days."

My mother sniffs. "I am crocheting a shower curtain for the wedding gift."

"Oh, boy," Rosie says under her breath.

"But the *shower* gift is a collage. It's a room divider."

"Oh," Rosie says carefully. "What room am I meant to divide?"

"Pick one!" Mom says. "Macklin, help me."

I reach into the car and carefully grab a set of three boards. The room divider folds accordion style. I open it to reveal the three-paneled work of art. It's covered in hundreds—maybe thousands—of photos. "Jesus, Mom." This thing must have taken months. It's a true photo collage, whereby each little photo snippet is combined to make a larger picture.

"Wow," my sister says in a hushed tone. "That's seriously impressive."

Mom beams.

"Who are..." my sister breaks off. The main image shows six people. Two of them are easy to identify—Rosie and her fiancé are depicted with eerie perfection. Rosie's face is made from snips of hundreds of bathing photos (to get that skin color just right.) I think I recognize my bare four-year-old ass among other photos.

That's an interesting choice.

But it's the subject matter that's really breathtaking. Rosie and Kwan are accompanied in this artwork by four children of various ages. The youngest one is a baby in Rosie's arms.

"Four grandchildren!" my mother bellows. "It took me seven gallons of Mod Podge to make this sucker. And seventy-six trips to CVS for photo printing. And as many months to make as it will take you to gestate an actual grandchild."

"Wow," Rosie says, but her tone is glum. "Four, though? You only had three kids. And you started younger."

"That is not my fault," she says. "I think you've got it in you. Now." She turns to me. "Now let's address your situation."

"My situation?" I echo, as a feeling of doom settles over me. It's the way she said "situation." Like she was saying "tumor."

"He brought a girlfriend to the party!" Rosie squawks. "Her name is Meg and she's adorable."

Mom gasps.

Dad tugs on the short sweater sleeve.

Shit. Now I'm going to have to murder my sister. I give Rosie a glare, but she only smiles back at me with a crazed gleam in her eye. Maybe the poor girl couldn't help herself. My mother basically demanded that she bear four grandchildren, starting today. I guess I'd change the topic, too.

"Let's eat chicken salad," I suggest, hoping Mom will forget all about Meg. I'm not ready for this discussion. I thought I wouldn't have to deal with this lie until the actual wedding. I thought I'd have some time to warm up to the idea and at least talk to Meg beforehand. How am I going to pull off convincing them that we're in love when I don't even know Meg's last name?

But Mom isn't listening anymore. She's marching toward the patio, determination etched into her features.

"I'm a little afraid for Meg," I grunt. "How could you throw me under the bus like this?"

"You never show up with a date! This is newsworthy. Also, Meg is lovely. So maybe you'd better tell me everything." She scrunches her eyes at me, like she's making it clear she can see through my bullshit.

Damn sister. How am I supposed to play Meg off as my adoring girlfriend now? In the span of two minutes, that whole idea seems crazy. I never could tell a lie to Rosie. It's her big eyes and their ability to see right through me.

"She's just a neighbor. Today I borrowed...some sugar...and she needed...a tire," I say slowly.

"Is that a euphemism for something?"

"No!"

Rosie is studying me. She could've been a cop too if she wanted, but instead she became a middle-school teacher. Come to think of it, the two jobs have a lot in common.

"I'm also bringing her to the wedding," I offer, thinking this might shut her up.

"Reallllly?" Rosie gives me an evil smile. "Because you're interested in her? Or because you are trying to shut down any family pity."

"Oh, for fuck's sake. She's my neighbor, and a friend, and I'm bringing her to the wedding, and she's going to play like she's madly in love with me so Mom and Dad will get off my back about having a girlfriend, and maybe Morris and Julie will realize I'm totally fine and over the whole ordeal. I'm better than fine. I'm with Meg who is gorgeous and smart and funny and..." It occurs to me I'm rambling.

So I stop.

And I just wait.

Rosie busts out a big old grin. "My wedding is going to be awesome! Can I say I introduced you two?"

"No," I say. "That would be a lie."

"You hypocrite! I want to be in on it. I already like her. She can be a bridesmaid if you want. You can have her on your arm. Make everyone swoon. She'll make you look even more studly than you usually do."

Whoa. "No! Don't put either of us in the ceremony. Just let me handle this. I don't want to *actively* lie. I'll tell everyone the truth on how we really met."

"And how was that?"

Now I'm really committed to this charade. "I was on shift, working a gas leak. She was waitressing for a bachelorette party. She, uh, thought I was the talent. So she tried to tear my clothes off. Literally."

And damn if I wasn't tempted to let her.

Rosie howls. Full out. From the belly. "I can't wait! And I'm so glad you're coming to the wedding. I know you don't want to, but it means the world to me."

She jumps up and gives me a quick hug. I lift her off the ground for a second because that's what we do.

Then she slugs me in the arm. Hard. "But maybe you should loan her some *sugar*," she says. "And that *is* a euphemism."

"Not gonna happen," I say immediately. "We're not like that."

"Then why are you staring at her right now?"

"I'm not." But I am, of course. And I'm so busted, because Meg picks that exact moment to catch my gaze, too. She takes a piece of lemon cake, pops it into her mouth, and then closes her eyes with delight. Then she licks her goddamn lips.

"Are you really trying to tell me that you two aren't a couple?" My sister sounds incredulous. "There's more spark between the two of you than a match and some kindling. All you need to get lit is a little rubbing."

"We're not a couple," I grumble. "We don't need to be *lit*. In the first place, I don't do relationships. And she's my neighbor."

"So?" My sister's eyes twinkle. "That sounds very convenient."

"Sure," I grunt. "Until I've had my fill. And then it's just awkward."

Rosie groans. "You are the most cynical man ever born."

I give her a smile, even though she's got it wrong. Cynical men are made, not born.

8 ALL THOSE TRAINING BRAS

Meg

I don't know how I ended up at this bridal shower, eating a piece of Maguire's excellent lemon cake, surrounded by smiling women who are hanging on my every word, but it's not a bad place to be. In the first place, Maguire's sister is all kinds of adorable. She's the bubbly kind of unicorn person. I'm usually more drawn to dark and twisted individuals, but she sort of makes it impossible not to like her.

The other women are just as nice, though. When I arrived with Maguire, a hundred female eyes turned in our direction. I expected to feel the white-hot heat of women judging me. But that's not how things played out. First there was a collective gasp and sigh as they took in the sight of Maguire standing at the edge of the patio. It's hard not to gasp and sigh at him. His T-shirt barely contains him and he's wearing tight slacks that cradle his ass.

If I can't have an acting job, I might settle for being his slacks. I could just hold his muscular buns all day, professionally. And it would still be a good life.

I'd expected those women to give me the collective stink eye, but that's not what happened. We were both embraced and ushered further onto the patio. Someone whisked the lemon bundt right out Maguire's hands. Before I knew it, Rosie was hugging me, then she and Maguire slipped into the kitchen, and I found myself plunked onto an outdoor glider, telling them the story of how we met.

Everyone thinks we're an item. I'm not sure how I feel about that, but I suppose it's good practice for the wedding. I did plan to help him out there, so why not get a little rehearsal in?

So I weave the tale. I fill them in on my old waitressing job, and the bridezilla who wanted to steal all the turkey legs, and then how I mistook Maguire for a stripper and tried to rip his clothes off.

There are howls and some genuine guffaws. Those are probably due to the mimosas.

The redhead sitting next to me puts her hand on my wrist. "That is such an amazing story. I met my last boyfriend in the dog food aisle at the grocery store, but your story is way better."

"Well, I mean dog food...is...kinda hot?" I offer.

"It isn't at all," she says. Then she leans in and whispers, "But do you see Leslie over there? She met her husband at a funeral."

"Yikes. I hope it wasn't anyone important."

The woman shrugs. "I'm Aubrey, by the way," she says. "Friend of Rosie and wedding planner extraordinaire."

"It's nice to have confidence," I say.

She smiles. "Oh, no. That's actually what my business card says. *Wedding Planner Extraordinaire.* I'm a better planner than I am a marketer."

She reaches into her Kate Spade bag, rummages around, and hands me a pink card. She's right. Her card says it all.

"Well, I'm Meg," I say. "I don't have a business card, but I'm a waitress extraordinaire. And sometimes an actor. But just a regular actor. Not extraordinaire."

"You are kidding me!" she says, delighted sounding.

"About which part? The waitress part? I'm totally serious."

She laughs and I like her. Why is everyone so friendly here? I forget sometimes that Michigan is weird.

"No! The actress part! That's amazing! Although, I can totally tell now that you mention it. You have the gift of storytelling. Is there...are you..." She seems like she's struggling to find the words. "I have a crazy question. Do you ever do freelance work?"

"Freelance? What, like stripping? It hasn't come to that." *Yet.*

"No!" Aubrey gasps. "Although I'm sure you could rock that. But I meant freelance acting. I'm in a serious bind with a client. He wants a flash mob to ask his girlfriend to marry him. And I told him I'd do it, because I hate to turn down work. But then I realized I have no idea how to pull it off. Directing people isn't the same as arranging flowers and..." She heaves a sigh. "Do you have actor friends? Could you help me pull this off?"

"Probably. Where is it supposed to take place?"

"At the farmers' market. She has a stall selling flowers. And he's the cheesemonger. That's where they met. Now he wants to propose while she's serenaded about... I don't know what. Love and birds and cheeses or something? He wants a big production. It should just unfold like..." Aubrey does jazz hands to indicate a big deal. But then her hands drop to her lap. "I don't know if I can pull this off. What if it turns out like a middle-school musical?"

Everyone within earshot looks suddenly uncomfortable. "There's nothing more cringeworthy than a middle-school musical," one woman says. "All those squeaky boy voices right as they're dropping."

"All those training bras," someone else says with a sigh.

"I can help you," I say with more vehemence than necessary. Because I have middle-school flashbacks, too. That shit is terrifying.

"Can you really?" Aubrey squeaks. "That's amazing. And he's paying five thousand dollars so..."

"Five—!" I yelp. "There must be a lot of money in mongering cheese!"

"That's what I thought, too." Aubrey shrugs. "I should peddle cheese if this wedding thing doesn't work out."

"Same," I agree. "If both the acting and the ass-holding fail."

"The...what-holding?" My new friend looks confused.

"Never mind," I say quickly because Maguire and Rosie are just joining us. There's also a woman with them who is round and soft and smiling, and a bald man behind her wearing the worst sweater I've ever seen. This dude has made some interesting fashion choices.

Rosie sits right next to me on the love seat, and then motions for Maguire to join us. "Come on, brother," she says. "Sit next to your *girlfriend*. There's plenty of space if you don't mind being cozy. Which you don't because you loooooooove each other and all."

Rosie's eyes are glittering. And Maguire has turned a peculiar shade of red.

And that woman and man who entered the room with Rosie and Mac...it occurs to me that there's a family resemblance.

And...

Oh. Oh! Rehearsal time is over, obviously. This is my premiere as Maguire's girlfriend. I think I've just met the parents.

I give Maguire a quick look and he gives me the slightest of nods. "Mom, Dad, this is Meg. Meg..."

He's not able to finish the sentence because his mom shoves him out of the way and bends down to give me an enormous hug. Suddenly I'm enveloped in mom-bosom and the scent of roses. And also some kind of scarf thing. I try to hold my breath, but then I just give in and breathe. It's actually kinda comforting. She must wear essential oils.

"Oh, Meg! I can't tell you what a pleasure it is to meet you! We thought Maguire would never get over..."

This time Maguire interrupts by gently moving his mom to the side and then snuggling in next to me on the glider. With Rosie on the other side of me, it's sort of like trying to shove your hand in a can of Pringles. There just isn't enough space. So in a fluid motion, he does some kind of maneuver and I'm suddenly sitting on him. On his lap. I wiggle a little bit. He coughs uncomfortably.

Maguire is not an actor. Maguire is as stiff as a board. Like his whole body is stiff. If we're going to pull off the whole we're-dating thing, this dude's got to loosen up.

So I grab his arms and wrap them around me. And then I lean back, turn a little bit, and lay a quick, soft kiss on his lips.

Well, it's supposed to be a quick one, but as soon as my lips touch his, his arms constrict a bit, as if he doesn't want me to go anywhere. The glider rocks gently, exaggerating our motion.

Holy shit. His lips feel good. His arms feel amazing. His lap is my new favorite place in the world. The glider sways beneath us. I think I actually moan a little bit.

Rosie applauds.

His mom sighs.

Maguire releases me.

Pity. I have to shake my head to escape the hormone haze. I almost forgot I was performing here. "What were we talking about?" It's a serious question. I feel breathless and flustered.

Suddenly, Aubrey is back, holding onto an enormous platter of food. I think she's brought that platter to share, but then she digs in and I realize, nope that's just for her. Gosh, I like her. "Meg was telling me that she's an actor extraordinaire and I was just about to hire her to do a flash mob thing for me," she gushes. "This needs to be an *event*."

"Do you do stuff like that?" Maguire asks, sounding genuinely interested.

"I haven't done this exact thing, but I could. I can totally do this."

This time it's Aubrey who claps. "I just knew when you two walked in the door that something big was going to happen!"

I laugh because there is something big that's happening right now under my ass. And that something is Maguire. At least part of him that's enjoying this charade. If I was really his girlfriend, we wouldn't even make it home. My panties would hit his car floor before we even pulled away from the curb. I'd make him pull over in a parking lot and then straddle him and...

"No whimpering, Meg," Maguire whispers. "You're laying it on too thick."

God. His gruff voice right in my ear! But he's right. I am moaning. So I stop.

Shake it off again.

Aubrey takes a look at her watch. "Oh!" she exclaims! "It's time for some shower games! I love shower games!"

"And that's our cue to head out," Maguire says. "Up, Trouble."

For a second, I don't realize that *Trouble* is me. So I don't get up. And the he pinches me on the ass. Is it weird that I like it? But I get up anyway.

"Thanks for the chicken salad," Maguire says stiffly.

"Hang on just a second," Maguire's mom says. "I need your help inflating the game I brought."

"The...what?" he asks, wary.

"It's inflatable. Like those pool toys you loved as a kid. And since all the Maguire men are full of hot air, I need your help with this. It's around back." She points to the corner of the house.

But he hesitates, looking from his mother to me and back again.

"Go on," she says, a strangely intense look on her face.

Tension shivers in the air between Maguire and his mom. I'm not sure of its source, but I'm sure of its potency. It's the kind of tension that's famous for ruining Thanksgiving meals.

Interesting.

"Be good, Mom," Maguire says, with an edge to his voice. Then he stalks off, toward the back of the house.

The moment he's gone, his mother swoops over to me, takes my arm, and drags me to the edge of the patio. It's a lot like that same zombie TV drama where I once worked. Only this time I'm the prey instead of the predator.

"It's lovely to meet you, Meg," Mrs. Maguire says, her face filled with more intensity than the moment requires.

"Likewise," I reply with a smile. If I were really Mac's girlfriend, I'd be terrified right now. Maybe she's one of those moms who thinks no woman is good enough for her baby boy. I bet I'm going to be grilled.

Bring it, bitch. The worse she is, the bigger my lies will be. If she's rude, I'll give her something to fret about. I'll convince her I have a lengthy rap sheet. Wait—her son the cop wouldn't go for that. I'll tell her I'm a visitor from the planet Zutron, here to study life on Earth. And marriage to an earthling is a goal of mine.

I'm very convincing.

His mom takes a giant breath as if she's winding up for something.

Here it comes.

"He wasn't always like this," she says. "He needs to laugh more. He needs to be less cagey. But I have faith in you."

Okay, that's not where I was expecting this to go. "Um...thanks?"

"He's held onto his anger for too long. Even when anger is justified, it hurts you. Don't you agree?"

"Usually," I hedge. I need to be very careful. Because I don't know *what the ever loving fuck this woman is saying.*

"Building bridges is harder than burning them," she says. "If you know what I mean."

"Right." I nod vehemently, hoping for even a small clue to what is happening right now. Honestly, a trip to the planet Zutron would make more sense than this conversation.

"I hope you're coming to the wedding," she blurts out.

"Oh, absolutely!" Finally a question I can answer.

"YAY!" her shout of joy is deafening. "He needs this. He needs *you*."

My smile is waxed on, and I have no idea how to reassure this woman. But luckily Rosie has come to my rescue. "Oh, come on, Mom! I can't believe you asked Mac to blow up a giant penis!"

That doesn't make sense, so I play the sentence back inside my head. Nope. I'm still befuddled. "A giant...what?"

"Look! You'll die." She hooks her arm in mine and tows me toward the backyard. The Maguires are all arm-towers. They just are.

But as we round the side of the house, I see what Rosie was so eager to show me. Mac and his father are both standing there, blowing air into giant inflatable...dicks. Cocks. Erections. There is nothing else those could be. They even have veins in all the right places.

I let out a snort of laughter so loud that it's actually painful. "What the heck?" I try to ask, but I can't quite get the words out. My belly is already shaking with laughter.

"It's a shower game!" Aubrey says cheerfully. "We're playing Penis Ring Toss! The head-to-head version."

I scream with laughter. "You just described my college years." I giggle. Not that anyone can understand me. I can't even breathe, I'm laughing so hard. The sight of Maguire with a giant penis projecting from his face is just too much to bear.

As I continue to howl, he drops his chin and glares at me. But that just makes the penis bob up and down.

I fall to the grass, laughing.

Maguire removes the XXL dick from his lips and closes the valve. "And I'm out of here. As much as I love amusing all of you with an inflated willy, I've got to get Meg home. We have a tire to change."

"I wish someone would change my tire," Aubrey sighs.

"Damn," Maguire says. "It's literally a tire. Can't anything be exactly what it looks like?"

"Apparently not," Rosie says cheerfully.

I reach out my hand. "Time to go, Copper," I say.

He reaches for me and our hands clasp. He pulls me to my feet. But laughter makes a girl clumsy, so I repay this bit of chivalry by bumping into him.

But he reacts in the sweetest way—by giving me a quick peck on the lips. I feel myself smile.

Rosie and her mother both sigh.

"So nice to meet you all," I say, and realize I'm not lying. His family is sweet and quirky and warm. I can't imagine why Maguire is so eager to trick them. But I look forward to finding out. I wouldn't mind knowing them all a little better.

Just maybe not his mother. At least not alone.

We leave the way we came in, with a flurry of squeals and well wishes.

But we also leave without the rest of the lemon bundt cake, and I have to admit, I'm a little disappointed about that.

9 NO CAKE THIS TIME

Maguire

It's the weekend again, and I'm baking. No cake this time, though. Today I'm kneading pizza dough. A good bread dough is a simple thing. So long as you have flour, yeast, and salt, you can make pizza dough.

Now, my grandma taught me to add a little olive oil and a little honey. The oil improves the texture, and the honey aids in browning. But you don't *need* those extras.

In other words, I can't think of a single reason why I'd have to knock on Meg's door today. The fact that I'm disappointed is something I'm trying hard not to analyze.

She made a bridal shower fun. How is that even possible?

Of course, if she was sitting on my lap, she could probably make anything fun.

I try not to think about that, either.

So it's back to shaping the dough, which is very therapeutic. I sprinkle a little more flour on the countertop, then fold the dough in half. Then I give it a satisfying little punch. The dough needs ten more minutes of kneading, which means I have lots of punches to dole out, and lots of time to think about all the crap in my life that needs attention.

For example, this morning my mother called to remind me to go get fitted for a tuxedo.

I give the dough an extra firm punch every time I think about the goddamn wedding. Wearing a tux is just an added punishment. My sister knows better than to put me in the wedding party. But I'm still an usher.

The lump of dough gets another smack.

After the kneading is done, the dough has to rise for a few hours. Later I'll fashion my dough into calzones. Calzones are great patrol food. You need something that can hold its shape for a few hours before I'm ready for my lunch break.

Once I made mini quiches, but my partner Lance found them funny. He laughed so hard he choked on his peanut butter and jelly sandwich. I don't see what's so funny about a quiche, but I almost had to give the man the hug of life. So quiches are out.

Another benefit of making calzones is that they bake on the grill, so I won't have to turn the oven on. It's another scorcher today. The humidity is about 99%, too. That's what you get for living thirty miles from Lake Michigan.

I give the dough one more punch. For luck. And then I shape it into a ball. I dust it with flour one more time, and then set it to rest in a lightly greased mixing bowl, with a damp cloth on top. Just like my granny taught me.

While I wait for the yeast to do its thing, I locate my pizza stone and carry it out to the grill. I lift the top of the grill and set the pizza stone inside, so I won't forget to preheat it later. A hot stone is how you get a nice crispy crust.

I'm just standing here thinking happy thoughts about Italian food when, out of nowhere, a shrill scream splits the air. And it's not just any scream. It's a sound that curdles blood, and it's coming from right next door.

Jesus Christ. I don't hesitate. I leap onto the overturned flower pot, brace a hand on top of the fence and vault right over.

Luckily, my neighbor has no furniture to trip on, so I land easily on the other side. Two seconds later I'm opening her kitchen door and checking the area for intruders.

I see nobody. Where the hell is the perp?

"Meg?" I call.

"Hot Cop?" Her voice comes from the bedroom. It doesn't sound strained. But maybe the perp is holding a gun on her and...

I ease toward the bedroom and then glance carefully around the door frame. My heart is in my throat, wondering what I'm gonna find.

But what I see does not match the terrors in my head. She's sitting cross-legged in the center of her carefully made-up bed, a laptop open in front of her.

"Jesus," I gasp. "Did you hear that scream? It wasn't you?" I step into the room.

"Why, Mac. How nice to see you! And how unexpected. Did you knock and I missed it?" She gives me a big happy smile.

Meanwhile, my heart rate is still 60 miles per hour above the legal limit. "You screamed," I insist. "Why?"

"Did I? I suppose I might have. I just received the best email."

"And email makes you scream like you're being flayed by the devil himself?"

"Well, actors, you know." She's shrugs as if to say *what can you do?* "We're dramatic."

Jesus Christ. "I just got an entire year older. But hey, as long as you got an email, it's all good."

"It wasn't *just* an email." She slides off the bed and stands up. "It was a great email. I'm in the mood to celebrate."

She takes a step closer to me and then does something dangerous. She steps into my personal space and hugs me. Like a real hug, with long arms wrapping around me and a tight body pressing against mine.

And then the vixen kisses me right on the jaw.

"Urrrumph," I grunt as my limbic system struggles to handle the sensory overload. I flash hot everywhere, and my heart is still pounding, although now for a different reason.

"Meg," I rasp, taking a step backward. "What is going on?"

"I'll tell you over lunch."

"Lunch?"

"Didn't I just say I'm in the mood to celebrate? Besides, you owe me a favor."

"Another favor?" When I named her Trouble, I knew what I was doing. "How do you figure?" Maybe Meg isn't good at math. "We're square. I helped you with your tire."

"The tire was in trade for the cup of sugar." She puts a hand on her hip and smiles. "And I'm still going to your sister's wedding."

"Right. Sure. But the wedding date is in trade for breaking into my apartment."

"Oh, I remember, and you gave me some bluster over how you could have had me arrested." She rolls her eyes.

"Well, I could have. So we're even." Obviously.

Her smile grows very wide, and I know that somehow I've missed a crucial detail. "We *would* be even. But you just broke into *my* apartment. And now I could have you arrested."

Oh, for fuck's sake. "But I was trying to save you!"

"And that really was kind of hot." She fans herself. "But here you are. No invitation..."

"I thought you were being killed."

"And that is adorable. But one misunderstanding cancels out another one, wouldn't you agree?" She bats her eyelashes. And they are very long eyelashes, lining a pair of impossibly large brown eyes.

This has always been a problem for me. Women start talking, and rationalizing, and reasoning with me, and I get befuddled. Meg's short shorts and pink lip gloss are robbing me of all my executive function.

"What sort of favor?" I croak.

"Take me out for lunch." I'm just about to agree when she adds, smiling, "On a date."

"A date?"

"For your favor, you asked me out on a fake date. I'm asking you for a real one."

That sobers me up. "Why?"

"What do you mean, why?" Her smile loses a little of its certainty. "Because that would be fun, Copper. And today, for once, anything seems possible. This TV role. You." She holds my gaze for a moment, daring me to disagree.

I don't want to let her down. But I have to. "I'm sorry. I don't date."

"Ever?"

"Never." And I never will again.

There's an awkward silence. I suppose I could leap in and say, "Just this once." It's not that I don't want to have lunch with Meg. But I don't believe in lying, and I'm not good at sugarcoating the truth. Ask anyone. I suppose I can at least try.

"Look," I say, wondering if I can save our friendship. "I like you. I like your attitude. I really like your smile." *And every part of your body*, I privately add. But I suppose she already knows that. "And if I was the dating kind of man, you'd already have aced the audition."

Her eyes dip. "It's okay, Copper. I have a thick skin." She looks up at me again. "Seriously. An actor knows how to take rejection. It's a life skill. But it makes me wonder if you're for real. Do you really not care that your friend with benefits was screwing another guy?"

"I didn't," I say immediately. "Except for the dog hair."

She actually rolls her eyes. "How could we forget that detail? If I had a dog would you have refrained from jumping over that fence to save me?"

I open my mouth and close it again. "That's unrelated. I was just doing my job."

"Right." She nods. "Who ripped your heart out, Mac? It must have been bad."

"It's not like that," I say immediately.

Although it's totally like that. Fucking actors. They are too empathetic for their own good. "Okay, Copper," she says, letting me off the hook. "Instead of a date, you can help me with research."

"Research?"

"About police work. That email I just got is from a Chicago cop show I auditioned for. It's called *Pierson of Interest*."

I snort. "That's cute, I guess. A TV cop show? They always get lots of shit wrong."

"Well here's your chance to correct that." She puts a hand on my shoulder, and now her shampoo is all I can smell. It's something a little fruity. Apples, maybe. "Whoever they cast in this role flaked out. So I'm invited back in two weeks for a screen test. This is big, Maguire. I'd play Pierson's sidekick. It's a real speaking role."

"Wow, Trouble. That's amazing." My hot neighbor, the famous actor.

She tilts her head and scrutinizes me. "Hey, are you all right? You look a little flushed."

Of course I do. When she gets close to me, my brain stops working. I really like Meg, but I still can't be the kind of guy she's looking for. I can't date her, because I don't do that. And we can't sleep together because I have a feeling it wouldn't be just a one-time deal with her, and that's a bad idea.

"Okay, I'll help you," I say, because I need to extract myself from this conversation. She smells like apples and I just want to bury my face in her bosom.

"You will?" She lets out another ear-piercing shriek. "See? You are still the best neighbor ever."

And then I get another goddamn hug. I can feel her breasts press against my chest. "Congratulations, Trouble," I say, easing back, and trying again to focus. "Does this mean you're going to be on TV?"

She shrugs. "Not yet. In fact, probably not. For a decade I've had these tiny breakthroughs that seem like something big is about to happen. And then it never does. This will probably be exactly the same story. That's why I have to celebrate right now. Before I'm disappointed again." She grabs her pocketbook off the bed. "I'm still going out to lunch. I know just the place."

Most of me wants to ask where. But I don't. Because it's none of my business.

"We'll talk research later," she says, leaving the bedroom. I follow her into the living room, where she's stepping into her shoes. "Maybe on the deck one night this week? I'll bring a notebook and interrogate you."

"I'm the cop. I do the interrogating," I say as a reflex.

She turns to me. "Where else do you like to be in charge?"

"Um..." Just the gleam in her eye makes my blood thicken. Oh hey, libido! Nice of you to drop by again. Fuck my life.

Meg just beams at me. "Speechless, much? It's a good thing you're not the one auditioning for a cop show." She opens her apartment door and shoos me outside into the hallway. "Bye, Copper! We'll talk soon!"

"Bye, Trouble," I mutter, watching her go.

It isn't until she disappears into the elevator that I realize I have a problem. Since I broke into Meg's apartment via the deck, my front door is locked. And I can't climb back over the fence because Meg is gone.

I let out a groan. "How much trouble can one woman make in my life?" I ask the hallway.

Plenty, obviously.

10 PASTY VS. PASTIES

Meg

"And how's my little Meggers?" my father asks, grinning at me from his corner of our four-way family video chat.

"Pretty good!" I reply. And it's true. Dad's ridiculous nicknames usually grate on me. But today I'm too happy to care.

"Hey, watch the hair!" my sister yelps from her corner, where she's holding little baby Alfred at her boob while the twins literally climb on her. I love my nieces and nephew, but when I see them crawling over her like puppies, I'm really grateful that I am nowhere near that phase of my life.

Eventually, I'd like to do the Mom Thing, but not today.

First, I'd like to do the Fall In Love For Real Thing.

And I'd also like to do the Get My Life Together Thing. These chats with my family are pretty good at reminding me that I'm supposed to have priorities.

"So..." My sister pries Alfred's tiny fingers off her hair. "You're pumped up about this audition?" Sadie asks. "Is this really a big break? You said it could be. But sometimes you..."

"Exaggerate?" I ask.

"Let's just say you've always had natural acting instincts," my mother chimes in.

This is why I don't spend more time chatting about my professional life with my parents. "This is the first time I've been so close to a real TV role. But you know what's weird? I ought to be spasming between hope and anxiety right now. But I feel kind of blasé about it. I don't know if that's maturity or if I'm finally just numb."

There's a silence while my parents consider this. Dad bites his lip, and Mom wrinkles up her nose.

"Acting is a hard road, Meg," my sister says, stroking the feathery hair on her baby's head as he nurses. "Numbness wouldn't be unfounded." My sister totally sounds like a therapist. Which makes sense, because she is actually a therapist.

My mother makes a noise of agreement. It's a sound like "*murm*" that she often makes when she knows I don't really want to hear her opinion but she can't keep her mouth completely sealed shut.

"Listen to this," I add. "I have another gig right now. I met a woman at my fake boyfriend's sister's bridal shower, and she hired me to do a flash mob."

Mom blinks. "Your fake boyfriend? Is this like your pretend friend Cheetah?"

"Oh!" Sadie giggles. "I forgot about Cheetah. You told us she had spotted hair."

"Come *on*!" I shriek. "I was *five* years old. Can we stop with the childhood memories? Or I'm going to tell Sadie's husband about the time she cut her own hair with Dad's weed whacker."

"Slow your roll, honey," Sadie says. "Let's get back to the fake boyfriend."

"How does that work, exactly?" Mom asks.

"He's a real *person*, he's just not really my boyfriend. It's a shame, though. You'd think so too if you could see his ass. And his face. They're both nice."

My father snorts. "But what about the flash mob? That sounds dangerous."

"No way, Dad!" Leave it to him to think a flash mob actually includes incendiary devices. "It's not dangerous," I say. "Unless you're worried about humiliating yourself. Which I'm not. It's singing and dancing in a crowd. It's about as dangerous as a bridal shower, but so much more exciting."

"It sounds stressful," my mother worries.

"That's the point! I've always loved how risky live theater is. A flash mob is like live theater on steroids. You have no idea whether it will work. But I'm not stressed. I'm *alive*. It's half *Sound of Music*, half *Mission Impossible*. I'm loving it so much."

"Hmmm," Sadie says, all therapist-like.

She doesn't understand, because she never understood why I wanted to be in theater. "What does that hmmm mean?"

Sadie unlatches Alfred. "Why do you think a flash mob is more exciting than a screen test for a part in a new television drama?"

Normally, I'd be a little annoyed that she's analyzing me. But it's a damn good question. Lately, the only things I've really been truly excited about are Hot Cop frisking me while we're in the shower (my fantasy), and when I've been planning this event. "Because it's not about me being *chosen*. Or getting ahead. It's creating something raw and impressive. I have one try to make this bride's day, and then the whole production fades away like Brigadoon. It's challenging."

"Well, there you have it."

"What?"

"You've always loved a challenge."

Huh. She's right. Before I can respond, Liam slips into view. He stands behind her, wraps his arms around her, and then kisses her neck. "Hey, Matthews clan," he says to us.

"Hey, professor," I say. He's not a professor, but he's wearing his glasses and I like to give him shit.

"How's our boy?" my mother asks. She loves Liam to pieces. And conversation shifts to his job and Sadie's twins.

And just like that, I'm out of the hot seat.

Until I glance at the clock. "Sorry, guys," I say, breaking into a conversation about building up little immune systems with sandbox play. "I gotta go. I'm off to make a marriage proposal happen."

"Proposal?" Liam asks. "Who..."

"I'll explain later," Sadie says.

We all blow kisses and I disconnect.

I really am excited about this. What I've got lined up is sort of epic. If I can pull it off...

I don't know exactly.

But if I can pull this off, I feel like something big could happen. Something big inside of me.

I'm not talking about Hot Cop inside of me, though that would be nice too.

It goes without saying that my flash mob might be a complete disaster. Rehearsal isn't foolproof. There are a million things that can still go wrong. Missed cues. Faulty props. Emergency interruptions.

I'm so nervous. But it's still the good kind of nervous. Butterflies and hope. I can't wait to see what happens next.

———

NINETY MINUTES LATER, Aubrey approaches me, clipboard in hand, messy bun tilting on top of her head, huge glasses sliding down her nose. She's wearing a cute, flouncy sundress covered in tiny champagne bottles. She's all sorts of adorable. "Okay. Are we ready?"

"Everyone is in place," I assure both of us.

"But are we *ready*, ready? Or just sort of ready?" I open my mouth to answer, but the poor thing just keeps going. "I mean, I really want to expand my business, you know? But this is terrifying. I'm not saying I don't trust you—I do. I saw all the work you put in. But there are *so* many people here! I can't tell who's part of the production and who's here for fresh zucchini flowers! Those are really tasty when fried and stuffed. I haven't had them in years and..."

I put my hands on her shoulder. Sort of to calm her down, but also to keep her from floating off into outer space. "We're ready," I say. "*Ready*, ready."

"Okay." She takes a deep breath. "Good."

We're standing in the middle of the farmers' market. It's noon on a Saturday, and the place is packed. I'm sure the weekends are always busy, but this is Next Level busy.

This is Flash Mob busy.

The farmers' market is a long, narrow space, with a huge metal roof covering the booths that line each side. In the center, people mill around with environmentally correct fabric shopping bags stuffed with fresh produce. There are mounds of fresh vegetables and herbs, and baskets of flowers.

But that's not all. There's handmade pottery, grass fed beef, and artisanal goat yogurt. (*From* goats. Not *for* goats.) There's also a guy who sells pasties, and every time I see his sign, I wonder if he knows that word has two definitions. One kind of pasty is a savory meat pie, and the other is what strippers use to cover their nipples.

I try not to confuse those.

A breeze brushes past my nose, and it's scented with flowers and dill. Sunshine filters in, dappling the merchandise with light. Really, if someone were proposing to me, this would be a pretty cool spot.

A quick peek at my watch tells me we're two minutes from go-time. I glance around. If you know what to look for, you can spot the theater people. They may be dressed like normal people, but they move with a curious fluidity.

Recruiting all my acting buddies for this gig wasn't easy. Hell, I recruited anyone who would agree to show up. But it was my awkward, nerdy theater friends who were the most delighted to be included in this little scheme. Every participant is getting paid for their time, but even after expenses and the rehearsal space, I'll still walk away with a couple grand.

Not bad for a week's worth of on-and-off work. I could get used to this.

Aubrey jumps. Literally jumps. She spins around, pressing her hand to her ear, where a discreet earbud is tucked. But she's about as discreet as the Secret Service at a political parade. "The target is back from her lunch break!" she yelps.

"That's good," I say in my most soothing voice. "Be chill, Aubrey. You have no chill."

"Chill. Right. Chill," she mutters. "Is the sky ready?"

Wordlessly, I point up at the ceiling, where the silk and ribbons are suspended.

"Right. Great. Okay. I'll tell everyone to *assume the position.*"

"The phrase you're looking for is *'places, everyone,'*" I point out. "This isn't a porn shoot."

"Yeah, okay." Aubrey raises a finger to her right nostril, closing it off, and takes a deep inhale. Then she switches sides.

"Are you okay?"

"Alternate nostril breathing calms me down." After a moment she taps her phone and gives the signal. "*Places everyone.*"

Finally!

I take a casual glance down the row of booths, toward Loon Lake Dairy. Our client is standing there selling cheese that retails for thirty bucks a pound. He's about to ask his girlfriend to make a lifelong commitment. If anyone should be nervous, it's him. But I guess he outsourced that to Aubrey.

Just across from him is the flower seller's stand. That's how these two met—gazing into each other's eyes during slow market days. As I watch, my high-school friend Lydia steps up to the booth and hands over forty dollars. She points at a bouquet of roses.

"What if she says no?" Aubrey whispers. "That will be so embarrassing. Besides, I need her to say yes. This wedding gig would be huge. His family owns the Groovy Brewery. They're loaded and the beer is really good."

"It'll work," I say. It has to work. Because my whole psyche is betting on it. That big thing I felt like was happening to me? It kind of hinges on this event. "She won't say no," I promise. The flower seller is in love with the cheesemonger. I know because I'm half in love with him myself. He makes homemade cheese, for fuck's sake. What's not to love about that?

Lydia takes the roses she's purchased and places them in a basket she wears over her arm. And it's time to cue the rest of my people. Quickly, I raise both of my arms in the air and wave them, as if landing a plane. And here comes the plane!

Not an actual plane, obviously. I don't have the budget for that. But I do have the budget for singers. Lydia steps back and sings the opening line from my favorite song from our old high-school musical, *Oliver.* "Who will buy these sweet red roses?"

Her voice is so beautiful. It's the kind of voice that's so clear and clean that you feel like there's hope somewhere in the world.

Our flower seller cocks her head, listening. A little smile plays on her face. She's not accustomed to her customers serenading her. But Lydia has such confidence that it almost doesn't seem weird.

Almost.

I get goosebumps as our friend Edward steps up beside Lydia and takes the next line of the song. He has a great voice, too. In another high-school production, Edward played Tony to my Maria.

The flower seller doesn't know that, though. At this point, Edward and Lydia might just be the kind of kooky couple who breaks into song at the farmers' market.

And my goosebumps double, because heads are starting to turn. It's thrilling. I've always thought of theater as something you have to walk into willingly. You buy a ticket and sit down and wait to be entertained.

But this is a different kind of magical brew. As curious customers lift their chins to the sound of my two friends harmonizing, they become part of the performance that's unfolding around them.

Two booths over, my friend Yashi gets up from where she's seated on a barrel. She lifts a quart of perfect strawberries into the air and sings a haunting line, asking, "*Who will buy?*"

Our flower seller's eyes widen. And then a hint of recognition dawns in her smile. She's starting to understand that something special is happening. But she still has no idea that it's all happening for her!

Even my goosebumps have goosebumps.

More singers join in. They're carrying baskets of roses—white and yellow ones. The crowd gapes. The song builds to a dozen singers. My performers walk the length of the market in a loop, before coming to stand in front of the flower seller.

And then you can see it on her face—the certainty that something wonderful is unfolding, and she's at the center of it. Her man has slipped out from behind his cheeses and moves to stand beside her.

That's when the violin comes in. It will be followed by more violins, and a mandolin, a harmonica, and even a cello. My friends are rocking it! This will be a story the couple will tell for years to come.

I have to admit that my eyes get a little misty. Maybe it's the beautiful music and the smile on her face. There's no time for crying though. I can't even spare a second to wonder why I'm never the girl in the middle of the circle. Because my bit part is coming up next. I slip between two market stalls and head for the flower seller.

11 GOOD PIPES

Maguire

"Why are we stopping here?" Lance asks from the passenger's seat as the cruiser approaches the farmers' market.

"Well..." That's a question not easily answered. Meg has a pull on me. It's sort of like what I imagine being pulled into the Bermuda Triangle is like. You just can't resist.

"I thought we were taking those photos of the bank lobby for the sergeant?"

"Snacks first," I grunt. Because Lance is always up for a snack.

"Righteous idea," he agrees. "But here?"

I pull into a parking spot. "They sell food here."

"They sell *kale,*" Lance snorts. "That's not food. That's what food eats."

"Dunno how you survive on burgers and peanut butter." I open the door and step out. "Look. Organic pastries. You're a cop. Go buy a donut."

"I hope they're not *healthy.*" He shudders and then stomps off.

At least he didn't ask me *why* I chose this stop. I'm not sure what answer I'd give him. The truth is that Meg is here somewhere. And when it comes to her, I have poor impulse control.

Honestly, I blame the laundry room. That's where I ran into her just the other day. While I separated my lights from my darks, she told me about the crazy musical number she's organized. She even asked me to participate.

I'd laughed out loud. "Nobody wants to hear me sing."

"Not true!" she'd argued. "You could wear your uniform! It would be so cool for a cop to suddenly join in."

"Cool for people without ears, maybe. Besides, I gotta work."

She'd waved a hand, dismissing both arguments. "You sing. Why are you pretending you don't?"

"You're high," I'd argued. "Should I frisk you for the bong you've obviously been hitting?"

That vixen only gave me a sexy smirk. "Frisk me already. And you're lying."

"Why would you say that?"

She'd opened her dryer and pulled out the tiniest pair of pink underwear I've ever seen. My brain activity dropped in half as I tried to picture them against her smooth, coppery skin. "Thin walls," she said.

"Uh, what?"

"Thin walls, Hot Cop. I've heard you singing in the shower. I've heard every noise you've made for the past six weeks. Especially when Nicole was staying with you."

This bit of insight blindsided me. And I was still staring at those panties. Meg could see it in my face, too. So she twirled them around on her finger. Then she took a step closer to me. All my warning bells started to ring. *Warning! Retreat! No hooking up with your neighbor! Too risky. Too close. Too much trouble.*

But I didn't budge. My brain was not the boss of me in that particular moment.

Meg leaned in close and said, "You have a nice baritone, Copper. Good pipes."

Her lips were so close to mine. It's been impossible to forget their softness. That fake kiss at the bridal shower is still burned into my consciousness.

Now Meg was offering me a chance at a real kiss. All it would have taken was the slightest turn of my chin. I could finally taste her. Slow and deep.

But we all know how that would play out. I'd probably hoist her up on the dryer, spread her legs, and go to town while the laundry shuddered under us.

But no. I didn't move. Discipline won, if only by a nose.

Meg hovered there for a beat, waiting. Then she tucked that thong into my front pocket, patted it, scooped the rest of her laundry into a bag, and disappeared. I just stood there. Dick nice and hard. Big stupid grin forming on my face. Trouble. Trouble. *Trouble*.

I can't get that girl out of my system. She keeps popping up, tempting me with her snark and her long arms that I want to feel wrapped around me, or even better, her long legs wrapped around me while I...

No, Maguire. Don't go toward the light.

It's been a hot summer so far, just saying. And all week I haven't done any singing in the shower, so she won't try to recruit me again.

Today's her big day, though. Even though I'm not willing to make an ass of myself by singing in public, I'm too curious to stay away. I mean, Lance and I were already in the neighborhood, so I'm just being a gentleman in swinging by to watch.

Lance is already halfway to the pastries, as I lock the car and approach the market. I can't pick out Meg in the crowd, but I can already hear the music. At least a dozen people are playing instruments. They're circling a smiling woman in the flower stall. She has her hands pressed to her face, and her eyes look shiny.

There's a nice feeling in the air right now. And I know that's all Meg's doing. She's the kind of person who weaves magic around people. She's like a firefly. She's lighter and brighter than everyone else. I can't help but smile a little whenever she's nearby.

And that woman in the flower stall? Now a man approaches her, hands thrust in his pockets. He's wearing a Loon Lake Dairy apron and a proud smile. Lucky guy. He's got all his shit figured out. He makes the world's most expensive cheese for a living, and he's made his girl tear up with music and attention.

I can tell by looking at this man that I'm never gonna have him in the back of a cruiser. Sometimes you just know. Some people are just plain made of light. But most of us have a dark side. Or at least a side the light can't reach.

I'm too much inside my head, maybe. I try to focus on the music instead.

The violins rise to a fevered pitch, and then another dozen people launch into song. And, wow. They've got some lungs. It's stunning to hear so many voices at once. I feel myself get very quiet inside.

When was the last time I heard live music? I'd forgotten what it felt like to be so close to a song that you can feel it in your chest. The fiddle has crawled down into my gut and given everything a tug.

I don't even recognize myself right now. But I'm not sure I care.

Then I finally spot Meg. She's actually climbing a ladder that's leaning against one of the beams holding up the metal roof. She's being subtle about it, like she doesn't want to draw attention to herself. She's wearing tight pants and Chuck T's, and her face is one hundred percent concentration.

When she reaches the top, she pauses up there, just watching the action. The expression on her face is pure joy. Just for a second I actually forget I'm me. I let the song pulse through my blood, and as I'm watching Meg, I hear myself sing along with the chorus.

The girl was right, anyway. I do like to sing. It's just that I haven't done so in a long time.

I'm not the only one watching Meg, though. I spot a security guard whose gaze is stuck on her like a tattoo. On her ass, specifically. But as she climbs even higher, he starts to frown. Like he's just remembered why he's here, and he can't figure out why she'd climb that ladder.

The little velvet box in her hand ought to be a clue, though. And there's some kind of prop affixed to the ceiling above her.

The security guy, though, is confused. And I'm sucked out of the music for a bit and straight into cop mode.

He's a young man, which is a red flag. An older security guard is usually a retired cop—a good guy with good instincts, who knows how to spot trouble brewing. But young guards are often hotheads who couldn't get a real law enforcement job. They crave the power of the uniform, but they don't have sufficient smarts or restraint. And sometimes they have a chip on their shoulder from not getting the job they think they deserve.

It's that chip I'm concerned about right now.

Sure enough, just as Meg gets to the top step of the ladder, he touches her ankle. "Hey!" he calls. I can't hear him over the music, but I can see his face. He's pinched and red-faced. And about two seconds from being a complete asshole.

She doesn't look at him. She's watching the action, and waiting for some kind of cue.

"Hey!" He grabs the ladder.

I'm already on the move, dodging bodies, trying to make it over there before he destabilizes that ladder and tips the whole thing over.

By the time I reach them, Meg is looking down at him, eyes wide with fear.

"Gotta ask you to step down," the guy shouts, oblivious.

"Sir," I growl, causing the guard to whirl around. "Step away from the ladder." I use my cop voice. Low. Quiet. And dead-as-fuck serious.

"But—"

I pull out my shield. He squints at it. "My badge is real. Now back off."

He sneers at me. "You gonna stop me from doing my job? I'm protecting the market from dangerous elements."

"You mean *her*?" I point up at Meg. "You gotta be kidding me."

"Well what's she doing up there?"

"No idea," I admit. "But it's part of this..." I wave my arms around. "And she has the proper permits," I lie. Meg doesn't strike me as a by-the-book kind of girl.

"Gotta see that," rent-a-cop says. He reaches for the ladder.

I knock his hand away.

"Hey!" He looks like he actually wants to punch a police officer.

Knew he was dumb. And the glare I give him is the same one that terrifies all the recruits. "You don't keep the peace by endangering someone on a ladder." I take a step forward, forcing him to take a step back. "And why, when there are so many people here, did you follow *her*?"

Meg looks about as threatening as a puppy wagging its tail. I look up and find her reaching over her head for a blue ribbon. And when she gives it a tug, a giant blue silk parachute unfurls, opening itself against the roofline. It's like there's a blue sky rippling above us. Now

Meg is affixing the little velvet box to a silk bird, which she's lowering with a pulley to the man in the apron.

Mr. Loon Lake catches it, then drops to one knee just as the singers hit their last chord.

As silence falls, he opens the box to reveal a ring. "Will you marry me, Gretchen?"

Gretchen is already nodding and squealing. "Yes!" The crowd lets out a collective gasp. They were here to buy lettuce, and they accidentally witnessed a small miracle.

Even I feel a twinge in my gut at this moment. I don't even have a name for the way this whole scene makes me feel.

Above me, Meg looks absolutely triumphant. And the applause is deafening. She climbs down a moment later, beaming. "Did you see the whole thing?" she squeals. "It was magic!"

"Saw some," I tell her. And the security guard has finally wised up and moved on. That fool is probably looking for someone else to bother.

Meg leaps to the ground and grabs me into a hug.

Goddammit, her hugs are gonna kill me. Today she smells like strawberries, roses, and every lustful thought I've ever had in my whole life. I step back, trying to keep my hunger off my face. "The music sounded great," I say, just to keep things normal.

"I know!" She claps her hands. "But it was more than just a performance. It was a big moment in somebody's life. And I made that. I'm *hooked*, Copper. I'm going to see if Aubrey wants to do more of these."

"Lookout, world," I say with an uneasy laugh. If she does more of these, we're going to have to have a chat about warning the security personnel. "I'd better get back to work."

"What are you doing here, anyway?" she thinks to ask.

"Just in the neighborhood."

"Great to see you." She gives me a flirty smile and darts away.

Just in the neighborhood. That's my general issue with Meg. She is literally my closest neighbor. I can't get away from her.

And I really don't want to.

12 THE EROTIC VERSION OF THE STAR WARS TRASH COMPACTOR SCENE

Meg

"Oh, can't you stay just a bit longer?" I whine. I'm drinking wine and whining at the same time, so everything is sorta rhyming and in perfect balance.

"I have to go," Cassidy sighs. "My Lyft is one minute away, and I have a plan to surprise Greg by dropping by tonight."

"But what about my needs?"

For the past hour, we've been celebrating on my little deck. By celebrating, I mean drinking cheap champagne and watching the moon rise. The moon is perfect tonight—full and golden. And although champagne gives me a headache, it tastes celebratory. *Here's to making a hefty sack of change! Here's to flash mobs! Here's to my new business ideas!*

"We've toasted everything but world peace, and it's barely eight o'clock," she says. "And this is my last chance to see Greg before he goes out of town."

"Wait." I grab Cassidy's knee. "Is tonight The Night?"

"I dunno." She stands up and shakes off my hand, which I was basically using to hold her down. "Maybe."

"Did you wear sexy underwear?" I pry.

She bites her lip. "So what if I did?"

"Oh, honey. Don't sleep with him just because you're wearing lingerie that has to be hand-washed. Make sure he's worth it."

"Get out of my brain," she complains. "I hate hand-washing silk. And we've already been on three dates."

I laugh out loud. "But you seem about as physically drawn to him as you are in fucking your tax return."

"Well, that's apropos because he *is* an accountant," she says. "I mean on paper he's perfect. Handsome. Educated. Good family. Rich..."

"And...?" I wait for her to admit the truth.

"Fine—incredibly boring. There's no passion there. We've kissed and his lips were cold. Actually cold! Like a pickled fish."

"See?" I bellow, maybe a little loudly. *Hello, champagne.* "Do not sleep with him! Tonight is not the night to say, *make dirty love to me.* Because I don't think he's capable of it. Tonight is the night you say *ta ta for now, pickle.*"

"You're drunk," she says, laughing. "At least I'm out there looking."

"Oh, I'm looking. I'm just not finding. And you aren't either. Seriously, Cassidy, wait for the guy that you just can't keep your hands off of. The one who wakes you up at night. The one you imagine tasting. The one who you just want to unzip and crawl inside."

She stares at me. "I was with you until that last bit."

"Sorry," I say. "I'm a little..."

"Drunk?"

"Happy," I say. Because it's true.

"Gotta go. I'll figure it out." She makes a move toward my kitchen. "I'll let myself out. And don't worry! I'll call you if I need you, or text you from the bathroom if I need you to rescue me."

"Okay. Deal."

She steps back toward me, refills my glass one more time, and then heads out.

Ten bucks says that Greg wears tighty whities to bed. But at least Cassidy is having sex tonight. That makes one of us.

I sit here a while longer, rocking gently in the nighttime air on the love-seat glider I bought today. It's a gift to myself. It isn't the hippest piece of outdoor furniture. But it was on sale for ninety-nine dollars. And that's a good enough reason. Now I can sit out here on my deck in comfort, watching the rising moon.

When I was younger I had dreams of becoming a rich, famous actress. But this year I can feel my goal starting to shift. I still want to live my life creatively. I'm not about to go to accountant school and change my name to Greg. But it's just dawning on me that a creative life could take many forms. Today I put on a show in a way that pays the bills.

Today was a good day.

It's peaceful out here. I anchor my foot against the deck boards and give my glider a little swing. I've got my bubbly, what's left of the charcuterie board Cassidy brought, and two *Pierson of Interest* scripts in my lap. Cassidy was going to finish running lines with me, but we kept getting distracted. My audition is first thing Monday morning, so I really need to be prepared.

I've already got the lines memorized. But every time I practice, it just feels like something is missing. One of the scenes is a hot flirtation between the character I'd play, Elsa, and a dirty cop. I don't mean sexy dirty, but *dirty* dirty. He'll end up getting my character killed four episodes later. (Bastard!) And while it's a well-written scene, I just can't seem to grab a hold of it. I can't feel enough of Elsa in this scene. It's just...hollow.

Maybe I'm the hollow one, though. Maybe Sadie is right. I've been auditioning forever, and nothing's stuck. Maybe I'm just afraid to invest myself one more time. I may have reached the breaking point with my career. How long am I going to do something that only makes me feel inadequate and hollow?

I sure didn't feel inadequate this morning when I pulled off that flash mob. It was so satisfying to be the one pulling the strings for once, instead of being the puppet.

The script lays abandoned once again in my lap as I daydream about other flash mobs I could produce. I can't wait to talk with Aubrey again. I want to know if she feels like taking on a partner and building something new.

Speaking of partnering... I hear my neighbor's door open and close next door. Then I hear him moving about in his apartment. He sighs, and even that is sexy. It's a warm night, so naturally I hear him step outside to take in the breeze.

"You peeping over here at me, Copper?" I call out.

He peeks over the divider, all cute-like. "That depends. Are you topless?" He asks this somewhat hopefully.

"No, because I'm not in the mood to be arrested for indecent exposure."

"How do you feel about public drunkenness?" he asks. "I could bring over some beers."

I momentarily weigh the alcohol content of my blood and then decide a little more won't matter. "Let's give it a shot."

"Sure. Two seconds."

It takes him longer than two seconds. It takes him about ten minutes. I would've wondered why, but I hear the shower running. And now I'm picturing him naked in the hot stream of water, rubbing his soapy hands all over himself, and thinking how much I'd enjoy breaking into his apartment again to join him.

But I don't know if I could make it over the fence without killing myself right now.

It's the bubbly. It's made me tipsy. And that sound you just heard was *not* a burp. That was the bubbles effervescing. Out of me.

No fence jumping tonight. Or fence crawling. Both ideas are bad bad bad.

Instead, I make the twenty-step trip through my apartment to unlock my own door. Then I return to my glider chair and my champagne and my forgotten scripts.

The scripts. The scripts that could change my whole life and give me everything I want.

Everything I thought I wanted.

So why can't I seem to want it enough to fucking rehearse the scenes?

I pick one up again, like a good girl.

I'm rereading the familiar lines when I can *feel* Mac come in through my apartment. His approach makes the hair on the back of my neck stand up. Not with fear, though. Excitement. Then he's standing in front of me. And...

He's shirtless.

Holy shit.

He's wearing khaki shorts and nothing else. His feet are bare and he's holding a six-pack of beer to match the six-pack on his front. My brain freezes, and all I can really take in is how incredibly ripped he is. All those muscles I want to trace with my tongue. His chest isn't barren. He has just enough pale hair to sift my fingers through. And that V leading down to the bulge of his jeans...

I drain the rest of my drink, but it isn't cold enough to put out my fire. Then he sits next to me on the glider, smelling amazing. I don't know what products he uses in the shower, but I just want to bury my nose in his lap.

Focus, Meg!

"So...how was...work?" I finally ask, hoping I don't squeak like a middle-school girl with backstage passes to Shawn Mendes.

He takes a pull on his beer. Runs his hand through his still damp hair, which looks darker because it's still wet. "It was a rough day."

He doesn't elaborate. Typical Maguire. Usually I don't mind, but if he doesn't speak right this minute, I'm going to hop on him and start humping. I need a little conversation here. "That's it? That's all I get? How about some details?"

He thinks it over.

"Come on, Copper, you can talk to me you know. I don't bite." I pause. "Unless I'm aroused."

He snorts.

He thinks I'm kidding.

He takes another long drink, sets the bottle down, and then adjusts himself! Oh, what a man! What a delicious hunk of man. "I'm trying to get promoted." Five words. But he sits back like that should do it.

"And?" I coax. "Maguire, seriously, you are a shit storyteller."

He snorts again. "I know. Let's just say I'm a man of action, not words."

"Oh, I can imagine. But you're the one who said we can't date. We can't fool around. And yet here you sit half naked on my new deck furniture. And there's alcohol. So you'd better start talking before I think up some other things for us to do."

He snickers. Then he takes a deep drink from his beer. "Fine, Trouble. You can hear all about my issues, if you're so keen."

"Spill."

He sighs. "I'm trying to get a promotion at work, where I'd be the head of a task force. I'd be helping victims of crime after the perp is arrested, when everyone's waiting for the trial date. There's a real opportunity to follow through. Because arresting the criminal isn't the end, you know? Victims need the tools to get past what happened and lead healthy lives."

He falls silent again. But that was already more words than I've ever heard him speak at once. "You are endlessly fascinating, Copper. Are you going to get this promotion? Why was it a bad day?"

He sighs. "It's down to me and this assface. Tommy. I've got more cred than Tommy. More street time. More arrests. More respect. But you know what Tommy has that I don't?"

"I can't imagine," I say. "A third nipple?"

This wins me a wry smile. "Tommy has the ability to kiss our captain's ass. I don't have time for that. I don't want to talk about the captain's golf game or his daughter's 18th birthday in the Bahamas that he's planning. But that's Tommy's game. Chat up the boss, and win the promotion. It's so insincere, but it seems to be working. I don't think he gives a rat's ass about the victims he'd be helping. He just wants a bigger paycheck and a little more respect. I think he'd actually do more harm than good."

Another lengthy speech from Mac. That's two in one night! I let his words sink in while he sips his beer.

"So you need some help with ass-kissing."

"Naw," he scoffs. "I need some help in convincing the captain that I'm the best man for the job."

"Exactly. That's what I said. Ass-kissing."

"Never. There's only one kind of ass-kissing I do..." I can hear the smirk in his voice.

Suddenly my lady bits are on high alert. Better change the subject. "Okay. Look. I think I can help you with this."

"How? You gonna kiss the captain's ass on my behalf?"

I shake my head. I need to think on it before I offer him my services. "Never mind for now. Can you give me a hand with something?"

"What's that?"

"I need you to read this scene with me."

He full out laughs. "No way. I'm no actor."

"You don't have to act it out. Just read it like a cop. This scene is for that TV audition I told you about. I've got a callback to play a character who has a torrid affair with a cop and..."

"Oh! Am I helping you with a sex scene? Because I could totally do that." There's a little bit of a pause here and then he seems to catch himself. "You know. If we weren't neighbors."

Now it's my turn to laugh. *Hell yes, Copper! Help me with a sex scene. Let's rehearse it right now.* "Sadly, there aren't any lines to rehearse in that scene. Just a lot of grunting. I need help with these lines."

He takes the script that I thrust at him.

"So the scene is pretty basic. You've come over for dinner and you're telling me all about a collar you just did." I stand up and offer him my hand. "Come on, then."

He gets up. But then he leaves the deck, heading into my apartment. I hear my front door open a moment later.

Wait, what? Did he just walk out? At least he left the beer...

A moment later, though, I hear the door open again. He reappears wearing a pair of reading glasses, solid black frames, and I spontaneously combust. Maguire with glasses? Hot and sweet at the same time? It's too much.

The alcohol I've consumed does another lap around my bloodstream. If he's actually going to run lines with me, I wonder if I will even be able to remember my part.

He holds up the script, and using the light that bleeds onto the deck from my kitchen, reads to himself for a minute. "Okay. This is garbage. Nobody makes a collar this way."

"He's not making a collar," I point out. "He's bragging about making one."

"So he's a tool. He's mansplaining a collar to a female cop?" He peers at me through those glasses, and I have the urge to pull them off his face and kiss him.

"That's the sum of it," I admit. "He's also the son of the police commissioner."

Maguire rolls his eyes. "Of course he is. Maybe this isn't so inaccurate after all."

"Are you going to read it?" I ask. "Or just stand there making me sexually frustrated."

He barks out a laugh. "Fine. I'll pretend to be this douchecanoe. But remember that you asked for it."

"Yes, *sir*."

His eyes darken. He holds my gaze for a moment. Then his eyes drop to the script, and he begins to read in a gravelly voice. "You shoulda been there, Elsa. I had this guy's nuts in a vice. I put him in the van, and then it's just me and the girl."

"Let me guess," I say, giving him the next line. "You let her go out of the kindness of your heart?"

"Not possible." Maguire suddenly moves his hand down to cover his fly. "I'm all dick and no heart."

"So I've heard." It comes out breathy. When I was practicing this with Cassidy, we were giggling too much for me to take any of this seriously. But with Mac, it's a different story. Everything with Mac is different. That strong hand cupping himself over his jeans? I can't find the will to look away.

He throws the script onto the deck and stalks toward me, where I'm standing by the fence. He takes both my hands in one of his larger ones and raises them over my head, pinning me. "*Stay right there, Miss*, I said to her. *I need to frisk you.*"

Oh my. I never imagined he'd do the blocking as well as read the lines. And now I'm sandwiched between the fence boards and his washboard abs. The scent of his shampoo wafts over me as he glares down at me with a fierce expression.

And I forget my next line.

Silence ticks by while I try to remember what my character is supposed to say. Oh! I got it. "How'd she take it?" I finally ask, trying to maintain my bravado. That's in the script, too.

"She took it like a girl who didn't want to spend the night in a holding cell. She took it on her knees, while I frisked her mouth with my cock." He even snarls the line, like an asshole. Like a good actor, too.

"You're going to get caught," I say quietly. I lift my chin and let myself stare into his eyes. "One of these days it's all going to catch up with you."

"Not today, though," he rasps, nailing the line, then trapping my hips against his, pinning me in place. It's like the erotic version of the *Star Wars* trash compactor scene.

Don't judge my metaphors. It's a classic.

Meanwhile, my hormones are firing like crazy. And I'll be damned if this scene doesn't make more sense to me than it did an hour ago. This scene is about risky choices. About taking what you want but don't deserve.

"Meg?" he rasps.

"Yeah?" I whisper.

"I don't remember what happens next, and I tossed your script on the floor."

Oh, please. "Like we don't both know what happens next. You need a teleprompter?"

He makes a quiet growling sound and drops my wrists to capture the back of my head instead. We both pause for a moment, just a breath, as if suspended between this moment and the next. What's going to happen? Do we go forward or do we go back?

Then I'm kissed like I've never been kissed before.

Firm lips catch me and then claim me.

And I'm so ready.

I slide into the kiss like I was born to it. He tastes like beer and heat.

"Fuck," he says, tilting his head, changing the angle. As if he can't quite believe we're doing this. His lips slide against mine, and then deepen their pressure. His fingers tighten in my hair, and I open for him.

And, wow. His bossy tongue is right there against mine. I spar with him, tasting him. My hands—flailing from sensory overload—find his bare chest. And the contact with his skin is a shock. I feel myself tighten inside, the pressure mounting. My palms skim down his ribcage, my thumbs bumping over each muscular ripple.

Our mouths are locked together now, and the moment one kiss stops, another one begins. We struggle a little, both trying to figure out how to move even closer. He bats my hand off his tight tummy and then scoops a hand under my bottom, lifting me up, pinning me against the fence a little higher than I was before.

I wrap my legs around him on impulse. He groans, and our kiss becomes a dirty grind.

Holy hell. We're going to wind up on my bed, if we even make it to my bed. There is a spectacular erection trying its best to burst through Mac's shorts. And I'm in the mood to help it along. Except I don't ever want this kiss to end. I wrap my arms around him and press my breasts against all that skin and muscle.

This should have been a silk underwear night for me, too. *Who knew?*

"You did," he growls into my mouth.

Whoops. I guess I said that out loud.

"You and your sexy script and your wicked mouth. Do you know what entrapment is?"

"No," I purr against the corner of his mouth.

"Me neither. Not anymore. I can't think when you look at me like I'm a stolen dessert."

"I'm very devious." I lean in and bite his lower lip gently. "Maybe you should punish me."

"Oh you know it," he growls, lifting me higher up on his body. Then I'm truly airborne, and Mac is carrying me toward the door to the kitchen. He flips it open with impatience bordering on violence.

Two seconds later I'm set down on the kitchen counter. Good thing I cleaned up earlier today, because I'm seated right on the prep surface while Mac tugs down my tank top and bra all in one go, exposing my breast. Before I'm ready, he dips his head and applies his tongue to my nipple.

"Oh, damn," I gasp. "More." I pull his head closer. His hair slides between my fingers. And I feel like I can't get enough of him. Like I want him to fill me up and possess me from the inside out. I feel like I want to crawl inside him...like..."Yes!" I cry.

And then...

No.

Mac jumps off me, yanking my top up to cover my breast again. And I can't even figure out why for a moment. How can we go from me with my nipple in his mouth to me fully clothed in two seconds flat. And why? Whhhhhyyyyyyy?

Then Cassidy tumbles through the front door. "Meg! You won't *believe* this bullshit!" She stops to let out a sob. "By the time my Lyft pulled up at Greg's, he was already deep into someone else's hand-washables!"

Mac and I are both still gasping for breath. He's stepped back a goodly distance, and is playing it cool, leaning against my sofa. But our eyes are locked on each other, with identical expressions of shock and longing.

"Wait, am I interrupting?" Cassidy bleats.

"Not at all," Mac grumbles. "I really shoulda been out of here a while ago."

Well, ouch.

"Night, Meg," he says cooly.

"N-night," I stammer, trying to interpret his Mac-speak. Did he really not notice that Earth moved a little just now? Or is he just being Maguire?

A moment later my front door opens and shuts again. That door is seeing a lot more action than I am tonight.

My heart rate hasn't even slowed down yet. But now he's gone.

"Can you believe that?" Cassidy is saying, and I realize I missed the first part. "He said *I'm* boring! Me! I have two masters' degrees! I speak three languages! I can tell the difference between Californian wine and French in one sniff! That last thing isn't useful. Fine. But I am NOT the boring one in this relationship."

"Of course not, sweetie," I say, hopping off the countertop. "How dare he."

She bursts into tears.

13 USE YOUR GLUE STICK

Maguire

"So that's it? You kissed her and then left?" Lance asks me this while eating a meatball sub in the passenger's seat. I wish he'd asked me *after* he'd finished that sub, but no. He's mid-chew.

I can't believe I even brought it up. But it was either that or listen to him spout off more of his "research." He's currently binging an erotic motorcycle series. So I spent the morning hearing about the biker jacket with a patch on it that he just bought. Now he wants to find his old lady. The dude can't even ride a motorcycle. He has a Schwinn 10-speed.

Where was I?

"Come on! You kissed her and then what? Just walked out?" Lance has no patience, but I'm grateful for the reminder of the question.

"No I didn't just walk out. I kissed her and then we did some scrapbooking. What do you think? Yeah! I just left. She's my neighbor. You know my rules about that. I shouldn't have even touched her to begin with, but...I mean, you've seen her, right?"

Lance wiggles his eyebrows and I have the sudden urge to thrust that meatball sub down his throat. I don't like the idea of Lance anywhere near Meg.

I take a sophisticated slurp of my lemonade to calm myself. We need to get back on the road in a minute anyway.

"Oh, I've *seen* her all right," he pants. "Gorgeous. Amazing. She's smart too, which, don't tell anyone, I think is probably of higher value than the looks. I mean you want a girl you can grab ahold of and all, but you also want one who can solve *Wheel of Fortune* words better than you. Competition is good for the libido." He chews, swallows, and then crinkles up the spaghetti-stained paper. Thank God that's over. Maybe I'll get my appetite back. "Also, I was waiting for you to tell me scrapbooking was one of them whadayacallits? Eugenics or something."

"Euphemism?" I ask.

"Yeah. Euphemism. Like I could go home and do some *scrapbooking* right now."

"Are you going to use your *glue stick*?"

"Awwwww yeah!"

This is my life right now. How did I get here?

I should interrupt Lance right now because I can see he's thinking hard. And that is a scary thing on Lance. The wheels are turning in that pointy head. "So..."

I brace myself.

"What if you changed your rules? Be the author of your own story, Mac. Write your own next chapter. I think I saw that on Instagram. What I would've done in your situation is I would've banged her. Pushed her up against the wall and told her *I want you more than I want to breathe right now.* And then I'd kiss her some more, just to warm up. And then the good stuff happens. I read this string thing once in a book..."

I'm really trying to focus. Is Lance going to tell me something about String Theory?

"...It involves a complicated system of like ropes and pulleys and stuff so you tie her up, or she ties you up, whatever, and according to how you maneuver the pulley system, you can expose any part of her body...with her consent, mind you, I'm not a monster...and that's what I would've done next."

I know I shouldn't ask him any questions, but sometimes I just can't stop myself. "Where would you get the pulley system?"

"Oh, anywhere. Home Depot? And if I didn't have a pulley system handy, I'd make one out of a soup can and some duct tape."

"What?" I sputter.

"Yeah. Duct tape is fucking amazing. And I've got rope in my car. All the time. I'm prepared. So I'd create this intricate pulley system and I'd..."

I've had enough. "Let's go," I say.

Also, I'm ashamed to admit, I'm a little turned on by the idea of Meg in front of me, wrapped in rope. Or silk. Or just plain naked.

Wait. No. I will not think of Meg and how it felt to pin her up against the wall and finally kiss her, for real. I will not think of how instantly hard I was pressed up against her or how I felt actual thirst for her. I will not think of how much I wanted to take her to bed.

No. Nope. Nada.

Our radio squawks to life with a nearby call. Dispatch is looking for a unit to respond. So I grab that radio like it's a life raft and report that we're back on duty.

And just like that I'm back in cop mode. One thing this job has taught me is to be focused and disciplined. I need all the energy and focus I have to get the promotion I deserve.

So I'm not thinking about Meg at all this afternoon. Nope. For at least a solid hour, I'm Teflon. Or titanium. Whichever of those is stronger. It's working great until my cell phone lights up with a text that says I GOT THE FUCKING PART!

I immediately bust out with a stupid grin. I have to congratulate her, of course. That must be why I find myself pulling over to hit the dial button. Some things can't be texted. Good news has to be exchanged personally.

"Tell me," I say as soon as she answers.

"I'm in Chicago! And I did that same scene that you, um, helped me prepare..." Her voice has a smile in it. I like that. "And it took them all of three minutes to offer me the role. My agent said she's never had a callback that went so well."

"That's amazing!" There's a little smile in my voice too. I sound really freaking chipper, and Lance is giving me a look, so I dial back on that. But then it hits me, and it's like a cold bucket of water. "So when are you moving?" My neighbor is leaving my life as swiftly as she entered it. That's good, right? It's what I wished for.

I'm not sure why I feel a pain in my gut.

There's a pause. "Moving? What the fuck, Hot Cop. I'm not moving anywhere. I get killed off after six episodes. Plus, I've lived in Chicago before. I don't want that life anymore."

"Oh."

Ohhhh. I feel tremendous relief, and I don't even know why.

I clear my throat. "Well that's just great. And if you need some more help..." So much for discipline. What exactly can I offer her? We can practice that scene again? Naked? I can make love to you for hours? "You can do a ride-along with me," I blurt out. "For research. I'd have to get it approved, but we've done that for a couple of writers and a reporter once, so it shouldn't be an issue."

As soon as I say this, I realize it's a double-edged sword. If she was riding with me, I'd get a blessed break from Lance and his fucking soup-can pulley systems. On the other hand, she'd be sitting there looking cute and torturing me while I try to work.

But maybe she'll turn me down.

"Hell yes," Meg says immediately. "Ooh! This will also give me a chance to ask you a little bit more about this wedding we're going to. That's coming up, right?"

Hell. I try not to think about that. "Yeah. Soon."

"Awesome. I'll quiz you about what you're wearing, and who we're trying to make jealous."

All that energy I've spent not thinking about kissing Meg, or touching Meg, or fucking Meg, is out the window. And I'm thinking about all the shitty things in my life.

Then she asks a question that makes me freeze up a little inside. "Who do you want to make jealous anyway?"

I can't fucking breathe for a second. And not in a good way. "I gotta go," I wheeze. "We'll figure it out later."

"Okay—?"

"Talk soon." And I hang up. It's kind of a dick move and I feel bad about that, but I've got to maintain some boundaries. Meg gets me talking and somehow I turn into Silly Putty. It's not good.

I end the call, check the mirrors, and pull out into traffic again, hoping Lance will keep his mouth shut for a while.

No such luck.

"Hey! I've got another idea. If you don't have pulleys, there's always bungee cords."

It's going to be another long shift.

14 PEOPLE IN PAIRS

Meg

When I come back from Chicago, I have to work three shifts at the bar in two days. Pretty soon I'm going to have to tell The Hip Burger about the seven-week leave I'll need to play Elsa in *Pierson of Interest*. So that will be a fun conversation.

Speaking of fun, I don't manage to run into Mac at all, which is a bummer. He doesn't come out onto the deck when I'm out there. And he doesn't turn up in the laundry room on lingerie day.

I should call him Officer Hot and Cold. Sometimes he's lots of fun, and sometimes he clams up. I like a challenge. But he's an extreme case.

These are my thoughts as I head over to meet Aubrey and Cassidy at a bar for a rare night out. They're already at the table when I walk in, with a classic Hemingway Daiquiri in front of each of them. I know that they're drinking Hemingway Daiquiris because I introduced the drink to them last month. "Drink this," I'd demanded. "It's evil and good." It's basically grapefruit juice and rum, with a splash of attitude.

We can all use some attitude today, I think as I sit down.

Cassidy is still upset over Greg the Gorgon. "I saw his penis, and it looked like a snake," she's saying as I sit down at the table. "A really skinny snake."

"Oh, girl," I commiserate before even saying hello. "Then you didn't really miss out on anything."

"That's what I said!" Aubrey says and then immediately starts flapping her hands, sort of like a jazz dancer on cocaine. I'm really confused, until a Hemingway Daiquiri appears in front of me, its arrival timed perfectly and organized by our Wedding Planner Extraordinaire. I made good friend choices when I moved back to Michigan.

"I have a bit of a dilemma. Not a big dilemma. A mini dilemma," she says as I take my first sip. "I don't know what to do. Should I tell my newest bride-to-be-client that her groom made a pass at me? I mean—" she stops to take a breath—"I think it was a pass. Why else would he rub against me like that? Unless maybe he was trying to scratch a mosquito bite?"

"Not a mosquito bite," Cassidy says. "I have three brothers and they have no trouble scratching themselves."

"Ew. I guess that answers the question. I'll mention it to the bride-to-be."

There's a little bit of silence as we all take another calming sip of rum. Then I decide to ask Aubrey the question that's been weighing on me. "Okay, tell me the truth. In your line of work, how often do you just look at the couple and wonder why they're getting married?"

"Hmm." She taps her lip with an index finger. "Only about a quarter of the time."

"Yikes." Relationships are not for the faint of heart. "Well, I was going to ask you two how to convince a man who doesn't want to date to fall madly in love with me. And fuck me into tomorrow. Not necessarily in that order. I'm not even sure why I'm wondering this. I should be focused on I GOT THE FUCKING PART FOR THE TV SERIES!"

"Yes, you did!" Aubrey says. "Woo-hoo!"

"Okay, I'm confused," Cassidy admits. "Are we celebrating or are we depressed? Because I feel like I should be depressed, but I'm so happy for Meg that I want to celebrate."

She makes an excellent point. "We're still depressed for this first drink," I say. "When our glasses are empty, it's my turn to decide our feelings."

"No unhealthy psychological boundaries there," Aubrey says. We raise our glasses.

"To switching gears!" Cassidy says.

"To grooms who behave themselves!" Aubrey says.

"To getting my hot next-door neighbor to give me some on-the-job training," I smugly reply.

We toast.

"That last thing needs an explanation," says Cassidy.

So I tell them the story on how Mac offered to run lines with me, and then we ran a love scene, and then later he offered to extend the training to have me in a car with him. "He won't go out to lunch with me. But he's offered me a ride-along."

Is it me, or is "ride-along" a fun euphemism? I guess everything sounds like a fun euphemism when you've gone as long without sex as I have.

"Oh, gosh," Aubrey says. "That sounds dangerous. And delicious." Her face is flushed. I think a single Hemingway has caused her to slip to the dark side. Welcome, my friend. Welcome.

"You know," I say. "I've been single forever. And I'm good at it. I like it. But now I want something more."

"You mean you want a commitment? Someone who will date only you? Someone to fall in love with and who will love you back and who will put aloe vera on your boobs when you accidentally get sunburned the one and only time you've taken your top off at the pool when you were in Italy?" That's from Cassidy. Wistful Cassidy.

"Well..." I don't burn easily. So the aloe thing is probably moot. But is that what healthy relationships look like? My experience with those is close to zero. My messed-up and self-indulgent relationships are batting 100. Past boyfriends include: three-married-but-pretending-to-be-single men, an actor who was too good to be true and then I found out he was preparing for a role as a 1950s boyfriend for some made for TV movie, and a really nice guy who had about as much sex drive as a snail.

Then again, maybe snails have high sex drives. All that wetness.

At any rate, I have not been successful in love. And when I look around at Sadie, and her friends, and basically everyone everywhere, I just see people in pairs. And I want to be a pair. There's no shame in asking for what you want.

I realize Cassidy and Aubrey are staring at me. "Yes," I admit. "I want someone to rub soothing products onto my bazongas in a healthy, committed way."

There's a collective sigh.

"Look." Aubrey whips out a notebook. "I am a firm believer that anything can happen if you just make appropriate plans. And you exfoliate." Then she starts scribbling furiously.

I take a hefty drink, because I'm not quite used to the pink and rosy outlook on my new friends. My old actor friends always talked about the drama and despair in their lives. I'm still getting used to Aubrey who ends her signature with a heart.

Now she turns the notebook around and shows us what she's drawn.

"What the fuck is that?" I ask, feeling the Hemingway in me.

"It's a graph," Aubrey says.

Cassidy squints. "It's literally a line. It's just a single line."

"No. It's a line that *curves*. See? This is where you are." She draws a big dot at the start of the line. "This is where you end up." She follows the arch of the line and then ends with a big heart. "And in the middle is the good stuff."

"What good stuff?" I really want to know. Because I'm really confused.

"All the—" she looks around and leans in—"fucking." Then she laughs. You'd think that Aubrey would giggle or twinkle or snicker, but no, she's got a laugh like a marine. Like it's funny, but it's a laugh that causes pain. God, I love her. "One end is loneliness and the other is where you and Mac are together."

"I like the in-between part. I don't get the rest of it."

"It's so easy!" she says, all excited-like. "I can read couples. Like, who has chemistry. Who doesn't. But you and Mac totally do. You just need to get on the same fucking page. And do you know where more fucking happens than anywhere else?"

"Toronto?" Cassidy guesses.

Aubrey and I turn matching confused faces to her.

"What? Canada is cold and dark. Maybe they need to stay warm."

"Noooooo!" Aubrey says. "At weddings, dumbass!"

Then I get it. I look at the line and the dots. I think of the texts. Of the kiss. Of the scene I want to play out with Mac. The path is all right there in front of me.

Mac has already asked me to be his pretend date at this wedding. I just need to turn the pretend into the real. And how hard could that be? It's like I've trained my whole life for this! I'm an actress who specializes in making the pretend real. Or at least feel real.

"Aubrey, I think you're onto something," I admit. "I need a plan."

"Now she gets it!" Aubrey tears the page neatly from her notebook and hands it to me, along with the pen. "Add some detail."

At the bottom of the page, I write "props list." Because every good production needs props.

"Hand-washables!" Cassidy says. "That's first on the list. What kind of lingerie would your cop like?"

"Hmm." He's a strong, sensible man. Just the kind to like skimpy lingerie. I write "see-through lace" on the props list. And also, "book of Hemingway quotes."

"Ooh," Aubrey says. "Is that a gift for him?"

"No way. It's going to help me get into character. I love a challenge." I flap my hands like a jazz dancer on cocaine, and another round of drinks magically appears before us. "The happy portion of the evening starts now," I inform my friends.

"Oh, good!" Cassidy says. "Draw me a line! DO ME, AUBREY!"

Heads turn at nearby tables, because Cassidy isn't a quiet girl after she gets a drink up her. What the hell was Greg thinking? Cassidy is great. We all are.

And Mac Maguire better get with the program.

15 MOANIES

Meg

"Now cut them small, okay?" Liam says. "These should be only about an inch wide, so that you can pop the whole thing in your mouth." He hands me a knife to cut up the pan of brownies we just made.

Personally I think one-inch brownies sounds a little stingy, but Liam is a pretty smart guy, so I do as he says. "Like this?"

"Exactly. We call these *moanies*," my brother-in-law tells me as he squirts dish soap into the mixing bowl. "It's actually Brynn's recipe. She named them."

"Oh. Why *moanies*?" Except I already have my answer. Brynn is my sister Sadie's friend, and she gives lots of her recipes odd names.

"You'll see. Try one."

I pop a brownie into my mouth. "Ooohhhhhhh." I do see. You can't eat this without moaning.

"Yeah, but Brynn also thinks they have super powers."

"Will I be able to fly after I eat this?"

He snorts. "No. But have you ever heard that chocolate is an aphrodisiac? Brynn thinks there's something potent about this recipe. When I told her you needed something for that cop friend of yours, this was her pick."

"Innnteresting," I say, licking my lips. The brownies are a last minute treat for Mac. I'm bringing them on my ride-along, which starts in half an hour. "These are great, whatever they're called."

"True story."

"Can I leave some for you and your girls? Where'd Sadie go, by the way?"

"In there. Look," he says, nudging me toward the doorway to the den. "You'll see. Happens every night."

I poke my head into the den and see my sister asleep on the sofa, her baby son asleep on top of her, face down on her breast, where he'd been nursing before they both nodded off.

This is what domestic bliss looks like, I guess. Love and exhaustion in the same frame. I turn away, unsure how I feel about it. Do I want that someday?

Yes.

I go back to the kitchen, where Liam is stacking brownies into a tin for Maguire. "Great recipe. Thanks again," I say.

"It's no problem. Brownies are the easiest thing to bake."

"My baking game is weak," I remind him as I grab the mixing bowl and give it a quick scrub. "But I think I could pull these off on my own. Can I see the recipe? I could scan it with my phone."

"Of course." He points at a dog-eared piece of paper on the counter. The title is "Lisa's Better Than Sex Brownies."

I wipe off my hands and pull out my phone. "Moanies is a better name for them," I say, lining up my photo.

"Right?" He laughs. "I don't know why every recipe is suddenly called *better than sex*. I mean, they're great brownies. But I do wonder if Lisa's needs are being met."

My laugh is uncomfortable, because my needs have not been met in a long time. And I'm on my way to spend six hours with the guy who rules my fantasies. But, hey, at least there will be chocolate.

"You're the best." I give Liam a quick hug. "My love to Sadie. I shouldn't wake her up, right?"

"Nooooo," he says. "Not until I get that baby into his crib without waking him."

"Good luck with that."

"It's my super power. Have fun tonight, okay? But promise me you'll be careful."

"Of course," I promise. "This isn't dangerous. I'm supposed to stay in the car."

"Be careful anyway," he says as he walks me out.

When I pull away from their house, the brownies are already making my car smell like a chocolate heaven. But I'm actually starting to get a little nervous.

This isn't dangerous, I repeat to myself on the way to the police station.

This isn't dangerous, I tell myself under the harsh lighting at a busy reception desk. Two cops struggle past me, towing a snarling man in handcuffs.

This isn't dangerous, I repeat when the receptionist hands me a liability disclaimer form that's four pages long—both sides—and a pen.

I sign away my life at the bottom of the page. This is what I do for art.

"Here comes Trouble," a gruff voice says behind me.

I whirl around at the sound of Mac's voice, and see what passes for his smile—a lip twitch and a quick light in his eyes. He's wearing his uniform, which looks like it was designed specifically for his square shoulders. I don't know how many times I've seen him in his work gear, but every time is just like the first: I have an insane instinct to rip off his clothes. And let's not forget that one time I tried.

But wow. His gun is holstered neatly at his side, and his badge gleams under the fluorescent lights. He's still my sexy neighbor. He's still Mac. But he's like Mac *amplified*.

And all my apprehension leaves me at once. Because I'm perfectly safe with him. I already know it. "Hi, Copper. I just signed my life away so that I can catch some bad guys with you."

"You mean *watch* me catch bad guys," he says, giving me his familiar scowl. "You don't get out of the car. Didn't you read the document I sent you?"

"I skimmed it," I say, just to piss him off. "Those are just suggestions, right?"

Someone behind him erupts with laughter, and Mac's scowl deepens. "You see something funny?" he asks the other man.

"Every frickin' day," his friend says, grinning broadly.

"This is Lance, my summer intern."

Lance straightens up and smacks Mac on the shoulder. "I'm his partner. That's just his idea of a joke."

"Are we all going together?" I ask, trying not to let my disappointment show. I want to sit up front with Mac and watch him work.

"Yes and no," Mac says. "Lance will be driving another cruiser, and a trainee will ride shotgun with him."

"Oh. Good." I brighten up immediately. "I brought enough moanies for all of us."

"Moanies?" Lance asks. "Is that, like, food that makes you moan? I like it already."

"Yep. And moan *loudly*," I say. "They're right up Mac's alley. Did you know our apartment building has really thin walls?"

Lance practically keels over laughing, while Mac scowls. "Are we gonna stand around here all night or what?"

"Let's do this." I clap my hands. "Lead on, Coppers."

————

"THIS ONLY WORKS if you stay in the car," Mac says as we approach the cruiser. "I can't do my job and worry about you at the same time."

"Can I roll the window down?" I ask. "I need to hear you."

"Sure. Fine. So long as your butt is in that seat, it's all good."

"Fair enough." I watch him check the tires on the cruiser, then open the driver's side door. His posture is straight and forthright, and I feel my spine lengthening already. This is why research is so helpful with acting. When you see someone who lives it, it's easier to step into their shoes. Metaphorically, of course.

I climb into the passenger's seat, and a few minutes later we're cruising the southeast side of the city, listening to the radio. It's all gibberish to me—numbered codes passed from cop to cop.

Mac picks up the radio transmitter while we're stopped at a red light. He barks something like "This is 23. I'm 10-8," into it.

"What's 10-8?" I ask.

"In service. Available for assignment."

I scribble that down. "Okay, what other codes am I going to hear?

"Oh, some 10-28s."

"What's that?"

"A vehicle registration request. It's not all action, Meg. A lot of police work is deterrence. Cruising around, making your presence known. Without serious action."

"Just like my sex life," I point out.

He snorts. "When I work a daytime shift, there's more detective work. I'm often following up on investigations in progress. But this graveyard shift is all about helping people in trouble, and spotting drunks behind the wheel."

I'm still asking questions a few minutes later when the radio squawks with: "Available units south for a 10-31." Or something like that.

I notice Maguire's body language shift slightly. He's more alert. More engaged. Like something in him is cocked and ready.

"Unit 23," Maguire barks. And then they have a rapidfire back and forth that ends with Maguire stepping on the gas.

"What's a 10-31?" I ask as we accelerate.

"Possible breaking and entering in progress." He turns a corner quickly, handling the car like a speedway driver.

My heart rate kicks up as I experience an adrenaline surge. "This is so exciting!"

Maguire glances my way for a split second. "You're staying in the car."

"I won't forget." And I won't. You may notice that my response is not *quite* the same thing as saying I'll obey him.

He flips a switch on the dash, and immediately I see the reflection of the cruiser lights on the shiny hood of the car.

"Oh! Can we use the siren? I know there aren't that many cars on the road..." That's putting it mildly. There are two other cars in view at the moment, and both of them have pulled over to let us pass. "But it would mean the world to me. I'll give you an extra moanie later."

He sighs and then points at another switch. "Go ahead, you drama queen."

I am, in fact, a drama queen. So I flip that switch before he changes his mind. And the siren starts up right away. It's glorious.

Mac steps on the gas again, and the cruiser leaps forward. We fly for another quarter mile, until Mac turns left onto a residential street. He also kills the siren, but it was good while it lasted.

We make two more turns and pull up in front of a small house with a brightly lit bay window. I roll down my window immediately so I don't miss anything.

"Stay put," he says, getting out. A man steps out of the shadows and I open my mouth to scream.

But I can tell from Mac's body language that he already knew the man was there. And anyway, it's just an elderly man in a University of Michigan sweatshirt, and he's waving Mac down as if the cavalry has arrived. "He's still in there! I tried to look in the window but the drapes are closed."

"Okay, sir," Mac says calmly. "This is your home?"

"My son's. I'm dog-sitting for the weekend." He holds up a key.

"And where's the dog?" Maguire asks.

"Ooh, good question," I whisper to myself.

But that's when a furry dog emerges from the shrubberies, his tail waving happily. So Fido is unscathed.

"Start from the beginning," Mac says. "Did you see someone in the home?"

"I was nappin' in the chair." The old man points inside. I note that the Michigander accent is strong in this one. "When I woke up, the first thing I heard was a loud bump in the master bedroom. And the dog barked."

The hair on my arms stands up. This sounds serious. A little scary.

I freaking love it.

"I called out hello, you know? But nobody answered. That bumping kept happening, though. So I called 911 and then went outside, like they told me to do."

"You're sure you're home alone?" Mac asks.

"Of course I'm sure." He looks indignant. "My son took his lady to the lake for the weekend."

Another cruiser pulls up behind ours, and Lance and the rookie climb out. Maguire waves them over.

"No fair," I call out of the window. "Why does the trainee get to help and not me?"

Maguire doesn't even dignify this with an answer. The three of them spread out around the house, poking into the shadows and looking for a point of entry.

They're back in seconds, though. And when Mac and Lance enter the house to search it, the trainee gets stuck outside with the old man, holding the dog.

But as I watch Maguire ease into that house, his gaze scanning for trouble, his body moving like a cat's, I feel tension in my belly. Mac's the guy you summon when you hear a bump in the night. He pulls up, guns blazing (metaphorically, anyway), and does the scary thing you're not willing to do yourself.

Seriously. Is there anything hotter than that? No sir.

My hands are clenched with nerves as I watch the house, waiting to see what will happen.

Lucky for my poor heart, the wait isn't long. Mac appears in the doorway and beckons to the old man. I unclench every muscle in my body and sort of ooze back against the seat with relief. He wouldn't do that if there were any danger.

But as soon as my heart rate drops into the normal range, I get curious. So I open the car door and gallop across the lawn to see what they learned.

And I only have to get as far as the front porch, anyway. I can see Lance in the living room. His face is red, and he has all the signs of a man who is trying not to burst out laughing. Red face. Flashing eyes. Shaking shoulders.

He's holding a Roomba. You know—a robot vacuum.

"I've never seen one of those in my life," the old man says, shaking his head. "It sounded just like a robber bumping into the furniture. I thought maybe he forgot to put on his glasses or somethin'."

Mac's scowl is firmly in place. "Your son should have warned you, maybe," he says. "You have a good night, okay?"

I'm just leaping off the front stoop, laughing, when Mac comes out of the house. "I told you to stay in the car."

"Sorry." I giggle. "And you're right. Those Roombas are dangerous."

"I'm never gonna live this one down," he grumbles. "But you still have to stay in the car, okay? Next time the perp won't be a vacuum cleaner."

"Should I write that down in my notes?" I bat my eyelashes at him.

"You do that." He cranks the engine and then sighs. "A Roomba. What will it be next?"

————

I SORT OF wonder what will be next too. I'm actually a little apprehensive about it. I mean, what would happen if he got a call for a domestic disturbance or something. I love seeing Mac apprehend a Roomba, but I'm not sure how I'd feel about him apprehending someone who actually wanted to harm him. It suddenly occurs to me that Mac could get hurt doing this job. He could get worse than hurt. He could get dead.

I don't like this thought at all. In fact, it makes me a little angry. Also a little scared.

"You got quiet all of a sudden," he says.

"I'm sorry!" I blurt out.

"For being quiet? No need to apologize. Quiet is nice sometimes."

"No, not sorry for being quiet. Although that does feel a bit unnatural to me. I'm sorry I got out of the car when you said I shouldn't."

He nods.

"I thought you were just being bossy and I wasn't really thinking about the possible, um, ramifications."

"Of a Roomba?" he says, deadpan, but I can sense the smile just below the surface.

"Don't be a dick. I mean, what if it wasn't a Roomba? What if it'd been a homicidal maniac? Who bumped into furniture a lot? Because he had really bad vision?"

We both laugh at that.

"Seriously, Mac, you could've been hurt. Or worse. And I could've gotten in the way."

He nods again. "It's all right, Trouble. I knew what I was taking on when I agreed to let you do a ride-along with me. That's why I asked for this shift in particular. Usually, this is the time of day, that time between day and late night, where things don't get too bad. It's the next shift where things fall apart."

"So a Roomba isn't falling apart?"

"A Roomba is comic relief," he tells me.

We drive around for a while more. He answers some basic questions. We chitchat. It's nice and easy and I almost forget I'm researching a role. It's more like I'm researching Mac.

There's a twinge in my belly, because I like what I'm learning about him.

Stop it, Meg, I remind myself. *You're researching a role, not a romantic partner.*

Mac doesn't do romance.

Not yet, anyway.

16 CODE 415

Maguire

I knew I'd like having Meg in my car. But I like it way too much. And it's a slow night, so I can't even complain that she's too distracting.

At last, on Lake Drive, I spot a swerving Mini Cooper. "Hit the lights, Meg."

She lets out a squeal that's really fricking adorable, and then flips 'em on.

The driver doesn't fight it. She pulls right over, stopping abruptly. I pull in right behind her. "Same rules apply," I tell Meg. "You keep your cute butt in that seat."

"Yessir." But it isn't flirtatious. She looks nervous, watching me with tense eyes as I get out to approach the vehicle. And I'm cautious, even though this will probably shake out to be the world's least interesting drunk-driving incident. But you never know. And even run-of-the-mill drunks can become angry and volatile when they realize they're about to get arrested for a DUI.

Not this drunk, though. The vehicle's only occupant is a tearful college girl. She apologizes profusely all the way through her field sobriety test.

"My boyfriend ditched me!" she cries after failing to walk a straight line. "He went home with another girl!" Then she leans against my uniform shirt and sobs.

Oh, man. Tears! It's almost enough to make me feel sorry for her. Almost. "That's what Lyft is for," I say gently. "These gentlemen are going to take you down to the station." Lance and the trainee are just walking up to us.

"Don't throw me in the slammer, Officer!" she slurs.

I glance at Meg, who's rolling her eyes in the passenger seat. "I've seen better acting jobs in porn."

Lance chuckles as he leads the sad little perp to the back of his cruiser. "You can ride along with me any time, Meg."

I growl.

But then Lance drives off, and Meg and I are alone again. "You were so kind to her," Meg says softly. "Aren't you angry that she'd drive around that drunk?"

"Well, I don't like it." I shrug. "But, to paraphrase Hemingway, as a cop 'you should not judge, you should understand.'"

"What's there to understand, though? You don't get to see the reasons that people do things. She fed you that line about her boyfriend dumping her. But we don't even know if it's true."

"It doesn't matter," I tell her as we cruise around another quiet neighborhood. "The law doesn't care why she's driving drunk. And it's not my job to hate her for it. This might just be the wake-up call she needs, you know? To stop taking risks that endanger herself as well as others. Everyone makes mistakes, Meg."

She's very quiet for the next half hour, while I respond to a couple of calls that are canceled before I'm even on the scene.

"Are we having those brownies yet?" I ask. "Sounds like something that would go nicely with our coffee."

"Later," she says with a smug little smile.

"They're just brownies, right?" I have to ask. "Law-abiding brownies?"

"Oh, these brownies don't break any laws. But they are especially sinful."

I'm about to ask why when we get another call. Code 415. The dispatcher gives me an address in a nice enough neighborhood.

But my jaw tenses and then locks right up. "Fuuuuck," I murmur before I can stop myself. Why on God's green Earth does it have to be that address?

"Everything okay? What's a 415?"

"Disturbing the peace." *Especially mine.*

"And that wrecks your day?"

To distract her, I point at the switch for the flashing lights. "Go on. You know you want to."

She flips the switch. But she also gives me a look, like she knows I'm trying to change the subject.

And I am.

I drive in silence, feeling more dread with every block we pass. Of all the houses in a city of two hundred thousand, this is the one I would most like to avoid.

Because it belongs to my brother. The one I haven't spoken to in years. Please let it not be Morris who's disturbing the peace. Not again. Officers have responded to my brother's address before. He's a big drinker. And a mean drunk, sometimes.

But I've never been the one to get the call. And I can't imagine that it's me he wants to see turn up on his doorstep.

Meg is watching me from the passenger seat. She's the most observant civilian I know. Hell, I hope she can't read minds. Mine is full of regret, grumpiness, and horny thoughts about her.

She obviously can't read minds, or she wouldn't be sitting here.

On that wacko thought, I pull up to their house, followed by Lance, who's back already from booking the drunk girl.

"There are times when this job is boring as fuck, and times when you wish it was boring as fuck," I grumble.

"Which is this one?" she asks.

"Vote's still out."

I get out of the car, my senses locked and loaded. I just hope I don't have to get into it with my brother over his drinking.

But even as Lance walks over to meet me, I hear the ruckus from the neighbors next door. That other house is lit up like a Halloween pumpkin, lights flickering, the sound of their speaker bass an actual physical sensation. It's a throb that goes straight to the guts, and not in a fun way.

"I'm thinking I know the problem," Lance says.

"Agreed," I'm relieved to say. Still, I need to check in at my brother's to let them know we responded. I could make Lance do it, but that's a pussy move.

Meg pokes her head out of the open window. "This call is just about a loud party? That's all the action I'm getting?"

Lance chuckles at her choice of words, and I whack him in the arm to shut him up.

That's when I spot her. *Julie*. She's standing in the open door, her shape silhouetted by the lamplight behind her. Any other night, I might have lost my calm just seeing her. But tonight is different. I'm still wearing a half smile, courtesy of Meg. And as I walk toward the house, I'm wondering what Meg will get up to in my squad car while I'm gone. Is she touching any buttons she shouldn't be touching?

Which makes me immediately think of her touching *my* buttons, and most definitely in a good way. One specific button, in fact. The big one right between my legs.

First, Julie.

There were moments in my past when Julie was all I could think about. Julie and Morris. The betrayal. My nightmare come to life. Those were some really dark days.

But as I make my approach, I realize I haven't thought about her in a while, though. In fact, before this family wedding popped onto my radar, it had been months.

Interesting.

I give one last glance back at the squad car. It looks like Meg is behaving herself. I'm a little disappointed actually. Her sass is pretty damned irresistible. Luckily, I'm immune to that sort of thing. Or I try to be.

"Evening, Julie!" I call out, my voice surprisingly even.

She opens the door and steps out onto the porch. That's when my bravado starts to crumble. I'm looking at the woman who destroyed me. I used to be a happy guy who thought he had the whole world figured out. Until she twisted the knife.

And—fuck—I forget to breathe. Because the baby is on her hip. She's holding the nephew that I've never met. He has a round face, and one fat little hand is clutching his mother's hair.

Then he turns that chubby little face toward mine. And there's just enough light so that I can see his eyes widen. He opens his mouth and begins to babble. "Dadadadadada!" And his short arms reach for me.

Goosebumps. Suddenly. Everywhere.

Holy. Shit. I'm not prepared for this. The baby thinks I'm Morris. Just when I thought things were already weird. And I swear to God I thought I was done with all this. I thought I'd already felt all the feelings I had coming to me. Wrong again.

When will I learn?

I'm actually frozen, one foot on the first of three steps up to the front porch. Julie looks down at me, her jaw unhinged. We're both sort of locked inside our discomfort for a very long moment, while my nephew squeals and struggles to get to me.

So I do the only thing a guy in my shoes can do. I unstick myself, climb two steps, and reach for him.

Gaping, Julie transfers his weight to me. And then the baby is perched on my arm, looking up at me. He lets out a squawk, but then goes suddenly quiet. Like he's figured out that I don't have the right haircut or maybe the right clothes. I don't smell like his dad, probably. Not enough whiskey on my breath.

Okay, maybe that last thing isn't fair. My mother tells me Morris has finally got his shit together. At least some of it. And I hope it's true, if only for the sake of the fifteen-pound person who's peering at me like he's seen a ghost.

I clear my throat. "A few of the details are wrong, aren't they little guy?" And then I wish I'd kept my trap shut, because the words echo back inside my chest. *The details are wrong.* Julie obviously doesn't agree. She made her choice.

Now she looks at her hands, growing visibly more uncomfortable. A few more details start to sink in, too. Her hair is mussed, but not in a sexy way. It's unkempt. That just doesn't look like the Julie I know. Then again, I'm not sure I ever really knew her. "You okay?" I ask. "Can I assume your call to the station was about that party?"

"Oh, I'm fine!" she breathes. "I mean, can you believe how loud they are? That kid's parents are gone to Mackinac for the weekend, and they left him unsupervised and he's throwing a rager. Can you get them to quiet it down a little? The baby won't go to sleep. I haven't been able to watch the ending of *The Bachelor* and it's killing me. Every time I press play, the dialogue is totally drowned out by the twerps next door."

It's a whole lot of verbal diarrhea. And it just keeps on rolling.

"Morris is in Chicago. Business trip. Again," she says. That *again* is weighted, but I'm not taking the bait.

"Okay." The music thumps on into the silence between us. "My, uh, partner is going to shut 'em down next door." And that's when I run out of things to say. I look down at the baby, who's still gazing at me, puzzlement on his rounded features. "You have a good night, now. Don't keep mommy up."

"Bah," he says gravely. Then he drools a little.

"So..." I wait for Julie to come unstuck.

She blinks and then grabs him back. She looks like she wants to say more, but I'm not here to talk her down or ask her about *The Bachelor*, for chrissakes. I glance over at the neighbor's place, where Lance is currently scaring the shit out of some teenage kids. They're actually pouring out of windows, trying to escape.

Sometimes the uniform is enough. This is one of those times.

I turn back to Julie. I've got nothing more to do here. I just need to fill out the paperwork and take Meg home. Not with me, of course, although that sounds nice.

Then I feel Julie's soft hand on my arm. "It's good to see you," she says. "Weird, but good. How long has it been?"

"Let's not," I say abruptly. "Let's not do this. My shift is over. It's late."

She swallows hard and runs a hand through her hair. Next door, the music shuts off abruptly, like a needle ripped off a record. That's how Julie and I ended, too. One ugly day the music stopped and there was nothing left to do but pick up the overturned red plastic cups of my youth and carry on.

"I'm going off shift," I say, trying to figure out how to get off this porch. Lance should rescue me. Where is that guy?

"Okay," Julie says, and then sighs. "You could come inside and have a drink with your old sister-in-law. I don't bite."

"No thanks," I say quickly. Because that's the worst idea I've ever heard. "And I have to get this back to the station." I motion to my squad car.

Julie looks past me. "Oh! You've got a criminal in there?"

My reaction is immediate and visceral. Meg is sitting in the front seat, her bright eyes watching me. There's nothing remotely criminal about Meg, except for how hot she is.

"Are you kidding me right now? That's not a criminal. That's my *girlfriend*. Why would you assume that? Is it because of her skin color?" Funny how the word *girlfriend* comes out smooth and easy. Maybe it's because I'm mad.

"Oh, god." Julie puts a hand up to her cheek. "I'm sooooo sorry. What a stupid assumption I made!"

The baby lets out a squawk of agreement. I like this kid already.

"She's waiting for me," I say through gritted teeth.

"In your squad car? She's a cop?"

"No, she's a drama queen. Gotta go." I turn and hop off the stoop. *Smooth, Maguire.* Oh well. I never was smooth with Julie. Never could be. Everything about this night is stressful.

And now I know what my child would have looked like if I had had one with Julie.

I turn my back on the house where Morris and Julie live. It's like visiting a version of my life that could have been. An alternate universe. I walk toward what my life is now. My job...and Meg. Or just my job. And an apartment where there aren't any baby toys strewn around.

So I got that going for me. It's something.

———

I CAN FEEL Meg's eyes on me as we drive away. She's staring. Maybe it's because I'm driving out of Julie's neighborhood like zombies are chasing us and the car is on fire.

"So," she says.

I grunt.

"That woman. Who is she, Mac?"

"Why?"

"Because she looked wary. You didn't look happy to see her. But her baby freaked out. I can't make any sense of it."

"I'll bet," I snort. "What if I told you I'd never met that kid before?" And honestly, it's the only thing about the whole familial standoff that gives me pause. My family's betrayal cut me deep. And I feel no guilt for cutting them out of my life. But how long is too long? Does anger have an expiration date? Best if used before...

"Who is she, Mac?"

"My ex."

I hear Meg's sharp intake of breath. "Maguire. Do you have a child?"

"No!" I laugh. "But I have an identical twin."

3... 2...1... I can almost hear the cogs of Meg's mind turning. She's smart, so "HOLY shit!" explodes out of her mouth awfully fast. "Your *identical twin* has a baby with your ex."

"Yup," I sigh. This topic isn't any fun at all, and I'm tired.

"Just a wild guess here. But is she the reason you need a date for Rosie's wedding?"

I say nothing. But we both know she's right.

"Because..." Meg tries. "Because you broke up with her, and she was so heartbroken she took up with the only human on Earth who looks just like you?"

I stop at a traffic light. "That's a nice version of the story, Meg. But that is not what happened. I asked her to marry me. She said yes. Then I went away to school, and she started sleeping with my brother."

Meg groans. "And then you killed him?"

"To the best of my knowledge, he still lives." Although I did have some violent fantasies right after it happened.

"You haven't seen him either?" she yelps. "In how long?"

"Ten years." God, that sounds weird when you say it out loud. "We don't speak."

"Whoa. Not ever? But I met your parents. They seem normal."

I give her a look.

"Okay, not exactly normal," she amends. "There's the inflatable penises and the collage art to consider. But they're not monsters."

"No." I press the accelerator. "But they never seemed to care that Morris broke us up."

"Not at all?" she yelps.

"They sort of shrugged when it all went down."

"What happens on Christmas? Or Thanksgiving? I mean, there is not enough wine in the world for that meal, right?"

"I don't attend," I admit.

"Oh. I see."

We both lapse into silence. Even the radio is quiet while I drive back toward the police garage. I'm too far inside my head, wondering how it all ends. Do I ignore my brother's family forever? That seemed perfectly rational until a few minutes ago.

I experience another quick flash of hatred for Morris. For putting me in this situation. For making me feel guilty for something he did.

"So how do you spend the holidays?" Meg asks suddenly.

"I work. Nobody wants those shifts. You can make a lot of friends volunteering for those."

"Friends, but not family," she says under her breath.

"Trouble! Don't feel sorry for me. It's my choice."

"Really? It was your choice to have your brother move in on your fiancée? And then marry her?"

"Let's just forget about it," I grumble. "That's what I do most of the time." I pull into the cruiser lot and park the car.

"That explains a lot about you," she says, climbing out of the passenger's seat.

I want to argue the point. But she's right. It totally does. And anyway, I have to go inside and sign off on a few things.

Meg waits for me in her car. She's my ride home. I took my car in for a service because I knew she'd be around to drive me home tonight.

When I come out, she's sitting in the driver's seat, listening to some music. I open the passenger's door, and there's something on the seat. "What's this?"

"The treat I brought you. But you have to wait until we get home."

"Why?"

"Because I don't like crumbs in my car, Copper. Sit down already."

Her car smells like chocolate and heaven, though. It's a long fifteen minutes until we've pulled up in our lot. I get out of her car, and I'm just about to pull the lid off when Meg grabs the box out of my hands.

"Upstairs," she demands. "These would go better with a drink."

"Like milk?" I'm hungry all of a sudden.

"Like rum," she says. Then she turns on her heel and sashays into the building. All I can do is follow.

17 HARD-BOILED

Meg

I feel absolutely entirely too aware of Mac as he follows me into my apartment. I wonder where his eyes land as I flip on my mood lighting, which consists of strings of fairy lights and a single beaded lamp on the kitchen counter. It throws multicolored light around my kitchen.

What does he see when he looks at my apartment, with its kitschy fabrics and bright colors? I've been dressing the space up and it's starting to feel, dare I say it, like my artistic home. But I wonder what he thinks of the pillows and paintings. The large tapestry hanging by the bathroom. The blooming flowers in every feng shui corner there is. He makes me feel self-conscious, because his opinion matters to me. But I have no idea if he feels the same way about me.

"Sit," I tell Mac, pointing at a counter stool.

He obeys me. A man will do anything for chocolate.

But I make him wait.

I tap my phone a couple of times until my new favorite playlist comes over the speakers. Then I grab my favorite cocktail shaker and fill it with ice cubes.

"You don't have to go all out," he says.

"I told you I don't cook. But I love mixed drinks. And this one makes me think of you."

He glances up at me, and I forget what I'm doing. Because those gray eyes look so serious. "Why's that? Is it a drink for grumpy guys who won't date their hot neighbors?"

I let out a hoot of laughter as I reach for the limes on my counter-top. "Yes and no. It's a drink named after a famous old codger. I'm making you a Hemingway Daiquiri. Supposedly Papa drank these." After cutting it in half, I squeeze the first lime into the cocktail shaker. After lime juice comes a splash of grapefruit juice, some maraschino liqueur, and the white rum.

Mac watches all this with growing amusement. "You're telling me Papa drank fruity drinks?"

"Everyone likes a good cocktail. Some people—out of misguided ignorance or arrogance—pretend not to." I shake the shaker. "These are delicious. And Papa was known to like his alcohol. They didn't waste time with light beer in Cuba, Mac."

He gives me an appraising glance. And then, as I'm shaking up our cocktails, he reaches for the moanies in their container.

I smack his hand away. "No cheating! You think you're the only one who lives by an ironclad set of rules?"

"No, I suppose not," he says, showing me that arrogant smile of his. "You obviously have standards. Fresh squeezed lime juice, huh."

"Well, duh." I pour our drinks into two martini glasses and cut lime wheels for a garnish.

"Loud show tunes in the evenings—oh, wait. You play loud music *all* the time." He gives me a smirk. Then, before I have a chance to react, he reaches for the moanies again.

"Copper!" I set down the shaker and dart around the counter to where he sits, making a lunge for the dessert that I made for his grumpy ass anyway. Honestly I don't really care if he eats the whole box. But I do enjoy teasing him.

He raises his arm to escape my reach, but I fearlessly sacrifice my body by reaching up, leaning against his. This destabilizes him on the bar stool, and for one tricky moment I think I might actually tip the man over. But his solution is to grab me around the waist with his free hand.

And it works. It works a little too well. His iron-like arm wraps around my body, just where I'd always wanted it to be. Suddenly we're chest to chest, nose to nose. He goes absolutely still, and our eyes meet in a stare that's full of possibility.

"Careful, Mac," I whisper into the silence. "What would Hemingway do right now?"

Slowly, his grin turns sly. "Funny you should ask. Once he said, 'It is awfully easy to be hard-boiled about everything in the daytime, but at night it is another thing.'"

"Is it now?"

"Yeah," he grunts. "I don't think I really understood that quote until tonight. You undo me, Trouble. I don't make good decisions when I'm standing close to you."

We both study each other for another long moment. Then Maguire puts the moanies down on the counter with a decisive thud. He slides a big hand to the back of my neck. It's a maneuver filled with such control and confidence that I shiver. And then his mouth claims mine.

His kiss is shockingly hot and slow. As if he's giving me time to get used to the idea. Firm lips close over mine. This time, the kiss isn't a joke, or a ruse, or a mistake. It's just us. A hungry man and a smitten girl finally coming together because we need it so badly. His lips press and search. My mouth lifts and beckons.

He wraps his hand in my hair and gives it just a little tug so I'll tilt my head back to meet his lips more fully with my own. Our connection tightens, and so does my belly.

Nobody's laughing now. Because this is a kiss that's the start of something. Like a match flaring. All you need is a tiny flame to start a forest fire. I give his lip a little nibble, and he makes a sound deep inside his chest.

Then our tongues collide, and flames begin to lick at my insides. An aggressive tug pulls me more tightly against his chest as his tongue probes my mouth.

This. This is what I knew it would be like with him. I knew because I've heard him through my thin walls. He and...

No. I will not think about *her* or anyone else. I will not think about anything besides this kiss, and about the way his bossy hand is already cupping my ass. I'm flush against his big hard body. Tighter than a bumper sticker.

He doesn't date, though. It's only sex.

Shut up, brain! We don't have time for semantics because this feels too good. I'm going to mack on Mac right now. And worry later.

But then he gentles the kiss, which is not okay with me. I wrap both arms around his neck and lean in.

"Hey, slow down, Trouble," he whispers against my lips.

"Why?" I whimper. Every atom in me wants him to stay.

"We have all night."

"Do we?" I challenge. We study each other, his gray eyes boring into mine. We're both breathing heavily. I guess this is the moment where we decide. Are we crossing this line? Or does he head back to his apartment instead?

I make myself take a half step backward, though. If he wants to leave, I'm not going to beg. It's not my style.

Mac stands up from the bar stool, and my heart stops. He's about to leave. Again. But then he lifts the lid off the moanies, plucks one out, and breaks it in half. "I want to hear you moan. First with this," he says, placing the bit of brownie into my waiting mouth. Then he grabs my hand and puts it on the swell of his jeans. "And then I want to make you moan with *this*."

Sensory overload! I moan on command. Anybody would. There's chocolate in my mouth and a rock-hard dick under my palm.

That's it. My brain has entered complete shut-down mode.

I hurl myself at him.

He catches me, smiling. Our next kiss has the taste of chocolate. But I need more. My lips begin a patrol of their own, beginning on his roughened cheek, and traveling across the bristle of his jaw. Then I lick my way down his neck.

"Ungh," he says as his fingers find the first few buttons of my shirt. I love the slightly salty taste of his skin, and I show him how much with more kisses. Mac makes hasty work of my buttons. Broad hands slide up my tummy and work their way under my bra. A jolt of energy zings through me. That roughened hand on my breast is everything. I pull back and look up at him, my chest heaving.

He slides my shirt off my shoulders, tossing it down, revealing my lacy (hand-washable!) bra, my breasts heavy in the cups. He doesn't take time to mess with unclasping my bra, but just takes each breast and lifts it out, so that I'm spilling over my underwire. He teases one nipple with his thumb while his other hand cups my ass. Like he can't decide what to touch next.

And then—thank you universe—he lowers his mouth to exactly where I need him, licking my nipple. I shiver, and not from the cool air on my skin.

He plays me like an instrument, and I bite my lip to keep from moaning. Maybe he'd like to hear it, but I need to at least try to hold myself back. I run my hand through his thick hair, coasting further to the slope of his neck. God, Maguire looks sexy like this, bent over in service to my pleasure. Just as I'm about to say "the other one," he's already beat me to it by putting his warm, firm mouth on my other breast, licking and sucking, inhaling me, as if he can't get enough.

And neither can I. I'm close to begging, dammit. To shut myself up, I tug on his chin, until that wicked mouth is on mine again. And we are kissing as if there's no tomorrow, because right now, there isn't. It's my turn to unbutton his shirt. I want it off him, preferably yesterday. But as I unbutton his uniform shirt, it's just occurring to me that I can't undress him without help. He's wearing a heavy service belt and a *gun*, for fuck's sake. That's way above my pay grade.

Sensing my distress, Mac straightens up and winks at me. He opens several attaching loops on his belt, tossing them onto my countertop. Then he unclips his entire duty belt and carries it over to my refrigerator, where he lays it out of reach. "For safety's sake, I need to ask you not to touch this."

"I won't," I say quickly.

"Good girl," he whispers, rejoining me where I stand half naked and waiting for him. "That's the only thing you can't touch, though."

"Good to know," I whisper back, blinking up at him.

He takes my hands in his and places them on his shirt. "Better get started, then."

Right! I recommence unbuttoning him. And goddamn! His chest is glorious. I'd noticed before, of course, but it's even better when he's up close and personal. He has the perfect amount of hair on his chest, and his muscles flex when I touch him. "You really could be a stripper, you know," I tease.

He kisses me. Hard. Then I almost swallow my tongue as his

pants come off. He kicks off his socks, then drops his boxer briefs, too. Then he's standing there in front of me, his cock hard and proud.

I don't even think before I take him in hand. Thinking is so last season. We're way past that. His cock pulses in my hand, and then he's kissing my neck and my tits while I tease his cock with my hand. I give him a gentle squeeze, eliciting a sexy as fuck groan from him.

"Christ." He grabs my hand by the wrist. "What did I say about speeding? You're doing ninety in a fifty-five."

"I'm sorry, Officer. It won't happen again."

"Make sure of it." He puts those big hands on my shoulders and turns me around. When he speaks again, I feel his breath on the back of my neck. "I want this to last, Trouble."

Is it because it's the first time or the only time? I'm not going to ask. Not right now, anyway. Because Maguire has unbuttoned my denim skirt. It falls to the floor, and then he pulls me against him and I can feel his hard cock up lined against my ass. He presses the length against me, and I lean back a little. His hands are skimming my body, cupping my heavy breasts. I bow my head, and he sucks gently on the back of my neck.

This is why vampires are fucking sexy. I get it now!

Maguire doesn't draw blood of course. He probably won't even leave a mark. But I wish he would. I wish he'd mark me and claim me as his. And I'd claim him back.

But I'll take what I can get. And what I get is a hard cock against my ass, his hands on my tits, his tongue turning me into a puddle. And then one of his naughty hands slides down, invading my panties. I have never felt so much anticipation as when his hand dips lower. That clever hand fights the fabric and wins, until his thick fingers begin to circle my clit. I am warm and wet and waiting for him.

"Fuck, Meg," he breathes against my neck. "You're so hot and sweet."

I moan at just the idea, turning a little so that I can kiss him while he works my clit. But his thumb is not enough. A groan of frustration escapes me.

"Shh," he says. "I got you." Then, whoosh! My panties drop away. He whirls me around again, shoving everything on my counter aside.

The moanies, some bills, and a jar of peanut butter. The peanut butter actually falls off.

Whatever. Who cares. Because he lifts me up, my bare ass hitting the counter. And I'm naked and sitting in front of Maguire, who's also naked. There's a breeze from the door to the deck, and it brushes sweetly against my overheated body.

"Holy shit," Mac says, breathing heavy.

"Holy shit," I agree. We're really doing this. It's going to end badly, probably. But he's looking at me like I'm breakfast, lunch, and dinner. And then he puts both those roughened hands on my thighs, silently asking permission.

I don't even think. I just spread my legs.

18 A FIVE-ALARM FIRE

Maguire

I'm breaking all my rules tonight, and I don't know if I care. I'm too busy kissing my way down Meg's body and licking her smooth skin. Pausing to nuzzle her smooth stomach, I give myself one last chance to reconsider.

I live right next door. I shouldn't do this.

On the other hand, we're either about to have sex, or else spontaneously combust. Honestly, it's a public safety issue at this point. Either we do the deed, or the dispatcher is going to be sending units to a five-alarm fire.

Easy choice, then.

I lower my mouth and brush my lips across her mound. My reward is a hot gasp, followed by an eager cry. Her hands are in my hair, and they're shaking. The musky scent of her beckons. I flatten my tongue against her clit and she moans with gratitude. Goddamn. If I'm honest, I've wanted to do this since the first night I ever saw her.

My knees meet the floor as I settle in to worship her. Her breath hitches, then hitches again. There is nothing like making a woman mad with desire. I love the rush it gives me. I feel so powerful when I'm giving pleasure.

But Meg has a lot of power in this situation, too. She has beautiful long legs, and now they wrap around my body. She draws me in as I taste and tease her. A few minutes pass—or is it more? I lose track of time as I taste her. My cock is hard as a rail, but I enjoy teasing us both. She rolls her hips toward me, looking for release.

"Not yet," I whisper, easing back.

"You're mean," she complains as I rise to my feet.

"So mean," I agree, snagging my trousers off the floor and fishing the wallet out of the back pocket. I pull out the condom that I keep there. A man has to be prepared.

"Hurry," she says.

But I don't. If I'm going to break all my rules, I'm going to enjoy it. I unroll the condom while she watches hungrily. Then I take her pretty face in my hand and kiss her again.

"Oh," she moans against my tongue. "Now."

"Now what?" I rumble, sloppily kissing her cheek. Then sucking on her ear.

She shivers. "Now fuck me. Please."

"Well, since you said please." I spread her knees a little roughly, and she pants with anticipation. God, the sight of her is almost too much. I like a woman who knows what she wants. And Meg's face is half desire, half challenge. Like she can't wait to see what I'm going to do next.

Never one to let a lady down, I take myself in hand and line up. Then I pump my hips and enter her in one quick thrust.

"Yes!" She leans back on the counter and gasps, bracing herself for more.

But I have to pause and take in a slow breath. My heart is racing. I love sex, and I'm good at it. But tonight I feel a little wild. A little out of control. It's been a long time since I let myself get so carried away.

I reach an arm around her back and tighten our connection. It's shocking how perfectly we fit together. Like a well-made lock.

"Mac," she breathes. "Please."

My own groan startles me. And then I'm moving. Taking her in short, shallow thrusts. Her ankles link behind my ass and she yanks me closer on every one. Our mouths fuse. Our chests meet and slide together. It's hot and tight and amazing. I have the weirdest sensation that I've never been so close to anyone before in my life.

The short range of motion is just enough to torture us both. "I could do this all night, I think," I murmur to Meg. "There's no reason to ever stop." I always talk during sex, which is weird because I'm not much of a talker at other times.

Meg makes a happy noise that might or might not be "yes" and "more."

"Knew we'd be hot together," I rumble. "Can't wait to hear you come on my cock."

She whimpers and then gasps. And fuck me, Meg must have taken that to be a command. Because she bites my shoulder and moans so sweetly that goosebumps rise up on my back. Then I feel her shiver as her perfect body clenches around me.

And maybe I don't have all night after all. Because the sweet sound of her climax tightens my balls. "Fuck, Meg." I wrap my arms around her and lift her up.

Her limbs clasp around my body as I stagger toward the bedroom. She moans into my ear, and I'm desperate now. Somehow I find the bed and lower us both to the surface. It might be awkward. I don't even care. All I know is that I'm on top of her now, sinking into her again, kissing her like it's my sworn duty.

"Can you do that again?" I mumble against her lips. "Never heard anything sexier." I roll my hips. I'm practically drowning in pleasure.

"M-maybe," she gasps. "If anyone can pull it off, it's you."

Oh, hell. A challenge. I take both her hands and lift them over her head. "Fine. Just do as I say. Got that?"

She whimpers in reply.

I let go of her hands, and raise myself off her body a few inches. "Put your hands on your tits. Yeah. Like that. Pinch your nipples." She gasps as she does it.

Rolling back a little further, I tug her hips up until her legs fall open. "Aw, yeah. Just like that, baby. Never seen anything so hot."

She looks up at me then, her eyes bright. "Same. Here," she whispers as I pick up the pace. "We're in trouble now."

I know she's right. I just don't care very much right now. I dive down for another blazing kiss. And it's more than I can really stand. "Come now, baby," I beg. "You make me crazy and I can't hold back."

Truer words were never spoken. The moment she wraps her arms around me again, I feel my control slip. Then she moans, and I'm done like dinner. The orgasm hits me with a hurricane force. All I can do is hold on and roar my approval.

Her body tightens against mine, and she shudders deliciously beneath me. And then I slump down onto the bed, spent. Breathing hard.

Nobody says anything for a long time. But eventually my brain comes back online. Reluctantly I roll off of her and onto my back, still needing more oxygen. "What are you thinking about?" I ask when I can finally draw breath.

"Only happy thoughts," she says slowly. "Oh, and I'm wondering if the Hemingway Daiquiris are still good, or if they got too watery."

"I know a way we could find out." I slap her hip. "I think you promised me a drink."

"Sure, but I was only trying to get you into my bed."

I glance around. "Seems like that worked. Now get this tired man a drink."

"Yes, sir," she says cheekily before getting up to do just that.

I lay flat on my back and wait. I should be worrying right now. And beating myself up for breaking all my rules. But I'm too blissed out.

Worrying can wait.

———

IT'S the sunlight that wakes me up, a stretch of it spilling over my eyelids. Man, I slept great. I haven't slept this good in...

I bolt upright. Where. The. Fuck. Am. I? This is not my room. This is Meg's room.

The last thing I remember is moanies, then fucking Meg and both of us moaning, and then we were going to have a Hemingway Daiquiri.

What happened after the daiquiri? I must have had too much to drink. I must have blacked out.

Then it occurs to me. Nothing happened after the daiquiri. I didn't even drink it. I was intoxicated only by very, very good sex. And I fucking fell asleep.

Which means I've broken not one, but two of my signature rules. Thou shalt not fuck thy neighbor. Thou shalt not sleep over with any of your fuck buddies.

Although I've been a little squishy about that second rule lately.

Also, thinking of Meg as my fuck buddy just doesn't sit right in my gut. We're also friends, dammit. That oughtta be another rule for my rulebook: thou shalt not fuck thy cute friends. That way lies the kingdom of awkwardville. Man, what *was* I thinking?

Oh right. I wasn't.

And now isn't the time to ponder it either. Because I seem to be alone, which means I have an opportunity to get the fuck out of here. Even though my clothes are scattered around Meg's apartment, I still manage to dress faster than a fireman who has to go out on a call. I can't seem to spot my boxer briefs so I guess I'm going commando. I yank on my shirt, grab my belt, and am ready to hightail it out of the apartment. I hope Meg is at work, sparing me the awkward morning-after conversation.

But no luck. Just as I'm ready to lunge for the door, Meg steps back into the apartment from the deck, a watering can in her hands. "Morning," she says as I clutch my shoes like they're a life preserver. "Looks like you're at a level ten freak-out. That was fast. I thought you'd maybe just hover at a level eight."

I stand a little taller. Mentally cooling it all down. "Nah," I lie. "I'm totally a two."

She blinks. Then she takes a step closer, squints, and really examines me. It doesn't matter that I'm already wearing clothes, because I feel as though I'm standing here naked. I can't seem to lie to this woman. It's more than that. I can't seem to keep quiet around this woman. And keeping quiet is kind of my MO. "Fine," I say, dropping the shoes and shrugging. "I'm at a level eleven freak-out."

And what does she do? She fucking laughs! "Copper, you need to chill out. Did you have fun last night?"

"Well, duh."

She takes a step closer. "Did you like letting go for once?"

I try to nod, but mostly I just gulp. Memories of last night flood my poor little brain. Meg's hands in my hair as I kneel in the kitchen. The weight of Meg in my arms as I carry her to the bedroom. The feel of her underneath me as I thrust into her...

"Don't you want to do it again?"

Unfortunately, I don't have any words right now. All my words have flown out the window, leaving more space for my dick. My dick is now at an eleven too.

"Look," she says. "You can freak-out if you need to. I'll let you carry your shoes out that door. It's your call. But the genie isn't going back into the bottle, Mac. I know your libido has a souped-up engine. I'm familiar with your best work..." She crosses her smooth arms.

"...Basically, I see two choices. You can go home and we can be awkward and embarrassed and avoid each other. You can pretend not to notice me when I'm out on the deck. You can pretend not to spot my lacy underwear when we run into each other in the laundry room."

My throat goes dry just remembering the sight of her in lingerie.

"Or..." She pauses here and suddenly I notice she's wearing a flowered robe that hugs all her curves. I'm pretty sure she's naked under there. "Or," she repeats, "we can just skip to the part where you admit what you want."

Yup, this woman has my number. She has me all figured out. And now I feel like an ass, because she's a hundred percent right. "Look, Meg, I'm sorry." Immediately her face shutters, because of my poor choice of words. "No. I'm sorry I had a freak-out when there was no reason for one."

"Last night I asked you what Hemingway would do." She hugs herself a little. "That man broke a lot of hearts. So it's not like I expected a marriage proposal over coffee."

A sharp bark of laughter escapes me. "You're too smart for your own good. Did you know that?"

She rolls her deep brown eyes.

"Confession time. Is it terrible that I'm wondering if you're naked under that robe?"

"Hmm." Her arms remain locked around her midriff. "Is it terrible that I'm hoping you'll find out? But you'd have to put your shoes and your belt down first."

I glance down and see myself as Meg sees me. A fucking coward, with his shoes in his hands. I set everything down on the floor and then turn to her again. "Am I crazy, or did you say something about coffee?"

"Sure I did. I was about to make some."

"Can I trouble you for a mug? I somehow forgot to have that fruity drink with you last night."

She snorts. "You were passed out like a baby in my bed, Copper. I'll bet Hemingway could go all night."

"Is that a *challenge*, Trouble? Did you just question my manhood?"

She shrugs. "Take it however you will."

"Yeah, okay." I take a step forward and gently ease the fabric of her robe over her shoulder. She drops her arms, revealing only bare skin underneath the robe. I can't help myself. I have to drop my lips to the sleek curve of her neck where it meets her shoulder. When my mouth meets the warmth of her skin, I groan into the kiss.

I hear a low chuckle as her hands skim down my biceps.

"I just got played, didn't I?" I ask her shoulder. And then her breast. Because I forgot how to stop touching her sometime last night. And it's not clear that I'll ever remember.

"A little," she admits.

"Totally worth it. Unbutton my shirt. Again."

She laughs.

I guess some of my rules need adjusting. Right now, I want Meg more than I can possibly understand. So I just let my body take over.

And it is fucking *good*.

19 MMM BACON

Meg

"We *did* it! The fucking horizontal hula!" I exclaim. Well, I don't technically exclaim it because Cassidy and Aubrey and I are eating pancakes and bacon at Anna's House, which is a busy restaurant. And I don't want to offend the small children running around, or the dads, or grandparents. I don't worry about offending the moms because I can tell they swear all the time. I would if I were them.

So it's more like a stage whisper. But Cassidy and Aubrey light up anyway. "And?" Cassidy says.

"There are no words." I take a big bite of pancake and just hum. Or moan. I don't know.

"Did he..." Aubrey leans in. "You know. Call you a bad girl and use his cuffs on you?"

She sounds weirdly excited about that possibility. I shake my head. "There was no time. We were too busy inhaling each other to think about props. Next time, maybe, though."

"Next time?" Cassidy asks.

"I'm pretty sure there's going to be a next time. I can see there being a lot of next times, leading on for, I don't know, years. But I'm not sure that Maguire can picture that yet."

"You think you have feelings for him already?" Aubrey asks.

I think about it. Do I? Probably. When I met Maguire, it was like meeting a friend you hadn't seen in a long time. When I'm around him, things are easy. I want to talk to him, rile him up, get him exasperated, and then I want to crawl on top of him and ride him till he shivers. Are those feelings?

Whoops, they are.

"There are feelings. Maybe this is the start of something great. But I don't want to get my hopes up. He was pretty firm about not dating anyone."

"Well, you got your hopes up with landing a TV spot, and look how that turned out!" Cassidy is so supportive.

"Cassidy," I say slowly. Because she's on to something. "It took me a decade to land that gig. I don't want to wait ten years to land Maguire."

"Maybe you already have," says Aubrey. "But you've just got to let it breathe for a while. When is that wedding coming up?"

"Soon," I say. "Two weeks."

"Perfect," Aubrey says. "Weddings make people feel romantic."

"Maybe," I hedge. On the other hand, last night I learned a little something about why Mac is so buttoned up. I won't tell my friends about his ex marrying his twin brother. I'm not a gossip. But that's a deep wound. And some people just never get over a wound like that.

And I can totally picture myself getting strung along. Not that Mac would do that intentionally. He's only been honest with me. But sometimes when he looks at me, I feel like we could be magic. It would be hard to walk away from so much potential.

"So what's your strategy?" Aubrey asks. "You should really play up the girlfriend thing without being creepy. Maybe it'll be good training for him."

"Right!" Cassidy agrees. "The one thing I've learned from my brothers is that boys need a lot of training. Don't give up on Maguire yet. Maybe the emotional piece will fall into place. And until then, you can keep having lots of sex. By all means, get as much of that as you can so that your life doesn't become a sexual desert."

"I thought it was just a drought for you?"

"No," she says sadly. "It's an actual desert. Like with tumbleweeds."

The conversation moves on to other things. Such as: what is

tumbleweed, exactly? And why can't Cassidy find a decent man to date?

"They're afraid of your big brain," Aubrey insists. "Is there a dating app for geniuses? I mean, there's a dating app just for farmers. And there's one just for men with beards."

"It gets weirder than that," I point out. "There's a dating app for people who like *Star Trek*. And an app for people who like to eat bacon together."

"Mmm bacon," Aubrey says with a sigh. "I've heard worse ideas."

I pick up a slice of mine and take a big bite. It's nice to be out with friends. But I can't stop my traitorous mind from serving up flashbacks of last night. I think about how good it felt to hold Maguire, too. And I wonder how many licks it will take to get to his emotional center.

20 REALLY PROFOUND

Maguire

Breakfast with Lance was a mistake. Sometimes I wonder if he's my best friend by choice or by default. I'm sitting at his kitchen counter and he's just whipped us up some breakfast that is 99% meat 1% tomato.

I'm okay with this. We've got coffees and are shoveling the food in our mouths.

The bigger problem is that he's cruising an iPad and giggling. Jesus, the man *giggles*. We could not be more opposite if we tried. "There's a quiz that I think can help you. It's called 'Am I In Love?'"

The What The Fuck look must clearly show on my face.

"What?" Lance asks. "I've been doing some sexual research. And I found that *Cosmo* has all these awesome quizzes about sex toys and positions. I'm good at the sex toys one already, and my score keeps improving on the positions. Some of the information is really profound." He says this without an ounce of sarcasm.

The dude is...goddammit. He's just a delight. But I'm never telling him that. "Are you seriously going to have me take a quiz in *Cosmo*?"

"Just answer the questions, okay?" Number one wants to know whether I enjoy talking to her, or just having sex with her."

"Both," I say. "This is stupid. I don't need to know if I'm in love with her. I'm not. Not ever. I just want to know how long I can sleep with her before she wants a commitment and I have to move out. Please let the answer be a very, very long time."

"But that's why this quiz is appropriate. If you have no feelings for her, then you're safe for six months. Maybe even a year."

A year of fucking Meg and drinking beer with her and hanging out and eating food and then fucking her again? I could be good with that. "What if this...quiz...says I do have some, whatever, feelings for her?"

"Then you're doomed."

"I can't be doomed. I'm taking her to my sister's wedding and she's agreed to fall all over me and make my family think I don't give a shit about my brother and sister-in-law."

"That's a healthy idea for sure," says Lance.

"Just give me question 2," I bark.

"What initially drew her to you?"

Okay, this one is more confusing. How does a guy explain that kind of magnetic pull? Or that I didn't even mind when she tried to undress me within thirty seconds of meeting me? Or the way one hot look or smart-ass comment from her makes something inside me light up?

"She had a plant that was too big," is what I go with.

Lance squints at the tablet. "That's not one of the options."

"There are options?"

"Well, yeah. It's a quiz, dipshit. Not a therapy session."

"Oh. Whoops." It feels like a therapy session.

"These are your choices. A) That ass in those jeans. B) Her bright smile. C) She said something that made you laugh. D) All of the above."

"D," I admit reluctantly. "Is that bad?"

"Let's see..." He scrolls and scrolls to get to the bottom of the quiz. "So far you're maxing out on the possible points."

"And what does that mean?"

He reads. "Headed for the altar! It's time to get down on one knee, Romeo. Click here to read Four Ingenious Methods For Discovering Your Girlfriend's Ring Size."

"Oh, please," I complain. "This is stupid."

"No, I think they might know a thing or two."

"For fuck's sake, Lance. Use your cop brain. Who writes this magazine? Women, that's who. And they have an agenda. We're being railroaded right now."

Lance just shakes his head. "I am using my cop brain. And I'm using it to understand what women really want. And when I get my chance to try the Freaky Monkey, I'm taking it."

"The Freaky Monkey?"

"It's this sex position where you lean her left ankle and her right hand against the wall, and then pound into her on the diagonal..."

"That sounds dangerous," I point out.

"I know." He rubs his hands together. "Hey, let me show you the sex-toy quiz. You might learn something useful."

He's wrong, though. The sex part is easy for me. It's the relationship part that gives me the cold sweats. I don't need a "Do You Love Her" quiz. I need a "Are You Crazy Enough to Go There" quiz.

Sure, there's something there between Meg and me. Something nice. But everything in me wants to bail. I'm not proud of that, but that's what my gut is telling me. It doesn't matter that the rest of me wants to go over to her apartment right now and kiss her harder and deeper than I've kissed anyone before. My gut is right, because my gut remembers what happened last time I let myself get carried away with romantic optimism. I asked a girl to marry me. Now she's my brother's wife.

"What are you thinking about so hard?" Lance asks.

"Morris," I admit. "Julie. That whole shit show."

Lance shoves a sausage in his mouth and makes a face. "I feel ya. That must have been a really bad day. You walked in on 'em, right?"

I just grunt in response. This right here is why I don't do talking. Who'd want to relive that day? During my first semester studying criminal law, I drove home from Indiana to surprise Julie. Five hours in the car without stopping. I drove straight to the apartment that Julie shared with a new roommate.

That girl had opened the door. "Oh, hey! Did you step out?"

"What?" I'd asked, not understanding the question from someone I'd never meant. "Is Julie home?"

"Of course she is!" She'd given me a look like I was crazy.

But I suspected nothing. And, wearing the smile of someone who expects to enjoy a visit with his fiancée, I opened Julie's bedroom door.

Everybody who knows my story assumes that I caught them in the act. But that's only partly true. I caught them in bed all right. My brother was shirtless. But I can't even remember what Julie was or wasn't wearing. Because bare skin wasn't the shocking thing, and they weren't even kissing.

It was so much worse than that.

They were *cuddling* in bed. What stunned me was how cozy they looked. How *coupled up*. They were curled up under the quilt, peering at something on my brother's phone, heads together. There's no mistaking the way a couple looks—like they're on exactly the same wavelength. Like they're about to finish each other's sentences.

And when they both looked up, it took a moment for their duplicate happy faces to fail. That's how blissful their evening had been before I'd interrupted it. I was literally the last thing on either of their minds.

Julie was my whole life. I was taking an epic course load at school, because she wanted me to graduate early and come home.

Yet she was curled up in bed with my Judas of a brother.

Heartbreak is supposed to be a metaphor. But the pain I felt at that moment was absolutely excruciating. And I never want to feel it again.

I can't wait to see you, Julie had said, and I'd believed her. *I love you*.

Maybe she did. It's just that she loved Morris more. And she didn't bother to tell me.

Reeling with shock, I'd turned right around and walked out of the room. "Macklin, wait!" Julie had shrieked. "Let me explain." As if she ever could.

"Oh my God, there's *two* of you?" the new roommate had gasped.

"Not anymore," I'd said. And then I just left. I went to a buddy's house and let him get me drunk. The next day I drove back to Indiana, and I literally didn't come home to Michigan for almost three more years. A job offer was the only thing that could entice me back. That and my sister begging me to take it.

As for Morris, I never even punched him in the face. All my friends expected me to. I think Morris himself expected it. But that would only be stooping to his level, and I didn't want to give him the satisfaction. My only option was swallowing the pain and trying to prove what shitty people Morris and Julie were by being the better man.

They didn't notice, as far as I can tell. They got married six months later. Everyone was relieved when I didn't show up for the wedding. Or Christmas, or Thanksgiving. Ever. Their betrayal cost me so much.

It's not that surprising that I've written off relationships. And I don't see how that could ever change. I can't hand that much power over to anyone again. I'm not even capable of it.

Anyway. It's a moot point. I've got this other wedding to go to. Meg will accompany me, and I'll make sure she has a good time. After that, I'll have to break things off.

It doesn't matter what the quiz in the magazine says. They don't know me. Very few people do. And I like to keep it that way.

The shit inside my head ain't pretty. But it's home.

Meg

"Mac," I chide as his hand wanders down my thigh.

"What?" He cups the curve of my knee, and I shiver.

"Not now," I insist. "I'm trying to talk to you."

"I'm not a talker. I'm a man of action."

"You sure talk a lot while we're naked."

"That's dirty talk. Dirty talk *is* action."

I laugh. He makes me orgasm and he makes me laugh, sometimes at the same time. There are moments when I think Maguire might really be a keeper. A lot of moments. In fact, we've spent many, many moments together since the night of my ride-along.

These past couple of weeks we've invented quite a few new meanings for the word "ride-along." Ahem.

"No, listen. For real." I prop myself up on one elbow. We're both totally naked, sheets be damned, and tossed aside. I feel completely at ease talking to him like this. Clothes flung off. My hair a curly mess. It's easy to be comfortable with a man who's just tasted every part of you and then come back for more.

"Your sister's wedding is tomorrow and we haven't even talked about…"

"I don't want to talk about it," he groans. Then he reaches for the sheet to cover up his slowly softening cock. That's a pity. Both the softening and the covering.

"You don't have to talk about the whys or the history of it all. I just need to know the what kind."

He studies me. "I have no idea what you just said. It's either post-orgasm fog and I still don't have enough blood rushing to my brain, or you just made no sense. The whys, the history, the what kind?"

"Focus!" I say. "I just need to know—what kind of girlfriend do you want me to be?"

I can actually feel him start to choke. And there's a flush to his cheeks.

"Maguire!" I say and snap my fingers inches from his face. "Breathe. I mean, what kind of girlfriend do you want me to *pretend* to be for your sister's wedding? Remember?"

"Oh!" His relief is so obvious that I feel a pinch in my chest.

"I don't need to know all the history, unless you want to tell me. But I just need to know what you want. From me."

He shrugs. "I'm no good at hypotheticals. Give me some examples."

"Okay, sure." It's actually a great idea. So I jump up and run, buck ass naked to my little closet where I haul myself into it. Literally.

"Meg?" Maguire calls as I disappear, sounding concerned that maybe a demigorgon has sucked me into another dimension. Not to worry. That only happens on Netflix. I emerge holding onto an outfit straight from the puritan 80s. Or my mother's puritan 80s wardrobe. It's a pastel pink power suit with shoulder pads to die for. "Do you want me to be vintage and weirdly subservient?" I put on a sweet-sounding voice, "Yes, Maguire. Anything you say, sweetie. Or...." I drop the hanger onto the doorknob and jump back into the closet.

This next idea takes a couple of minutes, because I need to put on this outfit, instead of holding it up in front of me. And these fucking garters take a while to connect to the pantyhose.

When I finally emerge, I'm wearing barely anything. I'm clad in a black leather bra with my nipples exposed, a chain that connects from my bra to my garter, thong underwear, a garter belt, and mesh stockings. I've also slid into a pair of stilettos.

"Holy shit..." he breathes.

And then I crack the whip. Literally.

Every actress needs an assortment of props. Every woman, really.

"Do you want me to be the one in charge?" I ask, strutting toward him. *Stomp stomp stomp.* I fold the whip, using just the tip to trace a line down his chest down to his... *Hello, sailor!* At least part of Mac likes this getup. "You'd have to be my subordinate if we go with this outfit, okay? Try saying: 'Yes, Mistress. Your wish is my command.'"

Mac blinks back at me with half-dilated eyes. "That one might be a little...much..." he manages to say. "Maybe save that one for later."

Sure. Gotcha. Back to the closet I go. I pull on a T-shirt and some Daisy Dukes.

"How about this? I could play the girlfriend from the wrong side of the tracks who listens to Billy Idol and wants to fight the system."

"So we're back in the 80s?" he asks.

"What of it? It was a good decade and I didn't get to experience much of it."

"Maybe you could be from the right side of the tracks. But still want to fight the system?"

"I could, huh?"

He smiles up at me, his body spread out like a relaxed cat taking in the sun. I wonder if this little exercise is making Mac think about what he'd like in a *real* girlfriend. And I wonder if he can see me in that role.

"Let me try on something else," I offer. "While I'm dressing, you tell me the kind of girlfriend you want me to be. I can pretty much be anyone you want. Except Australian. That's an accent I just can't manage."

"Hmm," he says as I go back to the closet.

I find the perfect dress, peel off the Wrong Side of the Tracks outfit and slip a new dress over my head. No bra needed. And I wait to see if Maguire will start talking. Sometimes, I've found, if I leave his line of sight, the words come a little easier.

After a whole lot of silence that's starting to verge on the awkward, he calls, "Why do you have to be any certain thing? Why can't you just...be Meg?"

"Yeah, but which Meg?"

"All the Meg!" he says. "You're perfect just as you are." He says those words. Out loud. And I hear them.

I could do a lot of things right now. I could call him on it. Point it out. I could celebrate.

But that's not the way to go with Maguire. He has to come to realizations on his own, and that could take some time.

Still, the compliment hits me right in the tits. I'm perfect just as I am, huh? I smile to myself just as he starts to backtrack. He's a little on the frantic side now when he says: "I mean, you don't have to *be* anything really. I asked you to go originally to make my brother and sister-in-law a little, I dunno, jealous. But that's not really the point now, I guess. Really, I just want you there..."

It sounds like he could stop right there. Put a period on the sentence. *I just want you there* would be lovely. But no. The ass has to keep going.

"...I just want you there to take some of the pressure off. Show my parents and my siblings that I'm doing just fine."

I poke my head out the door so he can't see me yet. "You are doing just fine."

"I know, I know. But I could be finer."

I decide now is the time for the big reveal. I walk out and twirl around. I'm wearing a soft marigold-colored dress, made of a crepey silk that catches the air when I twirl. It's got spaghetti straps and I'm not being vain when I say my tits look amazing in this dress. That's just a fact. It glides around my waist and then flares out. This is a dress that I spent hours searching for and when I stepped out of the dressing room, Aubrey and Cassidy both sighed. I think Aubrey cried a little. This dress is that good.

"Be the Meg that wears that dress," he says. His voice is a little less frantic now, and has more than a hint of desire in it. Then he reaches for me. "Come here," he says.

"You cannot touch this dress. Not until the wedding."

"Come *here*," he pleads. "Let me touch you in that dress."

"Nope," I say.

"Meg, dammit. I have to touch you now. Can you see what you do to me?" He nods to his cock. It's magnificent standing straight up like that.

"You can't touch the dress," I say, "but you can touch me. But only with that." Now I nod to his cock.

"Fair," he says. He spreads his arms and legs and just waits for me to climb on.

So I do.

For the third time today.

————

MAGUIRE

Where is my brain? Where is it? I ask myself as we lie in bed together after sex.

Oh yeah. It exploded along with my third orgasm with Meg this morning.

I don't understand what she's doing to me, and I hope she never stops.

So when she asks me what kind of girlfriend I want for the wedding, I'm honestly confused. What kind of girlfriend? I just want Meg.

And that, my friend, kicks me in the gut. It has the ring of truth to it.

I need to backpedal the fuck out of this realization about wanting Meg, but how? I could tell her that she doesn't need to be my date for the wedding.

But honestly, I want her to come with me.

So I'm just going to do some breathing exercises like Lance suggested and see if I can just tamp those thoughts down. I don't need a girlfriend. I need a FWFB. (A friend with frisky benefits.) And Meg is the best one in the world. Hands down.

I finally leave her apartment and slink over to my place for a shower and a quick bite of breakfast before I start my shift. I made toast and a couple of eggs, and all the while I'm eating, I'm aware of Meg next door. What is she doing? Is she wearing one of her silky robes? Is she rearranging those damned decorative pillows? Is she touching herself, thinking about me?

Arggggg!!!

Why is she still in my brain?

I have things to do today. Big things. I'm actually meeting with my supervisor for the final interview for the promotion I want. I need to focus on that, and then I'll have the next four days off and I won't need to focus at all.

The interview will change my life. Or it won't.

And I need to think about the wedding too.

Maybe at the wedding, when she's pretending to be more than a friend, I can just pretend she's mine. Like a real couple. Maybe I can own that for a bit. Just, you know, to try it on.

Then again, that's not fair to Meg. None of this is. I'm not an idiot. She's hoping for more. I can see it in her eyes. She deserves it, too.

If I were capable of being the man she needs, I'd be that guy. I really would.

I finish my eggs and head to work. And I think about Meg the whole way there.

22 IS SOMEONE CUTTING AN ONION?

Maguire

"To love, honor, and cherish. As long as we both shall live," Rosie says in a pure, sweet voice. And I hastily wipe my eyes.

"Everything okay over there?" Meg whispers.

"Yep. Hay fever season or something." I sniff.

"You are so fucking cute," she whispers back to me. "Don't ever change."

As if I could.

And that's the special magic of weddings, right? Change. All that serious language about two souls joining into one. Irrevocably, forever and ever. There's no room in the wedding ceremony for uncertainty. That's why I'm never getting married. I'm not wired for that kind of optimism.

Not anymore, anyway.

I just watched my baby sister make the biggest decision of her life, and she did it with a big smile on her face. Some people make their own optimism, the way plants make sunshine into food.

Up in front, Rosie is still smiling. This marriage feels right to her, and who am I to argue? Man, my little sister is truly grown up now. I think I feel some more hay fever coming on. Or is someone in this church cutting an onion?

"Kwan, you may kiss the bride."

"She's so beautiful," my mother sobs from down the pew. "My baby!"

After a big smooch that I can't really watch (a big brother just can't) the newly married Rosie prances back up the aisle, hand in hand with the world's luckiest man. He doesn't deserve her, but only because nobody could.

"That was beautiful," Meg says with a sigh. Since she's on the end of the pew, she stands up first. "Weddings always make me feel so dreamy."

"That's how I feel about whiskey," I mutter, following her.

"I know, big guy." Meg pokes me in the side. "I've got you covered."

"Because it's time for the drinking?"

"No. Because it's time for the photography."

"So? A few photos won't kill me, right?"

She glances at me, her beautiful face knowing. "Oh, honey. Not if I have anything to say about it. But the photos are always a trial."

"Why?"

"You'll see. But here's something pleasant for you to think about while you're taking them." She leans close and whispers in my ear. "I'm not wearing any panties under this dress."

"Wait, really?" My eyes skim down her curves, clad in captivating silk, in a soft orange color. And, dammit, I can't tell if she's teasing.

Meg shrugs, smiling. "Let's go. Time for those photos."

———

MEG KNOWS things that I don't. Like how TV shows are filmed. How to survive on takeout food and mixed drinks. And, apparently, how weddings work.

Nothing in my life up to this point has prepared me for the hell that awaits me outside the church.

My mother had mentioned "a few photos" after the wedding. That's like calling an Iron Man race "a little stroll." First the photographer insists on a dozen shots of my sister with Kwan. And then with her bridesmaids. And his groomsmen. And then the whole lot of them.

And then there's the photographer, who seems to shout every word she says. The woman is like a walking megaphone. "BIG SMILES! GROOM, TILT YOUR CHIN TO THE LEFT!"

It hurts the ears.

The only saving grace is that my brother is nowhere in evidence. I'm no good at small talk with anyone, let alone the brother who betrayed me and the woman who was my fiancée before she became his wife.

"Knock knock," Meg says.

I give her a grumpy look.

"Come on, Mac. Go with it. The night won't be any easier when we're all stuck on a boat together. Knock knock."

"Who's there?" I say from between gritted teeth.

"Butch and Jimmy."

"Butch and Jimmy who?"

"Butch your arms around me and Jimmy a big kiss," she says, flinging her arms out to the sides.

I laugh in spite of myself. "That was the worst joke I've ever heard in my entire life." But the girl is waiting, so I grab her, lean her over backwards, and give her a big kiss while she shrieks.

When I stand up, suddenly Morris and Julie are right there, watching us.

My smile dies on my face. But Meg's smile only widens. "Well hello! Who could you be?" She holds out a hand to my asshole brother immediately, before there's time for an awkward pause to even develop.

Hell, did I pick the right date or what? Meg is magic. Morris and Julie sort of stare at Meg with slack-jawed wonder as she introduces herself and puts them both at ease.

I know I have to say something to them. So I guess now is as good a time as any. "Morris, Julie," I say stiffly. "How have you been?"

"Oh, fine," Julie says quickly, inspecting her hands.

"I'd catch you up," Morris says. "But it's tricky to summarize ten years, you know?"

And I am speechless. I wasn't expecting hostility from the guy who broke my life into shards and stomped on them.

"NOW THE BRIDE'S FAMILY!" the photographer yells from up front.

"Oh, that's you!" Meg chirps. She actually swats me on the ass. "Get up there, honey. Smile wide for Rosie's pictures."

I go, only because I can't wait to be done with this.

The first photo is of my parents, Rosie, and my brother and I on opposite sides. Not a big deal. Although they shoot it eight times anyway. "LOOK UP HERE! LOOK AT THE TREE! SAY 'POISON PICKLES'!"

"Dude, that is just wrong," Meg argues from just behind her.

"IT'S UNIQUE!" the photographer cries.

"YOU TERRIFY ME!" Meg shouts and my entire extended family laughs.

"NOW THE TWINS AND THE BRIDE!" the photographer screams.

I feel like screaming, too.

"ONE TWIN ON EITHER SIDE."

"That's the pose we need anyway," Morris says. "My brother wouldn't stand next to me."

"Morris," Julie gasps.

"What? It's just honest," my brother growls.

I sidestep my brother and slide over to Rosie's side. "You look beautiful," I tell her. "Your makeup is still perfect even after fifty pictures."

She takes my arm in hers. "Keep it up. Flattery works."

"SMILE, DAMMIT!" the photographer yells. "PRETEND YOU LOVE EACH OTHER."

"I'm sure that's a funny little joke in most families," Julie says from somewhere nearby. Then she heaves a sigh.

"Oh dear," Rosie whispers.

I smile like my life depends on it. Because I can't wait to get the fuck away from here. The shutter clicks eagerly, and the photographer dismisses us.

"BUT STAY CLOSE," she yells. "WE'RE NOT DONE."

Fuck.

My brother stomps a few feet away. He's actually shooting me angry looks.

My blood pressure doubles immediately.

That's when Meg's pinky finger hooks into mine. "Somebody needs a hug and a shot of whiskey."

"Since I can't have the second thing, I'll take a double of the first," I grumble.

"Why Macklin! You sweet talker." Meg steps into my personal space and wraps her luscious arms around me. "You're doing great," she whispers.

"No, you are," I whisper back, squeezing her a little tighter.

"I wasn't kidding about the whiskey," she returns. "I have a flask."

"Shut the front door!" I hiss.

"It's true."

"You are a total babe."

She releases me and then opens her purse. "Tell me something I don't know." She pulls out a flask that's studded with pink rhinestones. It looks like something that Miss Piggy might have designed.

"I think if you put whiskey in a flask like that, it changes into schnapps."

She slaps my hand. "Don't harsh on my flask. It amuses me."

I catch myself smiling even before I take a swig. "You amuse me." I tip the flask and take a swallow of single malt. "You're a genius as well as a total babe."

"NOW THE FAMILY AGAIN," bellows the photographer.

I trudge back into the fray and allow the loudmouthed photographer to arrange me next to my mother and Aunt Lucille.

"Show me some leg, Mac!" Meg cheers from the sidelines. "Work it, hot stuff!"

"I really like her," Aunt Lucille says with a sigh. "The next wedding will be yours. I predict it."

My laughter is explosive. "No fucking way. Because then we'd have to take more of these pictures."

"Good point, honey."

I steal another glance at Meg, and I'm surprised to see that Julie is speaking to her. She seems to be asking for something.

Meg removes the flask from her purse and passes it to Julie, who takes a gulp. And then another one.

Jesus Christ, Julie broke my life in half, and now she's drinking the whiskey that Meg brought as a gift for me. Will the girl stop at nothing?

"NOW WE'LL TRY A HUMAN PYRAMID."

Like I needed one more reason to never get married.

———

"YOU LOOK like you're marching to your doom," Meg chides as we walk toward the dock in Grand Haven. "It's just a party, Mac. You can get back to Hemingway in only a few hours."

"But I hate parties in general and this one in particular. I am going toward my doom."

"No, you're walking toward temporary discomfort. I bet you're a baby when you get a cold, too."

"Am not," I argue. But I totally am.

She smiles at me like she knows the truth.

"Can you believe that bullshit he spewed in the churchyard? Like it's my fault that we're never in the same place at the same time?" It took us thirty minutes to drive here from the church, and I thought I'd calmed down. But I'm not calm.

Meg's hand slips into mine. "My mother has this thing she says whenever my sister or I get upset at someone else's bullshit. She says, 'There are other paradigms of logic.'"

"What does that even mean?" I grumble as we approach the line of people waiting to walk up the ramp and onto our floating jail.

"It means that everyone thinks he's the good guy, even when he's not. You can't change your brother. You can only change how upset you are at him."

"Your mother doesn't know how angry I still am." Usually I can just ignore it. But today it's like a hot coal in the center of my chest.

"I do, though. Honestly when Mom used to say that, I used to slam a few doors to get back at her. Fuck that noise."

I let out an uncomfortable bark of laughter. "Meg." I stop on the sidewalk, a few yards short of the ramp.

"What? We're not bailing now."

"No," I admit, turning to her and taking both of her hands in mine. "We're not bailing. But I just wanted to say thank you ahead of time. Thank you for going to this shit show with me."

Meg's eyes go soft. "Hey, you're welcome. It's my pleasure."

"I also need you to know something important." I lean forward and kiss her on the nose. "The best bail bondsman in the city is Biff's, on Fuller Street."

Meg giggles. "It won't come to that."

"You don't know for certain."

She leans against my chest and laughs. "I do, Mac. Let's go eat some expensive appetizers and drink Hemingway Daiquiris."

"He liked a nice dry martini, too. Just saying."

"Fine. Whatever. Just get your very tight butt onto that boat. There's dancing later."

"I don't dance."

"Tonight you do," she says, wrapping her arms around me. "I told Julie that we were taking ballroom lessons from a nice teacher named Ernesto. And that your pachanga is particularly smooth."

"What?" I yelp. "I don't even know what a pachanga is."

"Me neither! And neither does Julie. So I don't think it matters." She beams at me.

"What did you go and do that for?"

"Because I want to dance with you, and this was the only thing I could think of to make that happen."

"But..."

We are interrupted by a very loud cat whistle. Both of us look up at the deck of the party boat, where my sister is standing in her wedding dress, two fingers in her mouth. "Get on the boat, Mac! Let's get this party started."

That's when I realize that everyone else has boarded already. And so many people are standing up there watching Meg and me that the boat might actually list from their efforts. Fuck. I hate attention.

Meg, however, does not. She holds up one finger in the universal sign for *wait a second*. Then she stands on her toes and kisses me deeply.

I forget all about the boat for a nice long moment, as Meg's kiss shifts my mind to other thoughts. Namely—all the fun things we can do after the stupid party is over. I'm going to unzip her silky dress and let it fall to my bedroom floor. I'm going to find out if she was teasing me about going commando under there. Is that really true? Or just a trick to make me wonder...

Before I've sorted it out, she steps back. "Let's go, Copper. Boat's waiting."

I follow her on board like a hungry dog. Just like she knew I would.

23 WEIRD SILENCE

Meg

Okay. I have been to a lot of weddings. Sometimes as a guest, some-times as a performer, but mostly as a server. But I have never been cruising around Grand Haven on a giant paddle boat that's festooned with flowers, mylar balloons, and sparkling disco balls. This has Aubrey written all over it. She's like some kind of unicorn pixie, sprinkling love dust and magic everywhere she goes...which is funny because her own love life is a disaster.

Anyway.

Tucked among the flowers and sparkling streamers are tiny white lights, as if we've stepped into a small floral universe under twinkling stars. I'm not lying when I breathe, "This is amazing!" I squeeze Mac's arm for emphasis.

I can feel his muscles flex. Damn his muscles. I sort of wish we could skip the reception and head straight to bed. Actually, I don't even need a bed with him. Just a dark corner where he can push me up against a wall, hoist my dress and leg up, and...

Mac kills the mood a little when he whispers, "This may sound paranoid. But I think Rosie put her reception on a boat entirely so that I can't escape."

At that moment, I catch Rosie's eye in the receiving line. Both she and her husband give us matching cheesy thumbs up. First of all, this confirms they're soul mates. And secondly, I realize Mac is totally right. Rosie did plan this boat reception as a way to force the family together.

Rosie is an evil genius.

She's fucking fantastic.

We make our way through the receiving line. "You are a beautiful bride!" I tell Rosie. Because it's true.

"As will you be someday!" she sings. The girl is clearly high on wedding-day exhilaration. Or maybe she inhaled some of the helium in the balloons. Either way, I wait while her brother gives her a squeeze. And then Mac and I go up to the top deck, where the dining tables are beautifully set. There will be dinner and then dancing. If we're lucky, we'll get a spectacular sunset too. This whole reception-on-a-boat thing is starting to really grow on me. Not that I'll ever get married. But if I did...

At the sound of Mac's sigh, I turn my attention to the table in front of us. I don't even have to read the names on the place cards to know what's coming. Family drama. But that's okay, because I know my role. This is what Mac brought me here for, after all: to be the girlfriend buffer.

Serve it up, Maguire family! This girl is ready.

Our table is just in front of the wedding party, and with a view of Lake Michigan sparkling over the railing. It's the Family Table, and it's just me, Mac, Mac's parents, and Morris and Julie.

"How cozy!" I say with a smile, while Mac scowls.

We're not the first to arrive at our table, though. Mac's parents are already seated. His dad, God bless him, is wearing a red crocheted sweater vest over his shirt and tie. And either Bob has really odd shoulders, or Mac's mom has incorporated shoulder pads into her design. Bob gives me a little finger wave and a smile. I finger wave back. And then I wait. Mac is frozen about two paces from the table.

So. This is awkward.

After a moment or two of weird silence, Eleanor, Mac's mom, says, "For Pete's sake, kiddo, pull out her chair!"

Mac shakes himself. "Sorry, darling," he says.

For a second I wonder who the darling is. Then I realize it's me. So Mac is in full-on This Is My Girlfriend mode.

I have to admit, I sort of like it.

After he pulls out the chair for me, I feel his hand trail down to the small of my back. I shiver and then slide into the seat.

Okay, fine. I don't just sort of like it. I love it. So much. It's a subtle way of telling everyone that you're a couple. I wonder if he even knows he's doing that. I hope it's just a reflex. Maybe that means I'm growing on him.

A moment later, Mac drops into the seat next to mine. His jaw is as tight as spandex on a pig. "Breathe, Copper," I whisper to him.

He adjusts his collar.

"Meg," Eleanor says in a dreamy voice. "I am so glad you're here. I thought for sure you were going to be a one-time fling, but here you are! I've dreamed of this day!" Then she whirls on Mac. "So...." She leans forward. "When are you going to pop the question?"

"Mom! Come on!" Mac says. Maybe a little too forcefully.

"What?" she asks innocently. "I've found out I'm really good at being a grandma. And Rosie should be pregnant soon. Give her a four months' start, and then you two should get started. I've been knitting booties."

"Booties," Bob echoes. I'm pretty sure that's a hint of despair in his voice.

I wonder if he's wearing a pair of booties right now. I don't get the chance to ask, though, when I look up to spot Mac's double, and Julie's Double Ds. The two of them slide into seats opposite us.

And, okay, it's a little bit like a *Twilight Zone* episode. Morris looks so much like Mac. And yet not the same at all. His face is rounder, his eyes a little tired and squinty. Maybe that's what happens the year after you have a baby, though. Or after you stab your twin in the back.

Then there's Julie. I have nothing nice to say about her at all. This is probably just a reflex. I can't possibly like a woman who betrayed Mac. That must be why I have a dozen mean thoughts about her immediately. Her dress is ill-fitting. Her breasts are about ready to make a run for it and pop the buttons right off her dress. She has lipstick on her teeth. I'm a terrible person for judging her so superficially.

But fuck it. She probably kicks puppies for fun.

"Nuts!" Julie exclaims suddenly. And I'm confused. Does she want to eat nuts, or is she regretting the way things ended with Mac? She better not be checking out Mac. Mac is mine.

Ohhhhh damn. Possessive much, Meg?

Just a bit, I tell myself.

Luckily it's not Mac that Julie is fixated on. A moment later I realize that it's the nuts on the table that have caught her attention. Bending over, she begins digging furiously through the bowl. She pulls out a fat Brazil nut, holding it up in the air like it's the Hope Diamond. Then she starts to nibble at it like she's eating a piece of baby corn.

I try to swallow the laugh that's bubbling up. Because Julie is *sloshed.* I squeeze Mac's thigh and he leans a little closer to me.

God, I love weddings. All that natural, unscripted drama just calls to me. I'm on the edge of my seat. It's only a little past seven, and already the tension at this table is as thick as tar, and Julie is floating above it like she's in La La Land.

This will only get more interesting, I decide as salads begin to land on the table, one in front of each of us. Morris hands Julie the bread basket. "Have a roll," he says to his wife.

"Too carby," Julie snips.

"I think you need to make an exception this time."

"What are you *saying?*" She swings her head toward her husband like a horse changing direction. "You're the one who thinks I need to lose the baby weight."

Eleanor flinches. "You look beautiful, dear. Try the rolls and let me know how they are."

Julie holds up a hand, as if she's about to swear an oath. "No, I shall refrain. And I won't tell you what I think about the rolls, or anything else. That's what the Maguire family does, right? We just hold it all inside. That's our way."

There is a deep silence. Everyone looks at his plate. Except for me, of course. I'm practically taking notes. It would be rude to pull out a pen and jot this down, right? This is drama *gold.*

Everyone picks up his fork and begins to eat salad. Even me. And it's a good salad, with candied pecans and sour cherries. "I love dried cherries," I say with a sigh. "Such a Michigan thing."

"Mmm," Bob agrees.

"Dried up like lil' raisins," Julie says. "Like our sex life, right, honey?"

Morris chokes on his sip of water.

The awkwardness congeals around us, like shredded cheese left out in the sun.

The tension is only broken when a waiter glides up with a tray full of champagne flutes. "It's bubbly time!"

"Excellent." Bob claps his hands together. "Champagne for my real friends. Real pain for my sham friends!"

"That one hits a little too close to home tonight," Mac mutters under his breath.

Now everyone who has ever been to a wedding knows you're not supposed to drink the champagne until after the toast. So we all set our glasses down on the table and wait.

Except for Julie. She tips hers into her mouth and glugs back the whole glass in a big fat hurry. Then she plunks the empty glass onto the table and belches. "Megggggh," she slurs. "I know this is awkward," she says, enunciating every word. "But I just want you to know that I'm so happy you're here. For Mac. He looks good with you. And I look good with Morris. And since they're identical, does that mean we look good together? By the transitive property. Isn't that weird?"

There's a silence at our table that practically throbs.

"It is weird," I agree, because fucking hell. It is.

"Have another drink," Morris says. He sounds tired. Maybe because he is. He stops a passing waiter and commandeers a fresh glass for his wife.

Julie immediately raises her glass. "Here's to a night off from the baby and nursing and all those late night Netflix binges. And here's to family harm." She giggles. "I mean, family harmony."

There's a pause when I don't know what his family is going to do. But then everyone picks up their glasses and clinks them together. Because, hey, what else do you do with your dysfunctional family but go along with the flow?

THE DINNER IS your typical wedding affair. Lots of toasts and speeches. Courses of food, and it's actually pretty tasty for 1) being served on a boat and 2) this being a wedding. There's Michigan whitefish that's been dredged in flour and then pan seared in locally churned butter. A summer medley of vegetables. And the biscuits! I don't understand how they did it, but they're so fluffy that it's clear someone's got some weird voodoo magic going on. I think I actually moan when I take a bite.

And then there's crème brûlée and tiramisu and chocolate cake, all served on individual spoons so you get just a bite. I could handle about a hundred bites, though.

"Do you think I can slip one of these into my purse?" I whisper to Mac.

"That would be stealing," he says without thinking.

"Then I guess you'd have to arrest me. Did you bring your cuffs?"

That brings a smile to his lips. He surprises me when he says, "I might have. Hold that thought."

"Oh, I'll be holding it."

Mac is bearing up pretty well, given the pressure. It helps that there's a lot of great food, and speeches, and eventually music.

What there isn't a lot of is conversation.

Mac's mom and dad look blissfully unaware of the tension. Or maybe they're just in denial. Julie is swaying to the instrumental jazz that's playing. Or maybe she's just swaying. Morris glances at his phone from time to time, but it's obvious that he can't figure out where to rest his gaze.

And Mac? He's just staring straight ahead, tense like a cable that's pulled taut, and about to snap.

"Sooooooo...." I say loudly to the table. Then I realize I've got nothing. No material. You'd think my training in improv would help with this sort of silence, but not so much. Everyone turns to look at me, and I have to admit, I panic a little. I say the first thing that pops into my head. "It's time for that dance you promised me."

There is a beat of silence. Then Mac says, "Right! Let's do it."

I almost fall out of my chair, I'm so surprised. But I scramble to my feet, not wanting to waste the moment. Catching Mac's hand, I pull him onto the dance floor, taking care to put some space between us and the Table of Doom.

"So this is what it takes to get you to dance?" I ask Mac as we come together, cheek to cheek. The band is playing "As Time Goes By."

"Apparently," he says, that gruff voice setting off fireworks all over my body. Maybe this is a fake date, but we're dancing for real. And the weight of his hand at my waist is divine. The sun is beginning to tint the sky pink.

"This is so nice," I hear myself say. "And look at Rosie. She looks so happy!"

Mac shifts to glance at his sister. "She does," he admits. "I guess a few hours of discomfort are worth it for Rosie."

"You're not uncomfortable right now," I say, pressing my luck. "You've been fed and you're dancing with me. So your life is basically perfect."

He chuckles, and the vibration does buzzy things to my belly. "You're a hell of a date, Meg."

"Well, you make it easy."

He smiles against my cheek, and I'm so happy. This is the *perfect* moment.

"Excuse me. Can I cut in?" There's a tap on my arm. And the tapper is Julie.

"No," I snap. "No. Just no. I was promised this dance, and I will finish this dance."

Julie's head jerks back, like I slapped her. "I thought we were going to be friends."

"Why did you think that?" I ask, genuinely curious.

"Well..." She looks confused. "We're both with men who share the same face."

That's not all you shared. Luckily, I manage not to say that out loud. "Julie, go back to your man. We're busy here."

"No!" She actually stomps her foot. "Don't take that tone with me. I need to talk to Mac!"

"Seems like you had plenty of chances to talk to him, and then decided to give that up," I point out.

"Meg..." Mac gives me a wry smile. I can tell he doesn't want me to escalate the situation.

But God. I'd like to escalate my fist into her throat. If only we were somewhere more private...

"I'm *getting* my chance to talk to him," she says, her eyes unfocused. "This night isn't over." She stomps away.

"Good grief," I whisper. "She isn't keeping her shit together."

"She never did," Mac says. "Always whining about something. Always trying to take more than her share."

"Then why were you going to marry her?" The question just pops out. And I feel Mac go still in my arms. "Sorry," I say quickly. "It's none of my business."

"Nah, it's funny," he says, gathering me closer again. "I don't remember. I mean, I know I loved her."

"Of course."

"But I've forgotten why."

"Doesn't matter now," I say, backpedaling like crazy. The last thing I want is for Mac to remember why he loves Julie. I step a little further into his embrace.

But then the song ends, and then the band announces that they're going to take a short break. Reluctantly, Mac and I move apart.

"Thanks for the dance." I bat my eyelashes at him, feeling suddenly shy. When the farce of this wedding is over, I'm the only one here who will be sad.

"Dancing isn't so bad," he says sheepishly. "Like rolling off a log."

"We haven't done the pachanga yet," I point out.

"Oh, we're doing that naked later."

I laugh. "Okay, but now what?"

"Want a beer?"

"Maybe..." I hesitate. "That depends on which of us is driving home tonight. It's okay if you'd rather drink. I don't mind being the designated driver."

"No way," Mac chides, cupping my shoulder. His thumb sweeps across my skin, and I fight off a shiver. "A man always gets his date home safe and sound. That's just how I roll."

This guy. I truly hate Julie right now. Who could turn away this guy? "I appreciate that," I tell him. "But tonight, I'm here for you in your hour of need. If your hour of need requires copious martinis, I'm down for that. I don't mind helping you."

Actually, I like it way too much.

"There's no need," Mac says, shooting me down. But then he puts his hand at the small of my back again, so it's almost okay. "I don't think drunkenness would really improve this party for me. And this boat doesn't dock for at least another hour, so I can have a beer."

We go to the bar, where the overworked bartender is busy dishing out drinks to the thirsty crowd.

"Macklin!" Eleanor booms while we're waiting for our drinks. "How's that promotion coming along?"

Mac makes a face. "No news. I expected to have a decision by now, but I think the chief is enjoying the process too much. Tommy is kissing his ass so hard his lips are going to be stuck there permanently."

"And you—what's your strategy?" his mother asks.

He shrugs. "I'm the best guy for the job. My strategy is good work and trying to stay out of the elevator with the chief. Because I'm no good at small talk."

"You want me to help you strategize?" Eleanor asks. "Hey—I could make him a gift!"

"No need," Mac says quickly. "Although I do appreciate it."

She looks mildly offended as she walks away.

"Oh, lord," Mac says with a sigh. "If she knits him a sweater vest I can kiss my career goodbye."

"Can I just say something?" I ask. Although who am I kidding? I am going to say it anyway. "You're better at small talk than you think."

"I bet you're wrong."

"Not hardly. Just try this one thing, okay? Do you watch TV?"

"Sometimes."

"Great. So tell me this—what's a character from a show that you find charming and a little bit slick? Pick someone who's charming, but you still respect."

Mac thinks this over. "I guess I'd go with Danny from *Downtown Blues*."

"Mac!" My heart flutters even more than it usually does when he's nearby. "You too, huh? I adore Danny. We should be watching this show together."

"Wasn't there a point you were trying to make?" He plucks our drinks off the bar and hands me mine.

"Right! Yes." His smile implies that I'm scatterbrained. Which I am. But I'm also onto something here. "All right, so next time you end up in the elevator with the chief, and he asks about your weekend, I want you to prompt yourself with—what would Danny from *Downtown Blue* say? And then say that."

Mac looks skeptical. "I'd sound like a poser."

"No way! You'll be the only one who's in on the joke. So what *would* Danny say?"

Mac clears his throat. "Had a couple of drinks at the bar, and then I entertained a lady friend."

"Mac!" I squeak. "That was perfect."

He gives me a grin.

"Come on, how hard was that?"

"Not hard, I guess."

"You sounded just like you, only slightly more charming. Come to think of it. I don't know if the world can handle a more charming Mac."

He starts to smile again, but then it dies. "Do you hear shouting?"

We both pause, listening.

"Julie! Get down! Get down right now! This isn't funny."

Oh shit. That's Morris's voice!

Mac darts toward the doorway, leading to the narrow deck that wraps around the tier of this boat. And I'm right on his heels. We have to weave and dodge, because this is a crowded boat. But after sliding past a few dozen people we reach the front deck, where Morris and Eleanor and Bob are all staring up at the roof of the boat.

And—hell—Julie is *standing* up there. No—she's swaying, and way too close to the edge. There is nothing to stop her from falling two stories into the lake.

"Sit down!" Morris yells. "You could fall!"

"I'm the queen of this boat!" she yodels. "Where is Leonardo DiCaprio when you need him?"

"Oh shit," I whisper. "We have to get her down from there before she tries to reenact the ending."

Mac is already removing his suit jacket. He thrusts it at me. "Hold this, babe. And this." He hands me his beer. Then he strides toward a ladder that I hadn't noticed before. That must be how Julie made it up to the roof.

Oh, God. I wanted drama. Now I've got more than I bargained for.

Mac

When I'm in a crisis situation, there are things that happen to me. Chalk it up to my training and to years on the job. Chalk it up to my natural disposition to always be a little bit leery of people and their impulses.

So when I spot Julie up on that roof, a professional calm descends on me. My body just takes over as I put all the tension of the night aside and climb the ladder. There's a very drunk woman up there. She's too inebriated to make good life choices.

I was made for this situation.

What I hadn't expected was Morris to be right behind me, his jacket off too.

"What the hell, Morris? Give me some room," I say, my hands grasping for the top of the ladder. I can visualize what I need to do—grab Julie by the waist and get her to safety. But I need room to maneuver.

Morris gives me a shove in the ass. "You always have to be the hero, don't you?" he asks.

And that stops me cold. Because I don't need two crazy people on this roof.

I turn around. "I'm a first responder. This is literally my job."

He blows out a breath and then looks away. And it's weird, but I could swear I see a flash of envy. It kinda throws me and I start wondering if all this time when I've been jealous of Morris and his marriage and his life, if he hasn't been jealous of me too. Wouldn't that be ridiculous?

I shake that off. Time to focus. "I'm a cop, Morris. I'm trained for this." I take the last step on the ladder.

"I'm her husband," he says. "I'm trained for this too."

He has a point. I reach the top, but then step aside to let Morris up, too.

And holy hell are we up high. The lake shimmers around us, and the sun is just starting to set. There's a slight breeze and a sway to the deck that I am not a fan of. I assess the situation and note that Julie is still safe so far. She's further from the edge of the deck than she was a moment ago. So long as she doesn't move too suddenly, I can get her downstairs. And get some coffee into her.

But then she moves. Of course she does.

"Mac! Morris! Don't you come near me! I've had enough. Enough enough *enough!*"

"But baby," Morris says. It's sweet the way he says it.

"Don't you *but baby* me!" Julie says. Then she repeats it, but yells it this time: "NO BUT BABY!"

It's at this point that I spot our large audience, because of course there's an audience. Not to mention loud hip-hop music playing over the sound system, which only adds to the tension of the moment. I scan the deck and my eyes go right to Meg, standing amidst the swarm of wedding guests, all looking up. She shoos me toward Julie, and I can't help but smirk a little. She's probably enjoying the drama and wants me back in scene.

"Julie," I say. I'm putting my cop voice on now. "You need to vacate this area immediately. This is not safe."

"You know what's not safe? Huh? Ten years of crazy!"

I'm not sure where she's going with this. And neither is Morris. "Come on, Julie, let's go down. I want to dance with you," he pleads.

"And I want this bullcrap to end!"

I honestly don't know what she's talking about. The cop part of me is measuring the distance between Julie and the edge of the roof. And does it slope downward at the edge? Yikes.

"You don't like this party?" asks Morris. "We can leave as soon as we dock. I'll make it up to you! I'll take you to a pancake house!"

I am getting a very real glimpse into their relationship. And all the envy I've been feeling for years is starting to slide right off me.

"No!" Julie screams and then inches ever closer to the slippery edge.

Morris and I both say, "JULIE!"

She tosses her hair and sighs, complete with an eye roll. She could compete with any teenager right now. "You two need to stop this shit now and talk to each other. I am sick of this constant tension. I want our little boy to grow up in a healthy family with his dad and his uncle there and you two are acting like little toddlers. AND I HAVE HAD ENOUGH!"

She wobbles a little, and the audience gasps.

"I'm fine!" she calls.

Someone from the crowd yells out a question. "Why aren't they talking to each other?"

Someone else calls out, "I'm a therapist that specializes in family counseling. I can give you my card!"

Julie takes a deep breath and I can just feel what's about to happen. She's about to become a living, breathing geyser of words. This cannot happen. We don't need to talk about this. Not now, on a pitching rooftop in front of the whole fucking world. Not ever. I start to move forward but Morris stops me. "Let her say it," he says.

I stop.

And wait.

"I slept with my fiancé's twin brother just after Mac proposed to me. And then I married Morris."

There's a pause, until someone below yelps, "Holy shitballs!"

"I know, I know!" Julie says. "It was wrong, but it was also inevitable. Look, I have a certain type. Big guys who are strong and ruggedly handsome. So when I met Maguire I was like, oh this is nice. And we were dating pretty steadily and things were okay and good and I just felt like...okay. Good. This is what love is supposed to be like and I guess this is enough. And *then* I met Mac's brother. He looked the same, sounded the same, but there was something significantly different."

"Did he have herpes?" some wiseacre calls.

"No!" We all yell in unison.

"He had *chemistry*. With me. Crazy, make you do stupid things, make your brain shut down, make your body light up chemistry."

I swear to God the whole crowd sighs.

"I tried to ignore it. Tried to go with the flow with Mac because I really did love him. I just loved him...like a brother." Julie says the next thing directly to me. "I'm sorry, Mac. I really am. I did my best to love you the way you deserve. But then you went to school and we weren't even talking and you weren't around and one night Morris came over to help me put together an entertainment center and then..."

"Chemistry," Morris breathed.

"What can I say? Love makes you do stupid things. It makes you crazy. It makes you set aside all the I shoulds and you just focus on what you want. No. Not what you *want*. What you NEED. And I need Morris."

"I need you too, sweetie."

The crowd sighs again.

Julie isn't done yet. "But I want you to know, Mac, that I understand how you feel. It must've been terrible for this to happen. Heart wrenching. And then to have your parents support Morris and me must've felt like everyone was freezing you out..."

Suddenly my allergies are kicking in. My eyes are all teary.

"And I'm sorry all of this happened the way it did, but I'm also not sorry it happened, because it led me to Morris. My other half. My puzzle piece. And it also left you open to find that person who makes you defy logic. Who makes you raw and open and vulnerable with emotion. The person you need."

An image of Meg flashes in my mind. Smiling at me. I try to shake it free but it's too late. It's there. Shit.

"And I guess it makes sense that there would be all kinds of family tension, but holy cow, is there ever a time when you can get over it? Life is short and should be savored and it's a shame to have a family that could be so great, but there's so much bullshit between you all that you're just mucking up all the potential love and joy!"

Now everyone is staring at *me*. Goddammit!

"Please, Mac? Morris misses you. He won't say so because he is a manly macho man just like you. But he misses you a lot and he's always looked up to you."

That can't possibly be true. But I glance at my brother, and his face is bright red.

"So!" Julie says. "I will get down off this roof if you two agree to a couple of things."

"What?" I grunt. "How about you get down and then you tell us your demands."

"No!" She holds up a hand like a supreme dictator. "I'm not falling for that. I'm not as think as you drunk I am."

My brother and I share a glance for the first time in ten years.

"One beer," she says, crossing her arms. "Together. By the end of next week. You two can pick a bar. Neutral territory."

"Fine," I snap. Because I will get her back on that deck or I will die trying. The only thing worse than a betrayal between my brother and me is a betrayal and a dead person.

"Sure, honey," Morris says with a sigh. "Now get down."

"You have to shake on it!" She yelps. Now she's drunk on power as well as on champagne. "Shake on it! And also you need to fix the garage door opener."

"Fine, fine!" Morris says, reaching for my hand. We might be on top of a swaying boat and desperate to put this behind us. But old habits die hard, and it's a short but bruising handshake.

Everyone on the deck below us cheers.

I take a step closer to Julie, wondering if I need to grab her or if she'll take my hand when it's offered.

But she isn't even watching me. "Thank you!" Julie shouts, addressing the crowd. "I'd like to thank you all for witnessing this moment of..."

She doesn't get to finish that thought. Because that's when a speedboat roars past, causing a huge wave to hit the *Grand Haven Queen*. We all feel the boat rock. And then we all watch as Julie pitches overboard.

25 THE BEST THEATRICAL
PERFORMANCE EVER

Meg

This has been the best live theatrical performance ever. I mean, everyone is riveted by the scene playing out above us. I wish I could run up there and help, but I don't really have any skills to offer that would be helpful. Unless they want me to rile up the crowd.

And I don't need to rile up the crowd, because the next few things happen very fast:

1. There's a rogue wave and the boat lurches.
2. There's a scream like "Wheeeeeeeee!" as Julie falls overboard.
3. We all run to the side of the boat to see where she landed.
4. All we see is the dark lake. And two hundred people hold their breath at the same time.
5. Mac does a beautiful swan dive off the roof as he launches in to save her.
6. We hear frantic footsteps as Morris nearly launches over the side of the boat, too, but about fifty people shout at once to stop him. "Get down, son," Bob shouts. "There's a rope here."
7. Time seems to slow to a complete halt as I scan the waves

for Mac and Julie. First he pops up. But then she does. She spits out lake water and then coughs, struggling.

8. Mac does his best Michael Phelps imitation as he slices through the water to Julie, grasping her from behind and steering her toward a dangling yellow rope with the flotation device on the end of it.

9. They are towed to the prow, where another ladder awaits. Mac hands Julie up into Morris's outstretched arms.

10. The crowd goes wild.

I don't really breathe properly until Mac climbs the ladder, too, emerging dripping wet, his shirt sticking to his muscular chest and totally see-through. It's like that classic *Pride and Prejudice* moment from the PBS series. And I am suddenly throbbing the way that Elizabeth Bennet was throbbing and Jane Austen just couldn't or wouldn't describe it.

Because, holy throb.

Mac looks at me for a minute and it's intense. I'm hoping he's about to grab me and kiss me, press his wet body against mine. And there's this second when I think that's just about to happen, and we stand trembling, waiting. But then Morris runs over to him, and I'm worried there's going to be a fist fight.

Instead, Morris hands him a stack of tiny napkins. "Thanks for rescuing my wife," he says. Mac takes the stack of napkins.

"What are these for?" Mac asks.

"To dry off. I wanted to help in some way and I, I don't know, there just aren't any towels."

There is pure Michigan silence for a moment. Even the music stops playing.

Then, all of a sudden, there's a different kind of music. Mac and Morris? They both start laughing.

26 DANNY BOY

Maguire

I'm feeling extra jolly on Monday. I have a lot to be happy about. My sister is happily married. Meg and I got a free pass to leave the reception early, owing to my soggy suit and tie. The boat docked early to let me and my brother off.

Meg and I barely made it into the shower at my place before we were all over each other.

The next day, Rosie called to check on me. I was a little worried that she'd feel like Julie's shenanigans ruined her reception. But not Rosie. She enjoyed every minute of it. She even took an action shot of me diving off the boat.

So I feel pretty good about that. And I feel okay about meeting my brother for a drink. Maybe someday I'll even decide that crazy Julie did us a favor. You never know.

But let's face it. The real reason I'm so chipper today is that the wedding is fucking *over*. I don't need to dread it any longer.

I'm actually whistling to myself as I step into the elevator at headquarters. And when the chief steps in after me, it doesn't even dent my mood. Much.

"Mac Maguire!" the older man booms. "How was the weekend?"

Here we go again, my subconscious complains. And for a second I just freeze. But then I remember something Meg asked me just before all the crazy shit went down at the wedding. *What would Danny from* Downtown Blues *say to the chief?*

"Great weekend, Chief," I say immediately. It just pops out, because I can picture Danny saying it.

The chief's eyes light up. "Really? Get into any trouble?"

I chuckle, because he has no idea. "Went to a wedding on a *boat*, for chrissakes. Had some beers. Tried to avoid the crazier members of my family."

The chief chuckles and shakes his head.

"Get this, Chief. One lady got a little tipsy and fell overboard. Guess who got his suit a little wet fishing her out?"

The chief lets out a great booming laugh, and I feel myself smiling. The chief doesn't need to know all the private stuff—my fucked-up family. My creaky heart. Ten years of silence between my brother and me.

That shit is private. But jumping into the lake? That's just a good story. Meg was onto something. Shooting the breeze isn't so bad. Like rolling off a log, really.

"There were no towels," I add, and the chief is beside himself now. "My brother handed me a cocktail napkin."

A tear runs down the man's face. He swats me on the arm. "Good story, kid."

The elevator door opens. He turns to leave. "Say, Chief?"

"Hmm?" he turns around.

"I know you haven't decided yet about the new victims' taskforce. My application has been complete for a few weeks already. But I just wanted you to know how much I *want* that job. I'd do good work. And I'm the right man for it."

He smiles. "Glad you finally spoke up," he said. "Thought you were going to make me give it to Tommy." He swats me on the arm again. "He keeps asking for it, but he's not the right fit."

"Uh..." All my new chatter deserts me.

"Sometimes you gotta speak up and ask for what you want, you know?" the chief says. "Otherwise I can't tell who really has the fire inside to make it work."

"I do," I sputter. "I want to help those people. I want to be the one they call when they're scared." It's not very eloquent, dammit.

What would Danny say? "I'm the right man for this job, and I won't let you down."

The chief nods. "Great. My assistant will have an offer in your box by the end of the week." Then he turns and walks away. And I just stand there in the hallway for a minute, blinking after him.

"Holy shit," I say after a minute. I walk toward the briefing room in a daze. I pull out my phone. **Holy shit**, I text to Meg. She's probably still sleeping. My girl likes to wake up late. *I used your trick.* ***What would Danny say? And it worked. Not just a little bit, either. I think I just got my promotion.***

We are going to have to celebrate. Right away.

———

AT TEN P.M. I'm bouncing around my apartment, waiting for Meg to get home from her shift at the bar. She didn't have to close tonight, at least. But I'm not a patient man.

I am, however, a hungry man who's made a kickass dinner and can't wait to eat it. I've marinated some fish filets, and the water is boiling for fresh Michigan sweet corn. The salad has a homemade dressing, and I even baked some rolls just so I'd have something to do with my hands while I waited for her.

The whole setup is awfully domestic. I'm waiting here in a freaking apron, for fuck's sake. But Meg doesn't scare me like so many other women do. She gets me. We have a good time. I still don't know if I'm capable of being someone's other half. But Meg makes me want to find out. Test the waters, as they say.

So here I am with my homemade meal, listening for her knock at the door.

When it finally comes, I almost don't hear it, because I'm singing along to some jazz on the radio.

"Maguire!" she yells through my thin front door. "I can hear you. How come you can't hear me?"

I run over to the door and fling it open. "Sorry, Trouble. Come in."

She does, and immediately flings herself into my arms. "Congratulations, Copper! I'm so excited for you!"

I grip her tightly to my chest, because she feels perfect there. "I'm pretty psyched," I admit. "He said all I had to do was ask."

"Some things are just that easy," she says, kissing my jaw.

"I guess." I'm not the kind of man to trust it, though. "Can I cook the fish, now? I'm dying here."

"Oh, sure. I suppose you can feed me a gourmet meal. If you really want to." She dances farther into my apartment. "Can I shuck the corn?"

"Already done. But if you want to peel some things off, you can start with your clothes." I give her a cheesy wink.

"Feed me first." She tosses her bag on my sofa. "And there must be something I could do to help."

"Pour the wine?" I grab my fish and carry it out onto the deck, where the grill is already hot. I carried a small table out here and set it for two. There's even a candle in the center, because I've clearly lost my mind.

I wonder if optimism is addictive? Am I gonna end up in a twelve-step program, jonesing for my next impossible hit of good news?

When I glance back into the kitchen to see Meg smiling at me as she pours the wine, I don't think I care that much.

———

"YUM!" Meg says for the tenth time. "This food is so good I want to marry it."

"Fine, but you *cannot* throw the reception on a boat."

We both crack up.

"Copper," she says, sliding her bare foot up my ankle. "I have a couple of key questions about your promotion."

"Shoot." I take a gulp of the wine. It's a nice, crisp white. The guy at the store did me a solid.

"Does your schedule change much?"

"Yup. I'll work more normal business hours." Honestly I've never minded the weird hours I had on patrol. A single guy doesn't care as much, I guess.

"Cool. More importantly, though, if you're out there helping victims all day, you won't have much need for your handcuffs."

I shrug. "Guess not."

"Huh." Her smile widens. "Might need to find other uses, then."

"*Really*," I say slowly. "You're into that?"

"I'm into you. And they're part of your persona. So..." She shrugs. "I guess I am."

The ladies always like the handcuffs. Meg never brought 'em up before, though, and for some reason I don't like this development. I guess I thought Meg saw me as more than just a cop.

But I try to shake it off. Restraining her would be fun, right? Who am I kidding. "More wine?"

"Thank you." She accepts another half glass. "I have some news, too, by the way."

I can tell by the tone of her voice that she's super excited with what she's about to tell me, and that adds a little more charm to a pretty good fucking day.

"You know how I'm going to Chicago to finally film *Pierson of Interest?*"

"Of course," I say. She talks about it every day. Every hour, really.

"This is so unreal, I almost can't believe it! Guess who they just cast as the evil dude who seduces me?"

My smile stays in place. But inside I feel suddenly cold. I don't like the idea of anyone seducing Meg but me. "Who?" I ask. If my luck holds, it'll be someone who's married. Or gay. Or both. Yeah, both married and gay. And even then I won't be able to watch the seduction scene.

This is very unsettling. I never used to be a jealous man. Where the hell did this come from?

"The actor is Peter O'Hare! Can you believe it?"

Peter O'Hare. "You mean...Danny from *Downtown Blues?*"

"Yes!" she squeaks. "The network is casting him against type, you know? It's a bit of a publicity stunt. They're trying to pull in new viewers. On my episodes! In a decade of acting I have never been so lucky."

"*Lucky*," I spit. My reaction to this news is full-on primal. If Meg had physically punched me in the gut, it would hurt less than what's just happening to me now.

Meg keeps going. "Can you just imagine that I'm going to get up close and personal with Danny...Mr. Playboy himself? Now we won't have to ask What Would Danny Do? We'll know!" She laughs. She actually laughs.

And that's the final kick. Straight to my groin this time. Perfect shot.

I don't just see red. Red floods my entire body.

Because I know how this story plays out. I've seen it all before. Meg will meet Danny, act with him, *kiss* him. And she'll realize he's like a better version of me. Same handcuffs, prettier face. Better connections.

I mean, she's told me that sometimes acting can feel very real and intense. So what Meg and I have had will pale in comparison. Hell, she won't even think about me at all. Because she'll be with someone who doesn't have to pretend to be charming. Someone she can't stay away from. Some famous dude who can give her everything she most desires, including love.

It's Julie and Morris all over again, because of course it is.

"You in there, Mac? You've gone ridiculously quiet, even for you."

Am I in here? Of course I'm fucking in here. I'm always in here.

"You know what," I say. "That's great, Meg." At this point I'm not really in control of what I'm saying. I'm just reacting. I see flashes in my head of Meg fucking good ol' Danny Boy. Because she will. And she'll love it. She'll moan in a way I haven't heard before. And what can I offer her really? I'm a simple, boring cop. I just got a promotion which will probably mean more hours, not less. I can't offer her a vacation home or trips abroad. With me, she'll just get everyday life. Maybe an occasional splurge for chili dogs.

Pathetic.

This is why I don't do relationships. They rip your heart out. Or at least they rip my heart out. What was left of it anyway.

The blackness that is sweeping over me is intense and I can't fight it. "Chicago is gonna be great for you, isn't it? But it's also probably a natural breaking point for us."

Meg blinks. "Breaking point," she repeats slowly.

"Yeah." We haven't talked about her time away. In my head I'd been assuming we'd pick up again when she came back. But why did I even think that? This is already the longest I've spent with anyone.

"What if I'm not looking for a breaking point?" she asks in a voice that's suddenly high and strained.

"Well I am," I grunt. "We had a deal. And the wedding is over."

"A *deal*," she hisses. "We are so far past that deal, Mac. You know it's true."

I shrug uncomfortably. I do know that. But it just doesn't matter. I never should have put myself in this position. "We're fuck buddies, right? I told you that's all I do." Even if—for a minute there—I might have been fooling myself into thinking we could have more.

A silence descends on us. Meg stares at her wine glass, like she's expecting it to do something interesting. And I expect her to start crying. To start yelling at me in hysterics.

Bring it on, Meg. I'm made of steel. Whatever you want to say, I can take.

But she doesn't react the way I expect. Instead, what she says is real quiet. And maybe that's worse. "It scares you that much?" she whispers. "Danny from *Downtown Blues* has to pretend to kiss me and push me down on a bed. Fifteen seconds of airtime, tops. It's acting, Mac. Not cheating."

"That's not it," I lie. And then I break out in a sweat, because I'm the worst actor in the world.

"You are so full of shit," she whispers. "I'm worth more than this, Macklin Maguire. I am. And maybe I should've listened to you when you said you didn't want a relationship. I get it. You like living in misery. Being the big strong hero, the man on the white horse. Only you know what? I don't need you to rescue me. I'm fine on my own. In fact, I'm terrific. And what we have, what we *had* was great. If you don't want me, that's fine. I'm outta here."

She pushes her chair back very gracefully. Then she stands up, snatches her purse off the sofa, and heads for the door. I sit stock-still. Coiled and ready for a fight. With whom, though, I don't know.

"Maybe, Mac, the person you should try to rescue is yourself." That's the last thing she says before walking out.

She doesn't bother slamming the door.

She just leaves it wide open.

Maybe that's worse.

She leaves without a sound, as if she doesn't care enough to even let me hear her walk away.

Meg

I am numb. Completely. I don't feel anything.

And this worries me.

Usually, I'm all about feelings. Emoting. Expressing. It's what drew me to acting. But this is different. This is real life, and if I had to say I feel anything, I'd say I feel pain.

I look back on my time with Mac and maybe it was all mapped out in front of me, and I just refused to see it. How I had to pull him into the relationship. Convince him to date me. Force him to open up.

Love shouldn't be like that. Healthy, balanced love shouldn't be like that. Love should be the way that my sister Sadie and her husband Liam have: effortless. Liam loves her with total surrender. And that's what I want. That's what I deserve.

I've got my car loaded. Chicago is just a two and a half hour drive, and couldn't come at a better time. What I need right now is complete and utter distance from Mac, and my apartment, and the reminders of all the things I thought I could have with him.

Am I crying? Maybe a little.

I'm sitting in my car. I can go early to Chicago. I can stay with a friend. We film next week. But there's no reason to stay here. In fact, the only obstacle to my departure right now is my feng shui plant. Someone has to water it while I'm away.

I could ask Sadie, but I don't think I can handle seeing her right now.

And I almost call Aubrey and Cassidy, but I also can't handle that right now. I know what they'll say. All the good things girlfriends are supposed to say when your heart is breaking. "He's such a douchebag!" "I never liked him." "He's an asshole for treating you this way." "You deserve better."

I do deserve better, but those aren't the things I want to hear right now.

I could chuck the plant on the curb and leave it forever. But none of this is the plant's fault. So I do something that surprises me a little. I pick up my phone, hit my contacts list, and press call.

"Hi, Rosie," I say. "Can I ask a tiny favor?"

ROSIE AND KWAN don't leave for their honeymoon for a week, so Rosie waves me in when I show up toting the plant.

When Kwan takes it from me, though, Rosie gets a good look at me.

"Oh, no," she breathes. "What did he do?"

"It's..." my eyes water again, dammit. "It's a long story."

"This calls for mimosas." She leads me straight to her comfy front porch with more pillows than they have on a home-decorating Instagram feed. It's very satisfying.

"I'm not really in the mood for champagne," I say.

"Nonsense," she says. "You know why there's so many bubbles in champagne?"

"Why is that?" I ask, sorta genuinely curious.

"To lift you up. And that's what you need. I can tell."

She's not wrong.

She pushes me gently down so I sit on a wicker couch, surrounded by a garden of pillows. Ten seconds later, mimosas in hand, she sits across from me.

"What did he do?" she demands.

I smile. She's made this so easy. So I just start talking. I tell her that I've dated a lot and never wanted anything more than that, but maybe it's turning thirty, or maybe when I met Mac, something just clicked.

"Like a puzzle piece," she says. And it reminds me of what Julie said at the boat, and how of course Rosie heard it all.

I nod. "I thought, maybe, after all this time and bad relationships, that I'd found the one I didn't know I was looking for."

"I agree," she says, nodding. "I think you and Mac are a fit. I've never seen him so at ease with someone. And the way he looks at you..."

I can't hear any more of that sentence so I say, "I know. I know." And then I tell her the rest. What happened after the wedding, the connection we had, the smooth ease of today and earlier, and then how everything went to hell.

"He said WHAT?" she says. "That fucker!" she explodes.

I'm a little taken aback. Rosie is usually, well, sort of like champagne herself. Bubbly. And you don't expect a glass of sparkling wine to drop the F Bomb. Only she's just getting started. "That motherfucker! Dipshit! Asshole. Smug, emotionally blocked son of a bitch..."

There's a pause. I can't help but laugh. "Are you done?" I ask.

"Dick needle swizzle stick ass munch!" She explodes. And then she just pants.

This. This is exactly what I needed to hear. And it's better coming from his own sister.

She takes the champagne out of my hand, sets it on the coffee table. Then she grabs both my hands in hers and looks me in the eyes. It's a little uncomfortable at first, but then, I don't know, it's sort of magical. Like everything else just kind of focuses and zooms in.

"Look," she says. "Mac has come a long way. And I can tell he loves you. I know it. This is going to work out."

I try to pull my hands back, but she squeezes them tighter.

"This. Is. Going. To. Work. Out," she says.

Somehow, I believe her.

Maguire

It's a Wednesday evening in mid-September when I walk into an unfamiliar hipster bar in Eastown. I give the place a quick scan. Groovy brick walls? Check. Alternative track playing on the sound system? Check. Eight page beer menu? Skinny bartender with tons of ink and a handlebar mustache? Check, check, check.

Morris isn't here yet, though. I wonder if he'll even show. But I grab a bar stool anyway.

The bartender hurries over before I can even pick up the menu. "Hey dude. The usual?"

I blink at him in confusion for a second. But then it hits me. He thinks I'm Morris.

That used to happen all the time. But for ten years I've been living my life as if I don't share my face with someone else. I've been apart from him long enough to forget that we're a matched set.

"Sure," I say, because it's the path of least resistance. It's rude, but Morris and I used to do that sometimes—play along when an unsus-pecting stranger confused us. Not in a creepy way, of course.

But what's the point of sharing your face if you can't goof with people a little now and then? Besides, this is a little window into Morris's life. I have to admit that I'm curious about what he drinks when he comes to this place.

I used to know him so well. And now that I'm sitting here, I can admit that I miss it.

The bartender walks past all twenty of the artisanal beer taps to pull a bottle and a chilled mug from the cooler. He opens the bottle and sets it down in front of me, along with the mug. And then he also slides a bowl of wasabi peas in my direction.

"Thank you," I mutter, feeling like an imposter. I pick up the bottle and glance at the label, which is in German. Huh. I pour the light yellow beer into the mug and take a tentative sip. And it's...just okay. A little bland. No, *really* bland. Unlike the rest of the world, my brother's taste in beer has not evolved toward hoppy, complicated brews.

I'm fascinated. I wonder why he comes to this snobby beer bar and orders this? It's a good thing I'm not a picky man.

I take another sip of the beer, which is wonderfully cold. And I relax my elbows on the bar. *Life is good*, I remind myself. Everything happening right now is more or less exactly what I wanted.

My new job is only three days old, and already interesting. Today I went on my first call to a crime victim's house. I visited a family who'd lost a daughter in a drunk-driving accident. The perpetrator is out on bail, and they wanted to know what's stopping the perp from killing more people.

"No one else should experience this," the victim's mother had said in a shaking voice. "How can we keep this from happening again?"

I spent a long time with the family, explaining that the driver of the car would not be behind the wheel of a car anytime soon. But also giving them a realistic vision of the criminal justice process. They had so many questions about sentencing, and about plea deals, and even about parole.

And I answered every single one as patiently as possible. It's a terrible thing that happened to them. I can't bring their daughter back. But I can make this small difference in their experience by listening and being available in their time of need.

It's goddamn humbling is what it is. "Bad shit happens in varying degrees to everyone," I'd explained to Lance just before the end of the day. "What matters is how you learn to cope with it."

"I dunno, dude," he'd said. "I just don't understand why you want to spend your days on crimes you aren't even allowed to solve."

That's only partly true, though. A calm, informed witness is a useful witness. But never mind. I prefer to think that Lance just misses me. I miss that crazy doofus, too.

But, let's face it, I miss Meg even more. I mean, our breakup is still for the best. But I shouldn't have lost my shit like that. I really wish I hadn't. We parted on bad terms, and it's all my fault.

I admitted as much to my sister Rosie, who is super mad at me. "You are *so much dumber* than you look!" had been her response. I'm still puzzling over whether or not that was a compliment.

Probably not. She's still so mad at me that I can't ask. And so is her friend Aubrey, and also my mother. Word gets around. Everybody keeps telling me they were "pulling for Meg," whatever that means. Like she and I were engaged in a battle, and they wanted her to come out on top.

But it wasn't a battle. She was never mine to win. Some people just can't change on a dime, and I'm one of them.

I take another sip from my cold but bland beer and wonder when my family will just get over it. I'm here, aren't I? At least I showed up for my date with Morris. Part of me wonders if my mother isn't standing outside, peering through the windows just to make sure.

Paranoid, I turn around and check.

Nope. I only see my brother pushing through the doors in a big fat hurry, his phone pressed to his ear. "I'll get the diapers, honey, I swear. Cross my heart. Gotta go!" He hangs up. "Jesus," he pants, flinging himself down beside me. "Shit. I'm sorry I'm late. That was rude."

Stunned, I check my watch. "It's two minutes after six, dude. I wasn't ready to send out the search party."

"Still. Not very thoughtful of me."

When were you ever thoughtful? I choke back that statement, but just barely.

"Honestly, I wasn't sure you were coming," Morris babbles. "I thought maybe you'd blow it off."

"I thought about it," I admit. "But obviously I'm too afraid of what Julie might climb up onto next."

He gives me a sideways glance, and then we both crack up.

The noise draws the bartender toward us. And when he sees Morris sitting there, he does a vicious double take. "Holy shitballs. Do you two know each other?"

Morris and I exchange a smirk. "Barely," he says slowly. And we both laugh again.

The guy looks at us like we're insane. Which, come on, we totally are. "You know I thought you looked a little off," he tells me, setting a cocktail napkin down in front of my brother.

"That's what everybody says," I mumble.

He brings Morris an identical beer and chilled mug, and then he leaves us alone.

Morris points at my beer. "He just brought you that without asking, didn't he?

"Basically. But I don't know. It's a little mild for my taste."

"Ah." My brother takes a sip. "That's because it's non-alcoholic."

"What?" I pick up the bottle and squint at it. Sure enough, it says *NA* in the corner. "Why are you drinking non-alcoholic beer?"

Morris gives his head a shake. "Now there's a long story. I don't want to make a big deal out of it. But I had to give up alcohol a few years ago."

"I had no idea." My brother is an alcoholic?

He shrugs. "I asked the family not to mention it to you."

"How come?" I know lots of people in recovery. And I'm not judgey.

"Well, it's embarrassing." He picks up his non-alcoholic beer and takes a sip. "I mean, you're the one who was wronged, and I'm the guy who couldn't handle it."

"What?"

Another shrug. "I was wracked with guilt, I guess. Julie and I almost called it quits after the first coupla years. She said I had to stop with the booze or she was leaving me. It was right around the time you were graduating with high honors and I was flunking out of community college." He shakes his head. "Water under the bridge, though."

My head is spinning, and I can't even blame the beer. It never occurred to me that Morris wasn't happy with the life he'd stolen from me. *Wracked with guilt.* "Is there any other use for the word *wracked?*" I ask suddenly. "Can you be wracked with joy? Wracked with hilarity?"

Morris laughs, and it's a funny sound. He laughs like Ernie from *Sesame Street.* It's so familiar that it makes my hair stand up.

I'd forgotten. I'd forgotten so much. "Mor."

"What?"

"Why didn't you and Julie just *tell* me." The question just pops out. But now it's here, and I have to follow through. "All those years ago. Why did you make me find out by accident? Like it was some sick joke you were playing on me."

His face drops. "I'm sorry about that. You have no idea how many times I tried to, like, rewind everything in my brain. I knew that Julie and I were meant to be together. But after our first big slip-up I wanted to hold off and figure out what to do. But she..." He cuts the sentence off, unsure what he ought to say.

"She didn't," I try.

He hangs his head. "She said she couldn't wait. And I was weak, man. I thought if I made it complicated, Julie wouldn't choose me. I loved her, but I wasn't confident. I really didn't understand why she'd pick me in the first place. And I wasn't willing to risk it. I'm sorry. I knew I fucked everything up. I knew it even before you walked in that night."

And I am speechless. That's a whole lot of honesty from a man that I thought wasn't capable of it. For ten years I made up my own stories to explain his behavior. That's a long time to live in your own reality. I'd gotten real good at it.

I clear my throat. "Well, I wasn't going to stand you up tonight. Because I want to know my nephew. I might be a shit boyfriend and I'm never having kids. But I could be a good uncle."

He swallows hard. "Okay," he says. "I want you to be that. We could hang out without Julie. You know, if that's weird."

"Eh." I shake my head. "Maybe it doesn't have to be weird. I can barely remember being twenty-five. It really feels like ancient history."

"Okay." We both take twin gulps of shitty beer, because that's a lot of talking for us. "You really think you're never getting married?"

"Nah. Old dog. No new tricks."

He sighs. "I don't believe that, though. If my dumb ass can stay married, surely you can give it a whirl."

I take a swig of the nonalcoholic beer. It's actually growing on me.

I could do a lot of things here. Change the subject. Joke around. Bring up things from childhood. But something in me fights against all that. My brother and I have already lost most of our adult lives to fighting. I don't want to lose another lifetime in not being honest with him. "I broke it off with Meg."

Morris nods. "She do something stupid?"

"Nah," I say.

"Then why'd you break it off with her?"

"Because she's..." I pause here. What am I supposed to say? Because things were getting too real? Because I wanted her too much? Because when I stopped long enough to envision a future life for myself, I envisioned waking up next to her? "I honestly don't know," I say. "I think she's just too perfect for me."

"That bitch!" Morris says, and he smiles.

"Yeah. She's kind and hot and passionate. And she's so much trouble." Now I'm smiling too.

"You always did like trouble."

"Yep."

Morris looks a little awkward. Something I'm not used to seeing. "You know, let me offer you a little advice here. As your big brother, I feel it's my duty to do so."

"You're my big brother by two minutes!"

"And so much wiser than you."

I shake my head. This is good. I've...missed this. "Okay, so what's your advice?"

"Apologize. Make it up to her. Do whatever you can to get her to come back to you, because if she's too perfect for you, then she's the one that's going to keep you on your toes. She's going to make you want to be a better person. She'll call you on your shit and she won't settle for anything less than the best. And that's what you need, Mac."

"I need to be challenged?"

"Yeah. You need someone to rescue *you*."

———

MY BROTHER and I shoot the shit some more. I have another beer, a real one this time, and we leave things with an impressive dude-hug and a promise to get together soon. And...it's easy. Surprisingly so.

When I get home, I'm looking forward to crawling into bed with Meg and then I remember. That's not an option anymore. And it's not even possible. She's not even here.

Nope.

She's in Chicago filming with that fucking superstar who's probably nuzzling her neck right now and promising to frisk her.

Dammit. That's my line. No one should say it to her but me.

I take a breath. I remind myself that it's better this way. Pretty nearly perfect. I've got my nice quiet apartment. My stack of books to read. I finished *The Sun Also Rises* again, and now I'm looking at the thrillers on the *New York Times* bestseller list. Maybe I'll read a police procedural just to pick apart all the details they get wrong.

I sit down on my couch. Get back up to heat up a frozen pizza in the oven. Sit back down. Open the book. Read. But not really.

Timer buzzes. I get up. Get the pizza. It's hot.

Head back to the couch.

Pick up the book.

Take a bite of pizza.

Still hot.

Read a page.

Read another page.

Take another bite. Swallow.

Damn.

It's fucking quiet in here.

Like, dead quiet. I can barely concentrate.

I used to sit here and listen to Meg next door. She sings full out all the time. Sometimes she doesn't know the words, but she sings shit anyway. I would hear her bump into things. Hear her practicing her lines. Sometimes she plays the other characters in the scene with her and it's hysterical to hear her voice go all deep and manly.

Sometimes I'd just knock on the wall. Four quick taps. And she'd come over. Slip inside my apartment, and then I'd pin her against the wall. Against the counter. On the bed. One time on the balcony outside. Cover her with kisses. My tongue lapping at the slight salt of her skin. I'd cup her breast in my hand, pull down her shirt, take her nipple in my mouth. She'd moan.

I'd bury my face between her legs and just taste her. Best fucking taste in the world. And when she pulled my hair and moaned my name, I'd stand. She'd open to me, and I'd just slide right up into her.

The last few times, we'd pause there. "Just stay," she breathed. "Stay right there. Nice and deep."

The shape of her smile. The sound of her voice. Her laughter. I can almost hear the echo in my heart.

Right now I just hear...me.

My stomach gurgles.

The stove ticks as it cools.

I turn the page.

———

"WHAT IS FUCKING WRONG WITH YOU?" Lance asks. Actually, first he tosses a roll at my forehead and *then* he asks me what's wrong with me. He's on desk duty today. I think he asked for it because he misses hanging out with me now that I've got my new position. Today, I'm on desk duty too. I'm not accomplishing much. Mostly filling out the endless stacks of paperwork.

He tosses another roll at me. This one lands right between my eyes with a thump.

"How old is that roll?" I ask. "That fucking hurt!"

"Awwwwww, poor wittle baby. You want me to kiss it to make it better?"

I think about it. "Nope. I'm okay," I decide.

"You're okay?" he asks. "No you're not! You know what you are?" He doesn't give me a chance to answer. "You're a moper! You're moping!"

"I am not!" I say.

"Are too!"

"Am not!"

And this, my friends, is how low I've sunk.

Lance just looks at me. "Moper," he says.

"If you reach for another damn roll and toss it at me, I'm going to arrest you."

It's not a threat. It's a promise.

Two minutes later, he tosses another fucking roll at me! This one hits my ear.

"Dammit!" I shout.

And then I just sit there.

And mope.

———

I HAVE HAD a long week at work. I'm helping people, yeah, and that's super satisfying and also super depressing. Because there shouldn't be this many people who need comfort and guidance after going through a traumatic experience. There shouldn't be this much pain in the world, and yet there is. I do the best I can. I'm making a difference, I think, a little at a time. One person, one family at a time.

When I get home at night, all I want to do is cook up something, pour a drink, and knock on my hot neighbor's door. I want to tell her about my week. Ask her what she's up to. If she's lining up another acting gig, or if she's ditched her restaurant work and has started somewhere new.

Only she's not my hot neighbor anymore. She's still hot, of course. But she's not my neighbor, and she's certainly not mine.

Ain't life grand, getting exactly the thing you wanted? This was what I asked for, isn't it? The beautiful and rich life of a single guy.

I grab a beer. Sit down. Grab a book.

This silence is killing me.

I look at my cell phone to confirm the date.

Meg's been gone for twenty days.

It feels like a year.

Why aren't I fucking someone new? I should be.

I open my phone, scroll through the contents. There's a dozen or so hookups I could call, but instead I just start deleting them. One by one.

I have another beer.

———

YOU KNOW WHAT? Now would be an excellent time to talk to Lance! I miss Lance! Lance is my friend! I could call Morris, but I'm not quite ready for that step of the healing process. Actually, I'm not quite ready for that because I had too many drinks and Morris doesn't drink.

I am, however, plenty drunk enough to call Lance.

The icons on my phone shimmy a little when I look at them. I hit the video call icon. It rings.

The screen is black, and then I get a nice big close up of Lance's armpit hair.

"Why are you in bed!" I scream. I meant to just say it, but hey, sometimes the vocal volume goes up when you're drinking alone.

"Cuz I'm in fucking bed you fucking moron!" he says.

"Hey. Hey, Lance. Hey," I say.

"Whhaaaaaaaat?" He's annoyed. I can tell.

"I want you to look up that *Cosmo* quiz thingamabob."

"Now?"

"Yes, NOW!" Oops. That was loud too.

"You do realize it's 3:30 in the morning?"

I contemplate that. Huh. No wonder it's so dark. "Dude. This is important. I need the *Cosmo*."

"Fine," Lance grumbles.

I watch him stumble out of the bed and get a quick flash of Lance in a thong. Arrrggghhh! It burns. IT BURNS!

Then the phone jerks a bit as he carries me, apparently, to his kitchen.

"Look," he says. "I'm pulling up the *Cosmo* questionnaire. Which one do you want? How Much Of An Asshole Am I For Waking Up My Friend? Or Love Me, Love Me Not?"

"That second one," I say. And then, in case he's wondering, "I love you, man."

"I love you too," he says. "Now drink some fucking coffee."

I nod. Excessively. And then I make the way to the coffee pot and shove in a pod and hit the button a few times. It keeps dodging out of my way. Little bugger is hard to catch but finally I do. There. The coffee gurgles.

"Okay. Hit me!" I say, and I pat my chest for emphasis.

"First you have to put on some clothes."

I look down surprised to hear this suggestion and then realize Lance is observant. I'm 100% buck naked. Huh. "You ask me the questions, and I'll get drunk." I pause. "I mean dressed."

He starts asking me the questions. I'm going to ace this test. "How often do you think about her? Once a week? Once a day? Once an hour?"

"What about once a minute?"

He scribbles something down on a pad of paper and keeps asking questions. I flop down on the couch when we reach question three. I already know how this ends. I knew it the first time I took the quiz, but I fudged my answers.

This time, I'm totally 100% honest.

"Okay dude. You ready to hear the result?" Lance asks me when we're done. "You got a lotta points. Hang on. I'm still adding them up. Carry the two... and then carry the four..." He scribbles madly.

"STOP!" I yell. "Don't add them up." I don't want to hear it.

Deep down, though, I already know.

And *Cosmo* knows.

"Then why did you wake me up?" Lance grumbles.

"Because I'm a goddamned idiot. I'm afraid it's a permanent condition."

"Dude," Lance says. "You think you're like Hemingway, with your short, choppy sentences and your manly wisdom. But he knew some things you need to learn."

"Like what?" I'm so groggy all of a sudden.

"Dude got married three, four times, right? He loved women and he loved falling in love."

Fucking Lance. Always psychoanalyzing me. "Sorry I woke you up," I grunt.

I set down the phone on the coffee table, stumble toward my bedroom, crawl under the sheets, and close my eyes.

———

THE NEXT TIME I regain consciousness, my sister Rosie is sitting on the bed, poking me in the side. "Mac, wake up. Everyone is worried about you. Lance says you've fallen into a pit of despair."

"I have not," I grumble into my pillow. "Men don't fall into pits of despair. They get up and go to work and..." Oh shit. I sit up really fast. "What time is it?"

My sister blinks. "It's Saturday o'clock."

"Oh!" I fall back down onto the pillow.

"No, Mac. Get up."

"No."

"Yes."

I'm sure we had more sophisticated arguments in grade school.

"Take a shower," she orders.

"No."

"I'll make coffee."

I waver. Because coffee sounds pretty good right now. My head is pounding.

"And there are doughnuts."

Well that's a game changer. I open one eye.

"Come on. You know I'm not going to give up on you. I never do."

Aw. I sit up. "See? You can catch more flies with honey."

"Coffee, coming up!" She bounces from the room, and I consider going back to sleep. But it will never work. So I drag my sorry carcass into the shower instead. The hot water pounds on my aching head. Why did I drink? What a lousy idea that was.

Eventually I'm showered and dressed. I scarf down a donut at the kitchen sink and gulp coffee out of a giant mug that Rosie has handed me.

Meanwhile, she's buzzing around my apartment, fluffing the pillows. Meg loves those pillows.

Whoops. I've been awake about twelve whole minutes before my mind goes straight to Meg. What would *Cosmo* say?

Rosie even goes into my room and makes the bed. "Now Mac, come here!" she calls.

With my coffee for support, I enter the bedroom where my sister is sitting cross-legged on the freshly made bed.

"Sit. We need to talk."

I was afraid of that. But I sit down anyway.

"Now tell me how you're going to fix things with Meg?"

This again. "I can't fix them without becoming a different person."

"So do that." She shrugs.

"Rosie!"

"Look, Mac. We're all sympathetic. You don't like to take chances with your heart."

"I can't," I explain. "It's just not how I'm built."

"Hmm," Rosie says, looking thoughtful. "Humor me for a moment, would you? There's something I want to show you. Try this: stretch both arms over your head. And take a deep breath."

I hesitate. "Is this, like, a yoga technique?"

"Something like that."

I consider my options. On the one hand, my sister brought me coffee and donuts. And she obviously cares. So I should humor her. On the other hand, this is a bunch of bullshit and I'd like to get on with my day.

My day full of moping.

"Mac. Come on. Just lift up your arms, you stubborn macho bonehead."

With a sigh, I set down my coffee mug and slowly raise my arms overhead.

"Good job," she says. "Stretch! Take a deep breath and hold it. Arch your back a little."

Huh. Yoga is getting weirder all the time.

Rosie lifts herself onto her knees and takes my wrists in one of her hands. She eases them closer to the metal bed frame. "You're doing great. Hold it right there."

Hold it right there. That's something a cop would say right before he...

Something cool slips around my wrist. *Click.* The sound of a handcuff closing makes me jerk that wrist. "What the—"

Click.

She's got the other one, too! "Rosie! What the everloving fuck?" I yank on my wrists, but they're cuffed together with my iron bedrail in between. "Are you shitting me right now!"

My sister smiles. "Calm down, Mac."

"I WILL NOT CALM DOWN." I can't lower my arms. She's cuffed me to my own bed with... "Are these my *own* handcuffs? This isn't funny at all."

"It's not supposed to be funny. It's supposed to make you uncomfortable."

"I AM VERY UNCOMFORTABLE, CAPTAIN OBVIOUS!"

"There is no need to shout." She crosses her arms. "Let's just take a few breaths and observe ourselves with curiosity, but not with judgment."

"Oh, I'm full of judgment!"

"For me, sure." Rosie shrugs. "But let's focus on you. Describe your discomfort. Do you feel vulnerable?"

"Yes, dammit. Congratulations. Now get these off me. Where did you find these, anyway?"

"In your sock drawer."

"You evil..." I bite my tongue, because I cannot insult the person who I need to set me free. "Where's the key?" Oh, God. If she lost it, the boys at the station will never let me live this down. Lance will show up here and take fifty photos before he lets me go.

"Mac, it's right there on top of the dresser. Look."

My frantic eyes go to that spot. Sure enough, I can just see the key at the edge of the dresser. So close but so far away. I let out a bellow of helpless rage.

"Good!" says Rosie, clapping her hands together. "This is very healthy. How uncomfortable are you right now on a scale of one to ten?"

"Dangerously uncomfortable," I spit. "Like a hundred and forty-two. Whatever you're trying to prove, it worked. Now uncuff me or —" I try to think of a suitable threat. My sister knows that I'd never actually hurt her. So I have to choose carefully. "Uncuff me right now, or there will be no triple decker devil's food cake on your birthday."

"Ohhhh! You *are* really mad." She begins to look slightly concerned.

"You think? And I'm *not* joking. If you don't let me out of here, you're going to be stuck with mom's cake. And it'll probably have crocheted frosting."

We both shudder. "Huh, well." Rosie takes a deep breath. "That's just a chance I'll have to take. Because I need you to listen to me for a minute."

"Like I have a choice."

"I cuffed you to the bed because this is how people feel when they're in love. Trapped, exposed. Isn't that how you feel right now?"

"To say the least. But you're not really selling it to me, are you? Who would do this willingly?"

"Meg would." She sits back on her heels. "This is what Meg was willing to feel for *you*. She put herself out there, even when it felt very uncomfortable. She showed you her heart, even when you'd told her that you don't date. Even when you showed her your ugly past, she wasn't afraid. She chained herself to a very uncomfortable place. She stood in front of the Macklin Maguire human bulldozer without anything to protect her heart. And she did it all for you."

"Fuck." I take a deep breath. And then another one. The coffee and sugar are starting to kick in. And I think about what Rosie is trying to tell me. Meg did all those things. It's true. I don't know if I'm worth the trouble.

Except Meg thinks I am.

"I dunno," I tell my sister. "I hear you. But I don't know if I'm there yet."

"You will be," she says kindly. "I have faith. I'd give it..." She pauses. Then she counts on her fingers.

"Ten years?" I joke.

"Nah. I give it two hours." She slides off the bed. Then she picks up her purse and puts it on her shoulder.

"Where are you going?" I ask, my voice getting high and weird. Because now my sister is striding toward the bedroom door.

"Grocery shopping!" she calls.

"But... *Rosie*! You forgot something, here!" I'm still cuffed to the bed. "I learned your lesson! Get back here!"

She turns around. "Do you love Meg?"

"I..." The word is right on the tip of my tongue. But it doesn't matter if I love Meg or not. She'll still get sick of me. I'm prickly. I have a dangerous job. I'm set in my ways.

Rosie sighs. Then she checks her watch. "Three hours, maybe. You're a tough case."

"Hey!" I yell as she disappears from the bedroom. "Get back here! No cake for you! Not on your birthday! Not at Christm—"

Slam. My sister has left me here. I'm gonna kill her.

29 I'D KNOW THAT THUD ANYWHERE

Meg

"Okay, troops!" I announce from the middle of Aubrey's living room. "We're settled on "Uptown Funk," two dozen dancers, and October twelfth. First rehearsal is October first!" That's the day after my last episode wraps. I'm going to have to hustle back here to make this work. But it's totally worth it.

"Sweet!" Aubrey says, and her assistant flips her notebook closed. "I'll let you both get back to your Saturday."

"Thanks, baby! Can't wait for this."

I'm not exaggerating either. I *really* can't wait for it. When Aubrey called me with another flash mob job, I didn't even think twice about jumping into my car and racing back to Michigan for the meeting.

I *loved* our farmers' market wedding proposal. I think I have a real future in creating small theatrical events that change people's lives. And nobody has opened a business like this in West Michigan yet. It's waiting for me! I feel all sunshiney inside when I think about it.

My stint in Chicago, on the other hand, has been a real eye-opener. It's a great experience, and I'm still excited to see my episodes air. But it's not fun. The producer and the director are fighting. One of the lead writers quit in front of me yesterday. They're not a happy bunch.

Oh, and now I know exactly what Danny-From-Downtown-Blues would do in various situations. Good Ol' Danny Boy would drink Scotch between takes and then fall asleep behind the sets. Also, Danny would kiss like a real loser. *Ugh*. My scenes with him require every bit of my acting talent.

I have three more episodes to shoot before my character is killed off. And then it's back to auditioning again. Back on the treadmill.

Or is it? I haven't decided if I want to keep auditioning. Right now I could literally go either way. And that alone says something significant. When you lose passion for something, isn't it time to try something new?

Like *Meg's Mobs*. My fledgling business already has a name. *Meg's Mobs* is totally going to happen. *Meg's Mobs* gets me all a flutter. I'll start my own business the minute I'm back from Chicago. Hell, it's pretty much already started. And I'll make all the casting decisions. I can't wait to be in charge, for once.

There are so many ways to be successful. And I'm done waiting for my flipping fairy godmother to show up and make me queen of Hollywood.

I kiss Aubrey goodbye and then head for my car. Just as I'm about to get in, she calls out her front door to me. "You're going home now, right? To your apartment?"

"Yeah," I say. "I want to grab some things."

There's an awkward pause and I think I see her tapping on her phone.

"Why?" I call.

"Oh, nothing. Just asking. In case I need to stop by later. But I probably won't. In fact, if I need to stop by later, I'll make sure I call first." She gives me a final wave and then closes her door.

That's weird.

But that's Aubrey.

I start up my car, and immediately my thoughts go back to *Meg's Mobs*. Can I start a business while also hustling for more on-screen work? What kind of life do I want? Who do I want to be, exactly?

These are my thoughts as I drive to my apartment for the first time in three weeks. When I pull into the lot, Mac's car is there. That's too bad, honestly. I hadn't wanted to think about him this weekend. It's almost tempting to turn around and go right back to Chicago.

I sit in my parking space for a moment, the engine idling.

But then I grab the key and twist it. Because fuck him. This is my home. And if he's so frightened of my love that he needs to put some distance between us, that's on him.

In fact, I'm going to let him know I'm here and I am totally fine without him.

A few minutes later I'm marching down our shared hallway and unlocking my door with a flourish. Since it's stuffy in my apartment, the first order of business is opening all the windows and welcoming in the fresh air.

The song "Uptown Funk" is stuck in my head, because we played it a few times at Aubrey's house just to get the feel of the beat. This new flash mob will kick off a surprise party. The birthday boy is supposed to think he's been sent to the mall for just an errand or two. But his boyfriend has orchestrated a surprise party at one of the restaurants. And the flash mob is just the beginning.

"Uptown funk gonna sing it to you!" Whoops. Those aren't the words, but I'm probably close. "Uptown funk gonna ring it for you. Bling it at you! Something-something and someTHING!"

Fine—lyrics aren't my strong suit. But this is my home and I can butcher tunes if I want to.

I find when I'm working out a new flash mob scene, it helps to butcher with aplomb. And volume. So I am singing to my heart's content when suddenly I hear a thud against the wall.

I immediately go silent. The only thing beating is my heart. I'd know that thud anywhere. It's Mac. My copper.

But he's not mine, is he?

My blood stops circulating. Because that thud might mean he's already someone else's.

I feel nauseous at the thought.

Welp. More singing then. Some sounds need to be drowned out. "Uptown junk gonna sling it at you!"

And now there's another sound! But it's not a headboard banging. Instead, Mac answers with four little knocks in quick succession. And those four knocks... That's our code. That means he wants me to come over!

For a hot second I'm elated. But then I put the brakes on. Of course I do. I can't run over there and throw myself at his feet. Not. Happening. If he wants to see me, he needs to come over here and apologize. Preferably on his knees.

An image of Mac crawling on his knees toward me is almost enough for me to lose my balance. So I start singing again.

But then I hear his voice. "Meg?" It's so soft, I can barely make it out. I tiptoe over to the wall and press my ear against it.

"*Meg,*" he calls again, louder this time.

I don't say anything. Because he doesn't deserve a response.

"I need..."

My heart stops for a second. *What do you need, Mac? Just say it!*

"I need you!" he calls. My traitorous heart leaps. Because that's all I ever wanted to hear him say.

Except I don't trust it. He could have called me to say so. I've been in Chicago, for craps sake. Not Ouagadougou.

"You need me," I say to the wall. "Because you chose this moment to realize it? Or because you're trapped under something heavy."

He chuckles, low and sultry, and the hair stands up on my arms. God, that laugh. I miss it so much. "It's a little of both," he says. "Come see."

"Maybe later." *Or never.* I have so many feelings for Mac. But I'm not sure he's capable of returning them. Some wounded people never get over their wounds. And I won't spend my life waiting to find out if he's one of them.

"*Now,* Meg," he says. "I need you now."

There's a definitive tone to his voice that I can't ignore. My feet point toward the hallway before I can even stop myself.

"You'll have to climb the fence," he says.

That stops me. "What? Why?"

There's that chuckle again. "You'll see."

"No I won't," I snap. "You can't play games with me, okay? I've had enough."

"I know you have." Because we have such thin walls, I can even hear his sigh. "The irony is pretty rich, but I need you to break in just one last time. I'll never ask you to again. My front door is probably locked, and I can't open it myself."

I feel a tingle at the base of my skull. "Why not?"

"You'll see in a minute. And maybe you're not ready to believe anything I'm saying. But ten bucks says you'll think the sight is worth a couple minutes of your time."

The sight of...?

Okay, fuck it. I'm intrigued. And something tells me that there's a setup at work.

"Hang on a sec!" I call. I think back to how awkward Aubrey was and how she wanted to make sure I was coming home.

So I text Aubrey...

ME: WTF is happening at Mac's apartment?

...

AUBREY: Oh, good! You're home!

ME: Yeah but???

AUBREY: Rosie told me to tell you happy birthday. She left something for you in Mac's apartment.

ME: Is it by any chance...Mac?

AUBREY: My lips are zipped. But maybe you should go over there really quick in case your birthday gift has to pee. Okay?

My friends are a strange crew. But I guess I'll worry about that later. Mac can't open his own door? I'm going to have to find out why. But on my own terms.

I clear my throat. "Mac?"

"Yes, Trouble?"

"I'm in the middle of alphabetizing my sock drawer. I'll swing by in a few."

He snorts. "I'm not going anywhere. Apparently."

I tiptoe to my closet. Mac hasn't seen me in three weeks. This is one of those moments that calls for something outrageous. I start plucking hangers off the bar, asking myself: what would a sexy cat burglar wear? If I'm already breaking and entering, I might as well do it in leather...

———

...TWENTY MINUTES LATER

"Meg," he demands as I'm checking out my bustier in the mirror. "If your sock drawer is in order, how about you come over."

"Soon!" I grin at my reflection. That's showing him.

"Just, please, come over. Were you waiting to hear the magic word?"

"Maybe," I admit. "But the magic words are: I am a stupid fucking asshole."

"Well then I am a stupid fucking asshole."

I blink. Because that was a little too easy. "You're not dying, right? You're not bleeding out, or anything?"

"No, Trouble. I don't have so much as a paper cut. My ass is numb but I'm sure it's not fatal. Nice of you to ask, though."

While it's tempting to leave him in whatever situation he's in, I'm also dying to see what Rosie's done. And—let's be honest—I'm also dying for him to see me in this getup I'm wearing. So he'll remember *exactly* what he's given up.

That's what gets me onto the patio, where I shimmy carefully over the divider (because leather isn't cheap) and make a very ungraceful plunk onto Mac's deck on the other side. Good thing that the director of *Pierson of Interest* didn't see me just pull that stunt. She'd make me do another take.

I'm moving stealthily, like any self-respecting bad-girl would. Mac's sliding glass door is already open. Almost as if someone left it this way, knowing I'd be walking through.

Hmm.

I tiptoe across the living room. The bedroom door is open, too. Taking care to stand back, out of sight, I peek into the room.

And there is Macklin Maguire, spread eagled on his bed, arms handcuffed overhead. He was right—he's not going anywhere like that. My mouth falls open, and I quickly catalog two problems with this whole scenario. 1) He's clothed, and 2) We're not together anymore.

I'm fairly sure I can change one of those things.

I clear my throat and Mac swings his rugged chin to catch me staring. "Holy shit," he breathes, because I'm wearing a leather bustier, leather pants, and my black stilettos. Okay, this may be an old costume leftover from summerstock when I played Sandy in *Grease*, but it's a fucking great outfit. "That getup is…"

He doesn't finish the sentence. He doesn't have to. One glance at his pants, and the bulge that pops up there says everything.

"You happy to see me?" I ask, even though I know the answer.

"God, yes," he says. His eyes take me in from head to toe. Then he closes his eyes. Maybe he just doesn't want to look at me. And that hurts a bit. It does.

"I don't know, Mac. It's nice that you're happy to see me. It's nice to hear you yelling for me. Except you're only yelling because you need someone to unlock you."

He shakes his head. "You're wrong."

"Am I?" I snort. "You're going to pull a Houdini and free yourself?"

"Nah," he says, and then a slow grin forms on that irresistible mouth. "I'm yelling for you because I need *you*. I get it now. The handcuffs are just a mild inconvenience."

"So you don't mind if I turn and leave again?" I yelp.

"Oh, I'd mind very much." His eyes are warm and lazy. "Come closer."

I hesitate. Maybe it's a trick.

Except I know better than that. Mac *never* tricked me. Even though he let me down, he never lied to me. *I don't do relationships*. I hadn't wanted to hear it.

I still don't.

"What do you want, Mac?" I need to cut my losses and go.

"You," he whispers. "Just you."

"For what?" I'm so confused right now.

"For everything. Dinner. Lunch. Breakfast. Hobbit-style snacks. Fruity drinks. Party dates." He looks up at the ceiling, as if considering. "Not *too* many parties. A man can only change so much. And I don't think karaoke will ever be on the table. I probably have a few limits."

"But none of that sounds like you."

"I know. But…" He actually tries to beckon, but the handcuffs clank against the metal bed frame, so it doesn't quite work. Instead of getting frustrated, he actually chuckles. "Come *here* already. Jesus. I need to kiss you so bad it hurts."

There's a new tightness in my chest, and I'm pretty sure this bustier is only half responsible. "Don't tease me, Mac. If you don't want a commitment, I have to let you go."

"Don't let me go," he says immediately. "I get it now. You make me crazy. You're a whole lot of trouble. You challenge me. You kick my ass. And I'm so fucking hungry for you right now my cock is about to rip out of my pants. And I'm not running anymore. You've caught me."

I think about it for a second. "What does that mean...exactly? I've caught you? This isn't a game of cat and mouse, Mac. I'm done with games. And I'm done with emotional drama. What are you offering me?" I take a step closer.

"I'm offering you everything you see before you. Which is, admittedly, just a guy who's chained to a bed. But I'm loyal, I can hold my liquor, and I always say what I mean."

"And what do you mean right now?" I press.

"I love you so fucking much, Meg. That's the bottom line. If we can't fix this right here and right now, then I'm going to do something really stupid."

I take another step closer to him so now I'm standing right next to him, looking down at him, all beautiful and defenseless before me. Like a caged animal. It's very *Ben Hur*. "What would you do?"

"I'll...gnaw off my hand so I can get at you."

"That's graphic," I say.

"Too much?"

"A little."

We both smile at each other.

"Meg. If we don't fix this right now, I'm going to be lost all over again. And it's been really nice to finally feel found."

"You feel found with me?" I lean over and put a hand in the center of his broad chest, because I have to touch him.

"I feel more than found. I feel like I'm finally whole. Like you're my missing..."

"Handcuff key?" I offer.

He tips his head back and laughs. "I was going to say missing *piece*.

But if you felt like unlocking these things, it would be easier for me to kiss you."

"Would it?" I kneel on the bed. "You don't kiss with your hands."

His handsome eyes get hot. "I kiss with my whole fucking body when it's you I'm kissing."

"Oh. Well. In that case." I smile. "In that case I'd like to see you try it without your hands." I throw a knee over his thighs, straddling him. "I always thought it would be fun if you cuffed me. But it might be even more fun to be in charge."

His clear eyes consider me. "You think you're in charge right now?"

"Of course."

He raises an eyebrow. "I can lead from any position. Just saying."

"Can you now?" Just to prove that I'm driving, I finally lean down and kiss him.

He groans as our lips meet, his mouth beckoning to mine. And he shifts his body in a way that makes me fall against his chest.

It's heaven. It's amazing. It's everything I've been missing. I wrap my arms around his shoulders and tilt my head to make our connection even more perfect.

It wasn't bluster when Mac insisted he was still in charge. As our kiss deepens, my thinking goes fuzzy. I let his bossy tongue rule mine. His kisses roll together like waves on the beach, and I can't find the willpower to pull back or stop.

Then he lifts his hips off the bed, showing me exactly how much he wants me. I'm suspended on his tight body. And there's a very ambitious erection between my legs. We grind into deeper, hotter kisses.

I moan against his mouth.

"Unzip me," he barks. "Do it now."

And I don't think: *hey, I'm in charge*. I think: *yay, unzipping!* But whatever. He can win on this point. It's a crime he's wearing that T-shirt, too. I don't think I'm strong enough to tear it off his body.

But there are other pleasures. I reach into his boxers and wrap my hand around his girth.

"Fuck yes," he snarls. "More. Tighter. Taste me."

Again, I do not play it cool. I lean down and take his tip against my tongue. And then I moan at the first salty-clean taste of his skin.

There's a clang of metal against metal. "Fuck. I want my hands in your hair."

I moan, because that sounds pretty good. Those cuffs are starting to be a drag.

"Suck it," he whispers. "Show me your pretty eyes."

I raise my head a few degrees until our gazes lock. And his expression goes from hot to warm and sweet.

"Love you," he says. The words just roll off his tongue. "Can't wait to show you how much. Now lose that leather. It'll probably show up in my dreams later anyhow. But right now it's in my way."

I'm unzipping it three seconds later.

"Good girl. You're going to have to find a condom. And untie all those laces across your tits."

You know what? Sex is more fun when nobody is chained to the bed. Or maybe it's just a matter of getting naked first. I'll have to find out some other time, though. "Where's the key, Mac?"

"What key?" He laughs. "It's on the dresser."

I pounce on it. In order to free Mac, I have to climb into his lap, stick my chest in his face and reach for his hands.

"Oooh, stay right there," he says, kissing my cleavage.

"Oh, man." I close my eyes a moment as his lips graze the swells of my breasts. "You'd better cut that out, though. If I drop this key behind the bed, we'll have issues."

He groans. "Hurry then. I already have issues. I'm going to burst unless we're using this headboard in a more exciting way."

Amen to that. Luckily, I'm able to free him quickly. The click of the cuff opening up is the best sound I've heard in weeks. Mac lets me free both his hands. But then he's a blur of motion—tossing the cuffs off the bed, whipping off his T-shirt, rolling the two of us over.

"You okay?" I ask from my back, staring up into his beautiful gray eyes.

"Never better. I can't feel my arms, but I'm thinking I don't care right now." He leans down and kisses me deeply, until we're both panting. "Now take this off," he says, tugging on the bustier. "I need all of you spread out underneath me."

"Do you now?"

"I do. Oh, and one last favor?" he asks. "If it's not too much trouble."

"Just one? I freed your ass from bondage, and you're still asking favors?"

"Deal with it." I get another kiss. "Can you leave the stilettos on?"

"Sure," I say, untying the leather strap at my breasts. "But you'll owe me a favor. Fair's fair."

He rolls his eyes. "We can't be back to this. I mean—I could still have you arrested."

"On what charge?"

"Driving me crazy without a license."

"I plead guilty, then."

He kisses me.

Maguire

I'm tugging my ill-fitting uniform into place when I hear Meg's voice out in the hallway. "Copper! Emergency! Help!"

I take off like a shot, darting through my apartment, flinging the door open. I'm at her side in less than five seconds. And I'm happy to say that the "emergency" at hand is just a matter of too many grocery bags. Meg has staggered out of the elevator, arms full. My first act of mercy is grabbing the bag that's perilously close to sliding out of her grip.

"Oh my God, thank you. I don't like to pull the helpless female card, but it would be a crime if one of these bottles of wine broke."

"I hear you, babe." I relieve her of two shopping bags, leaving her with just one to manage as she reaches for her keys.

"My hero." She gives me a grin and then a head-to-toe once-over. "New uniform? That's a funky shade of blue."

"Yeah," I grunt. Hopefully she won't look too close. The uniform is part of a surprise I have brewing. So I change the topic. "Feeling hungry? I think you bought out the store."

"I bought three kinds of chips. Grapes, cheese, and some fancy crackers..." She leads me into her apartment, where we deposit the bags on the counter. "...Red wine, white wine, rum, guacamole, and—

my piece de resistance—little frozen pigs in the blankets. All I have to do is put them on a cookie sheet and bake them for 22 minutes!"

"A miracle!" I chuckle. Meg still doesn't cook and it's doubtful that she ever will. She says that's why God invented frozen foods.

Let's just say that I do a lot of the cooking around here. And she mixes the drinks.

"I'm having a spur of the moment party." She's pulling a metric ton of snack foods out of those grocery bags. "Look—this is for Hemingway Daiquiris." She holds up a pink grapefruit. "Just in case I can entice you to blow off your event tonight."

"Ah." The very last of Meg's episodes on *Pierson of Interest* airs tonight. Meg and I watched the first five of them cuddled up on the sofa together.

But I don't plan to watch this one. Even if I haven't told her exactly why. Anyway, tonight there's a town meeting at City Hall that I plan to attend, because police relations is one of the items up for discussion. Meg knows this already, and she doesn't really blame me for missing her show.

Even so, I move around the kitchen island to a place where I can stand right behind her at the counter. I wrap my arms around her.

And because I can't help myself, I place a soft kiss on the back of her smooth neck. And then another one. She stops fiddling with the groceries and leans back into my embrace. We're quiet for a moment together. I'm used to this now—to being half a couple. It doesn't even feel strange anymore. She feels right in my arms.

Hemingway said once: "The best way to find out if you can trust somebody is to trust them." And he was a really smart man. I trust Meg, and I trust us. And I'm about to show her how much.

"Listen, Trouble," I whisper. "I'm sorry I can't watch your show tonight."

"I know you are. But you can watch later."

"No, I really can't."

"Of course you can! I'm recording the episode."

"I get that. But what I mean is that I really can't bring myself to watch it. I have no trouble watching the scenes where you chase down the bad guys. And I didn't even mind those scenes where that asshole put his hands all over you." Well, I minded. But I kept it to myself. "But I just cannot watch a scene where you get killed."

Meg turns around suddenly in my arms, and her face is full of surprise. "Mac, it's fake. I'm standing right here."

"Doesn't matter." I shake my head. "I don't want that image in my mind. I love you too much to watch that."

Her eyes fill. "You are really something else. Have I told you that?"

"Yeah." I clear my throat, because I hate making people cry. "Look, when are all of your friends coming over?"

"Not for an hour."

"Oh. Phew. Because I have a present to give you."

"Really?" She bats her damp eyelashes at me. "I love presents. Is this a literal present? Or a naked present?"

"Well..." It's honestly a little of both. "You need to sit on the couch and wait. I have to go get something. Or I guess we could do this later. I went out on a limb and I'm having second thoughts already."

"Pfft!" she brushes that idea away. "With that build up, you have to give it to me right now. I love danger."

Of course she does. "I'll be right back."

Now, I've done a little research into what's about to happen. And, yes, *a little research* means I asked Lance. The man drives me insane, but sometimes all those sexy books he's reading are full of suggestions. And I'm banking that this is a good suggestion. Or I'm going to punch him in the throat.

Maybe that's harsh.

If this doesn't work, he's buying me a meatball sub, at least.

It'll work though. Meg once asked me if I'd ever done anything really crazy for love. The truth is, I've never let go long enough to be crazy. But she makes me want to free fall.

So here I go.

I dim the lights.

"What's going on?" she calls.

Then I connect the mini disco ball to my iPhone, lean into the room and set it on the counter.

Then I hit PLAY on the song I've got queued up.

It's a raunchy, down and dirty hip-hop song.

I'm hoping she recognizes it.

Then I hear her laughing. "Oh my God!" she cries. "Is this the song from when I was a serving wench and I thought you were a..."

She doesn't finish the thought. She doesn't have to.

Because tonight, right now, I'm not a cop. Not a real cop.

Nope.

I'm a down and dirty stripper, and I'm gyrating to the music as if I'm trying to screw something to the floor. Maybe I am.

Meg's face lights up. "Over here, Copper! Me! Me!!"

I strut over to her and grind up close to her, but not touching. I can feel the music leading me. Or maybe it's just the pull I feel from Meg.

"Mac," she breathes. "Are those..."

I think maybe she's noticed that this is no regular cop's uniform.

Honestly, Lance is a wealth of information.

I stand in front of her and rip my shirt off. It literally rips off. There's velcro instead of buttons.

"Oh, oh!" she cries. "Please, please please tell me that your pants rip off too!"

I'm too busy flexing to do anything but wink at her. She reaches for me and I pause just long enough for her to grab ahold of my removable trousers and give one big tug.

This time, the pants fall right off of me.

Huh.

That is super handy. Easy access.

Meg is in hysterics. I get a little concerned that this is going all wrong and I stop for a second, then she cries out, "Don't you fucking stop dancing, Copper!"

And then she's giggling some more. "What on earth are you wearing? Shouldn't you be totally naked? What is covering your...junk?"

"Isn't it obvious?" I ask. And I thrust at her. If you're going to go free fall, you might as well be wearing a red thong that has a sling for your balls. I give a little jiggle. I turn a little so she can see the little pocket. "This is for you," I say.

"You're giving me your dick? This is the best day ever!" she squeals.

I'm still grinding.

"The POCKET," I say.

"Oh. Oh!" She grabs me by the hips and brings me close to her. Her eyes and mouth are at the perfect position. One quick grab of this thong and I'll be straight up against her lips.

"Reach in the pocket," I say, because if I don't say something, I'm going to rip her clothes off before I can get to the good part. And this is the good part.

She reaches for me. Digs in the pocket. And pulls out a key.

"To your handcuffs?" she asks.

I stop dancing. Run my hand through her hair. She's looking up at me and I don't think I've ever seen a more beautiful sight than her brown eyes looking into mine. "It's a key to my apartment," I say. "So you can stop breaking in. And maybe, you know, just stay."

"Are you asking me to move in with you?"

I nod. "I'm asking."

"So. Ask."

She never lets me off the hook.

I wouldn't have it any other way.

"I'm asking you to move in with me. But it's more than that. I want you to move that ridiculous plant over to my place. And your pillows. I want to help you when you're freaking out about all the stuff you need to organize for Meg's Mobs. I want you to take out all that anxiety on me at night. Or in the morning. Mid-afternoon. I want to cook for you. And I want you to pick up takeout sometimes. I want you to stop being the girl next door, and be the girl who stays. I want you to move in. And never, not ever, move away. So I guess what this key is, is me. Asking you for forever."

Anything could happen right now. Anything.

She gives me her hand, and I tug her upwards. She answers me with her kiss. Her arms are around me and her lips are against me and there are no words for a few moments.

"You know," she says, "if you ever ask me to marry you, you're going to have to come up with a proposal that will top this. That's going to be difficult."

I smile at her. Taste her lips one more time. "I'll think of something."

"I know you will, Mac. Now shut up and dance with me. And without that ridiculous thong."

I take the thong off.

I take everything off.

From here on out, it's just me and Meg, naked and vulnerable as can be.

And you know what?

I fucking love it.

Because I fucking love her.

Trouble and all.

THE
END

ACKNOWLEDGMENTS

We would like to acknowledge the amazing editorial help we received from Nana Malone. Thank you so much for helping us keep Meg real!

Thank you Bernard Schaffer for your police officer wisdom.

Thank you also to Christine Coffey for your terrific design work! It's been so much fun to do these covers with you!

Thank you to Jo P. and Claudia F. S. for your proofreading!